PROLOGUE

When I was a little girl, I loved Nancy Drew.

When I grew up, I became her. I even have a little red roadster, a Triumph TR-6.

It sounds so simple, straightforward and happily ever after that way. Naturally, it's not.

ALIBI FOR AN ACTRESS

Gillian B. Farrell

POCKET BOOKS
New York   London   Toronto   Sydney   Tokyo   Singapore

*To Bo, Buddy, McNally, Barna, and
the Guys—*

*They gave me a chance when the casting
directors wouldn't and taught me a new way
of looking at the world.*

*I've never met more extraordinary people per
capita. I never laughed so hard or listened to
so many Frank Sinatra songs or heard so
many swear words per sentence.*

This book is a work of fiction. Names, characters, places, and
incidents are either products of the author's imagination or are
used fictitiously. Any resemblance to actual events or locales or
persons, living or dead, is entirely coincidental.

POCKET BOOKS, a division of Simon & Schuster Inc.
1230 Avenue of the Americas, New York, NY 10020

Copyright © 1992 by Gillian B. Farrell

All rights reserved, including the right to reproduce
this book or portions thereof in any form whatsoever.
For information address Pocket Books, 1230 Avenue
of the Americas, New York, NY 10020

ISBN: 0-671-75708-3

First Pocket Books paperback printing July 1993

10 9 8 7 6 5 4 3 2 1

POCKET and colophon are registered trademarks of
Simon & Schuster Inc.

Cover art by Honi Werner

Printed in the U.S.A.

CHAPTER ONE

Zest-Time Cola was doing a new series of commercials. The theme was human warmth and youthful excitement.

Human warmth and youthful excitement means a lot of different things; this time it meant squealing on a beach and loving the feel of an ice-cold bottle of Zest-Time Cola against my lips—I spent five hours shopping for a bathing suit that was flattering without being obscene, that I could afford, and that I might actually wear in public. Thank God it was September and bathing suits were deeply, deeply discounted. Nice Price on Columbus at Eighty-fourth Street had some serious possibilities, with the Bloomingdale's labels still in them. They also had a raw silk jumpsuit in a muted green that goes really well with my red hair and brings out the green in my eyes. My eyes are elusive. Sometimes blue, sometimes green, sometimes gray. They reflect what's around me and what I'm feeling, but they can be influenced by my eyeliner and what I wear. I'd seen the suit at Altman's just a month before for over four hundred dollars and here it was, just $79.95. The only one in green—which was the only good color—was my size. Some would call it fate, some would call it kismet, I put it on my Visa card. Either I was still under

1

my limit or someone, somewhere made a clerical error, and the charge went through. I contemplated getting my hair done, but the tip would have had to be in cash and that left that out. So I did it myself. The weather was good, cool and dry, which meant I could take a bus and save cab fare.

All the time I was doing this, it was not what I wanted to be doing. I wanted to be unraveling the secrets of Beckett. I wanted to be rehearsing Lady Macbeth. I wanted to be on stage as any one of Strindberg's destroyer women.

Advertising agencies do the casting for TV commercials, but they are not really set up for it. At least not from the actor's point of view. The waiting room is usually the lobby by the elevators and the ashtrays. At least that's the way it is at SSB&G. I don't know, but it seems to me that numbers must be important to these people. "Yes, Mr. Jones, we saw 4,852 girls in each category, sir. Had them do the bathing suit competition and the talent test, too. Our L.A. office saw just as many. The report's right here, and we have them on tape." So if it doesn't sell enough sugar or scent or soft drinks, you can blame the actors but you can't blame the agency for not looking hard enough. So there we are, twelve to twenty-five girls in a space designed for four or five, sitting on modern formed-foam almost couches in comfort-free shapes, by the elevators, all of us dressed to kill, the models with their big leather portfolios full of photos and stuff that will prove that they have appeared elsewhere and have money to spend on photos and stuff and all of us with our bags with our change of clothes for other auditions plus our regular pocketbooks with money and bank cards and change and phone books, filofaxes, makeup kits, magazines and paperbacks to pass the time, pads, tampons, emergency deodorant, tissues, brushes, combs, an odd relic from a current boyfriend or husband, and something for courage—the Bible, breath mints, an Est self-realization handbook, a note from our acting teacher, Valium, a joint.

There is no such thing as a dressing room.

There are two choices. One is to wear your bathing suit underneath your street clothes, then strip as part of your audition. The other is to go to the ladies' room.

I chose the latter. There were three girls in there in front of me. Plus two girls from the agency. One was using the toilet. The other was just taking a makeup break. She was using a green eyeliner with brown eyes and a magenta blush over a sallow complexion. It was all wrong for her and I could have told her so, but it's really hard to tell certain things to people, even if it's for their own good. I knew one of the other actors, slightly. A girl named Irene. It had been a year since I'd seen her—that had been in L.A.—but she looked like it might be ten. Don't get me wrong, she didn't look old. Last year she'd been a twenty-two-year-old who looked fourteen, now she was a twenty-three-year-old who looked twenty-eight. She said "hi!" while she checked her makeup in the mirror. I said "hi" back and asked if she was working. She said of course she was, she had to pay the rent. I meant acting and I said so. "It's all acting, isn't it, Annie," she said, giving the line both sting and mystery. Not a great reading, but definitely an intriguing one.

"What's all acting?" I said.

She looked around rapidly, nervously. The other actress had gone and the agency girl working on her makeup was on her way out. There was still a girl in a stall, but Irene decided to risk being caught, or wanted to be caught, or assumed it didn't matter if she was caught. She took out a small bottle of cocaine and snorted from it.

"I didn't think anyone did that anymore," I said. A few years ago it was ubiquitous, like dieting, but by the time I left Los Angeles the two top clubs in town were NarAnon and CA.

She looked at me in my one-piece, critically. "Do you have a scar or something?" she said.

"I do not," I said. My skin is very fair and almost flawless, if you don't count freckles and one very well placed mole.

"Let me show you something," she said. She meant me well and was sincerely trying to be helpful. She was much more impressive than me, up front. As casually as you please she unhooked the top of her bikini and revealed herself. She was not much more bounteously endowed than I was—I am on the slender side, all over. She had pads in the bathing-suit top that pushed her together and made it all seem much bigger. "Boobs in their wild state, never cleavage make," she said and put herself back together.

It was remarkable how many ad agency men had so little else to do that they could be staring out their cubicle doors or hanging out in the corridor to watch while we walked in our suits from the ladies' room to the conference room. Was I the only one who was bothered by it? I like to think not.

There was the Art Director, the Creative Director, the Writer, the Account Executive, the Assistant Account Executive, three Client People, and the Director, who is the person, once he gets on set, who is in charge of doing what all those other people tell him to do. Not that I was given the courtesy of an introduction. I deduced who they were by their wardrobe code. The Art Director didn't wear a jacket and had a shirt with more than two colors in it, the Creative Director used to be arty but now he had a tie, the Writer actually had leather patches on the elbows of a corduroy jacket, the Account Executive had a well-worn Brooks Brothers suit, the Assistant Account Executive had a new Italian-style suit, the Client People had suits that would play in Cincinnati, and the Director had Levis with a knife-edge crease and shined cowboy boots.

"What we see here, we see Summer Fun!" the Art Director said. Even though he had just said this at least thirty times to thirty girls before me, he looked around the room to see if they all thought he was saying it right.

"Youth. Essence of Youth," the Creative Director said with great solemnity.

"Now what I want you to do is pretend that you're in a volleyball game! Having the time of your life! You just love it. You're working up a great sweat in the sunshine and boy oh boy that icy Zest-Time Cola is gonna feel soooo great! Got it?"

I told myself that this was an acting exercise. A sense-memory exercise. That I could truly feel the heat of the sun on my skin, the grit of the sand on my feet. Hear the surf, radios blaring, girls shrieking—fun shrieks—guys cheering. That I could find the one nugget of character that would make the scene real. I tried not to think that I was seminaked—though more dressed than most of the other girls might have been—in a room full of fully dressed men and they didn't really care that I had studied with Vera Vlasova of the Moscow Art Theater, with Jeff Corey, that Geraldine Page had recommended me to play opposite her in *The Trip to Bountiful*, I tried not to think about the cold hard lines of a glass tower and the angular gray leatherette conference room all set for slick business and that this so-called audition was designed for nothing more than to see girls jiggle. And if the guys liked the jiggle, then they would gather around to watch her suck on a bottle.

They had me "play volleyball" facing them, in profile, and facing away.

I'd only been in New York six months, but one of the first things that I'd noticed was that a lot of people are Actually Actors. "Hi, my name is Tod, I'm your waitperson tonight, but I'm *actually an actor*. Our specials tonight are cold braised parrot with a delicate Chablis and prune sauce." "Yes, I work here," the receptionist behind the desk reluctantly admits, "but I'm just a temp. I'm *actually an actor*." Any cab driver who speaks English as a first language is *actually an actor*. That wasn't what I'd come here looking for. I was looking for actors making a living doing Brecht, Vaclav Havel, Sophocles, or New Young Playwrights.

The Willie of Willie's on Tenth, the best old-fashioned saloon in New York, is really Connie Jean Snyder of Peculiar, Missouri, and one of my best friends. Not one of my hundred best friends, one of my three best friends. She's not one of my three best friends just because her place is kind of a home away from home, now that I don't have a home, at least not in the way I used to, not so long ago, or because she is someone that I knew from the West Coast when I came East. She's a friend because she behaves like one. Listening and loyal and caring. Willie is the name she used when she was Actually an Actor. She was quite good, and she's equally good as a saloon keeper and hostess, and her place reminds people a lot of the way they thought New York would be when they saw it in a movie.

Willie greeted me with a big hug and a kiss, a

"Whatchya been doin'?" and a "Ya want somethin' to eat? Or to drink?"

"Just a glass of seltzer," I said, as if I merely had a mild thirst, dust in my throat from the debris in the air in the city, not as if my case of poverty had finally become terminal.

"Oh, bull!" Willie said as she sat me down at a table. "I have a really good split pea soup today, with Virginia ham. Then you should have some shrimp with saffron rice. And a beer. Beer is good for you, it's got a lot of those B vitamins."

"I'm not really hungry," I said, salivating.

"How are you, Annie, honey!" Andrew said. He's a Willie's waitperson who's Actually an Actor but shouldn't be. He should be a Working Actor. He's good. He gave me a kiss on the cheek.

"Andrew, you look wonderful," I said.

"I have got to thank you," Andrew said.

"Get her a beer and a soup and the shrimp special—it's on the house," Willie said.

Andrew sat down. "I got a call-back, actually I have two this week, but one of them is for 'Forever and Ever.' " I had helped him prepare his audition and I was happy for him, in spite of the experience I had just had with Zest-Time Cola. "The other is for a dinner theater in Tampa. It's a rep company concept," he said, dead-pan, "alternating *Hello, Dolly!* with *Taming of the Shrew.* Both in one-hour versions."

"Who are you, the shrew?" Willie said.

Andrew ignored her. "They loved me, those 'Forever and Ever' people. I had just the quality of insidious evil which they were seeking, they said."

"What's the part?" Willie asked.

"A sly killer from a Middle Eastern country to be named later."

"Like Iraq or Iran," I said.

"Like Libya or Lebanon," Andrew said, "depending on who's the bad guy on the news the week my character's place of origin is revealed. 'Forever and Ever' is *très au courant*, tackling the issues of the day, in a soapy way, and *très* proud of it."

"Bad guys are good," I said.

"You're perfect for it," Willie said. "Back stabbing and betrayal. The same qualities I look for in a waiter." She wasn't afraid of losing him, even though he was popular and reliable; there was an eternal line of Actually Actors ready to take his place.

"What I did was, I played it really appealing. Sort of seductive. Instead of one of those ranting, raving Middle East fanatic-type killers. Which is what *you* told me to do," Andrew said, giving me credit where credit was due. "They loved it.

"If I get it, and if America's consumers, those women who actually buy America's diapers, like me as Rasheed Rashad Abdullah, I will turn out to be the long-lost bastard son of Beaumont Ridley, that's the old guy who made his millions in oil. I am back for revenge because he abandoned my mother to the ravages of the Ayatollah, who had her publicly whipped and stripped for the crime of lifting her veil for a sip of anisette while wearing Western dress, a lovely light gold frock from Valentino. Of course if I am really loved by the Huggies and Luvs crowd, then it will turn out that Ridley didn't know about me, I will forgive him, we will be reconciled, my contract will be renewed for a year, and I will turn into a good guy."

"They told you all this?" Willie asked him, surprised. The future of soap plots are closely guarded secrets.

"Did you ever see a soap opera that didn't happen

8

that way?" He stood up. "At the dinner theater," he said to me, "I'm up for Petruchio, the lead, or Grummio, the comic servant. If I'm Grummio, the comic servant, I also have to move sets and work as a cocktail waitress between shows. Let me get you some sustenance."

"I'm going back to acting," Willie said. "There's an agent been coming in here, he used to be with CAA, he's dying to take me on. Once things settle down," she said, like she's been saying for years since she opened the place, "and I have some free time, I'm going to do it. Ted tells me I look better than ever. What do you think?"

What does one say to an actor? True or false, one says, "Better than ever."

Andrew was back before I realized he'd gone. He put down my soup and a basket of warm French bread. "How'd *your* audition go?"

"A cattle call," I said. "It's not about acting. It's about being a type. Today they wanted a T and A type."

"They should've called me," Willie said. She has a very impressive figure and was either born to or cultivated a very Marilyn Monroe persona, the breathy voice and curves that wiggle standing still. The bartender yelled over the din of voices and the beat of the jukebox that there was a phone call for her. "Gotta go," she said. A customer signaled for Andrew. He shrugged and went back to earning a living. Suddenly I was alone. I began to eat my soup. It was my first food since breakfast the day before.

When the soup disappeared I felt even more alone than before. I was totally broke. I had subway fare home, one credit card at the limit, one over, my rent due in a week, and thirty-seven cents in my bank account.

I was not going to look backward and wish that I still had a husband. Or a lover. That I was still with my

Los Angeles friends. That I still had the career I had back there, where I hardly ever had to audition or play the get-an-agent game and if a job didn't show up I had a spouse to cover the cash-flow problem.

I had given myself six months to restart my career. Actually, I knew that was about the farthest I could stretch my savings and residuals. It was time to face facts. It hadn't happened. For the first time in my life I was going to have to become Actually an Actor.

The question was as what? Actors need jobs that don't tie them down, that they can leave for an hour for an audition or a meeting, that they can leave for a month for a part, that they can leave forever as soon as they get the chance. I have no objection to hard work, but I did not want to be a waitress, office temp, bartender, house cleaner, or dog walker. I know perfectly well that there are other things some girls do to get by. Just enough to keep them in rent, meals, clothes, acting school, and makeup. I cast no aspersions, but that sort of arrangement is not for me.

I grew up in a small New England town with narrow horizons and little imagination. I went to Catholic school and to church every Sunday and made up sins to confess: "Father forgive me, I know I have sinned, it has been three hours since my last confession, I had two inpure thoughts." Actually I got to impure thoughts very late and even now I don't have them nearly as often as I think other people must, judging from some of the soap operas I have auditioned for.

I started going out with Patrick when I was fifteen— he was a year ahead of me at St. Mary's—and married him when I was twenty. We stayed married for eleven years. Even though we moved to Los Angeles and I worked quite a bit in *the business*, and many of my dearest friends were drug-enjoying, adulterous, debauched sophisticates, I remained, in many ways, the girl the nuns raised.

The best I can say of my married years is that they barely aged me. They left my complexion clear and my face without those little worry lines that drove so many of my friends to cosmetic surgery. Of course it may just be because I stayed out of the sun.

The worst I can say is that I did not find a very civilized and elegant way to break up my marriage.

But at least and at last I was on my own.

Andrew brought the shrimp. The sauce was rich and savory, buttery and spicy. It didn't make me feel less alone.

The people who had departed from the table next to mine had left a *Metropolitan* magazine behind. I picked it up to keep me company with my meal. I started with the theater reviews, then went on to the movie reviews.

When I finished eating I blew a good-bye kiss to a very busy Willie. I took the magazine with me to read in bed. I decided to walk home and left my last dollar on the table as a tip for Andrew.

The lead article in *Metro* magazine was about a couple who spent a lot of money. It promised to tell how much they spent and what they spent it on. The article after that was "Private Dick, *Metro* Style!" by Guido Pellegra, who did a lot of the cop, crime, and Mafia coverage for *Metro*. He always told a lively story, perhaps a little too colorful to be true, but who reads *Metro* for truth, people read *Metro* to know what to buy and where to eat.

The story was about "Duke" DeNobili, ex-cop turned P.I. According to Pellegra he had single-handed, using his own methods, solved some of New York's biggest and best crimes. Then he retired. Pellegra didn't say exactly why. Now he worked for Middle Eastern bank-

rs, flamboyant corporate raiders, and on the kind of
livorces that make millionaire lawyers. He was also
ery good-looking and had excellent, if somewhat
ashy, taste in clothes.

Somehow, I knew that this was the perfect job. I
gured out what I would say to him. I woke up three
imes in the night practicing my lines. The next morn-
ng I called.

"Mr. DeNobili," I said when I got through his recep-
ionist, "I just read all about you in *Metro* magazine and
am very impressed. I would like to work for you. I'm
n actress. I'm very good with disguises and accents. I
an walk down the street to be seen and I can walk
own the street and never be seen."

"Lissen, lady, dat's really nice," Duke said. "All de
uys dat work fuh me, dey been on the force for twen'y
ears, you know what I'm sayin'. What I'm talkin' 'bout,
m talking 'bout experience. You got a carry permit?"
m not being entirely fair to Duke, his accent wasn't
iat thick. But his attitude was.

"Well, if you ever have a case where you could use a
oman, I would very much like to be considered," I
iid. "I think there must be circumstances where a
oman might be more useful than a man. Following a
oman into an all-woman's health club, for example.
r interviewing another woman."

"An actress," he said, in speculative tones.

"Yes," I said. I gave it a little throat, to sound like
ie sort of girl who would create cleavage on demand.
Let me give you my number, and you give it some
iought."

His other lines were ringing. "Yeah, yeah, I'll give it
ome thought," he said. But he sounded like a man of
tion, not a ruminator.

Yes," I said, "we know the libertine's philosophy. Always ignore the consequences to the woman."

"The consequences, yes, they justify her fierce grip of the man," Ralph said, looking at me with those wonderful eyes. His eyes are Paul Newman blue. "But surely you do not call that attachment a sentimental one. As well call the policeman's attachment to his prisoner a love relation."

"I don't believe a word you're saying," I said, frustrated. I live in a brownstone. Ralph lives above me—to be specific, right over my kitchen—on the top floor.

"Is that in the script?" he said, easily bewildered.

"No," I said, harsh where I should be gentle.

"Then I think you're being a little harsh," he said.

Ralph had come to me for help. He wanted to get into a good acting class. That meant he needed a monologue to audition with. I was trying to find him one and then coach him through it. I was working on George Bernard Shaw's *Saint Joan* for myself, so I went to Shaw's *Man and Superman* for Ralph. If it was proving a little complex for him the mistake was mine. How was I to explain that to him without being more hurtful? Fortunately, the phone rang.

I said hello and Duke said "You ready to work?" It was three days after I'd called him.

"When did you have in mind?"

"Tonight," he said.

"Uh, what time tonight?"

"Seven o'clock," he said.

I looked at the clock. It said 5:10. I didn't know what the job was about. I didn't know anything about being a detective. I wondered what sort of training I was supposed to have. Didn't they have a trainee period? What about a license? A gun? A carry permit? There was so much to know. "What should I wear?" I asked him.

"Listen," he said, "this is easy. You go up Lexington, Seventy-seventh Street, that's 1191 Lex. You meet a guy there, name Sonny, that's Sonny Gandolfo. You'll recognize him, he looks like an ex-cop. Can't miss him. You introduce yourself. He'll tell you what to do. You got that?"

"Yes Mr. DeNobili," I said.

"I'll come by myself, I get a chance, maybe, check you out, understand? Just call me the Duke."

"Fine."

"One more thing, with the client, act like you been doin' this a long time, like you know what you're doin'. Tell 'em you been with the department or somethin'."

I couldn't do that, it would be a lie. "I'll take care of it," I said.

"I'll give you fifteen dollars an hour," Duke said.

"Fifteen," I said, impressed, but my line reading must've confused him because he started explaining why it was so little.

"A reg'lar guy, he gets twen'y. But he's got a lotta things going for him. First off, he's got twen'y years on the force. He's got his own gun, you gotta gun?"

"No," I said. And never would, thank you very much. Guns hurt people!

"So, they get the A scale, you get the B scale. I think that's pretty good."

"That's fine, Duke," I said.

Duke hung up. I had less than an hour to dress and get ready. Ignoring Ralph, who sat on the floor staring at his copy of *Man and Superman*, I flung open my meager closet. I always start at the bottom. I pushed my clothes back and looked for shoes.

"My first day as a detective," I said to Ralph, "and I don't have a clue what to wear." My (relatively) new lizard-look pumps from Fausto Santini (Rome) caught my eye.

"Not heels!" Ralph exclaimed. "Not if there's going to be a chase scene!"

"It's not a movie," I said. But he had a point, heels were out if I had to follow someone rapidly on foot. Comfortable shoes.

"Oh, not a movie," Ralph said. "What? A pilot?"

"Dress, skirt, slacks, or jeans?" I said. "Suppose I have to wait outside, like Gene Hackman in *The French Connection*, and it's drizzling and windy and chilly and I have nothing to eat but slimy old pizza? Not a skirt. Definitely not a skirt. But what if I'm smarter than Gene and go into the restaurant to watch the heroin traffickers? Do big-time narcotics dealers eat in places where jeans are acceptable?"

"Is this just an audition, or do you have the part?" Ralph asked.

"What sort of blouse?" I asked, holding up a print. Even as I put it in front of me, I realized it was much too busy.

"Are you doing a 'Cagney and Lacey' thing, or are they looking for a 'Charlie's Angels' bit?"

"This is real life, buster," I said.

"It's what?" Ralph said.

I chose my blue suede boots. They have a low heel, they're comfortable, and they dress up my jeans a lot, particularly since I have a belt that (almost) matches. A really good blouse from Bendel's, simple, white, 100 percent cotton. The thing for outerwear was a trench-coat, a good one, old, soft, and wrinkled, with years of mystery in it. Since I didn't have one, I selected my Canadian-army surplus overcoat. It's a dark teal blue. I got it for $10 when I was doing a movie of the week that shot in Manitoba because it was financed with Canadian tax write-offs.

I went into the bedroom to change, not that Ralph would have been interested. New York women are always complaining, and their complaint is that all the good men are already married and all the good-*looking* ones are gay. Ralph is very handsome indeed.

"It's what?" he called from the living room.

"It's a job. To pay the rent."

"You mean you've already got the part," he said, thinking he understood.

"No. I'm really going to be a real detective, like when someone goes out to be a waiter and they go to a restaurant, they take orders, serve food and collect the checks and all of that, and they're really a waiter."

"Oh," Ralph said.

"What should I do with my hair?" I said. There really wasn't time to do much so I decided to just brush it out.

"I didn't know you were a detective," Ralph said.

"I wasn't," I said. "But now I am."

"How can that be? That can't be."

"Well, it is," I said, and gave him a steely glance. It

seemed to work—I am a very good actress—and he believed me.

"How do you know what to do?"

"How many years of improvs have I done? How many roles have I played?" I said. "If there's a part, I can play it."

"But this is real life!" he said.

"All the better," I said, and it suddenly occurred to me that it might be true. I also realized that wearing my hair down was not working. I am a redhead and my hair is long—it was just too flamboyant for following people. So I put it up and put a hat on, a beret. Jewelry? Simple hoop earrings. I put on my favorite bracelet, a Navajo piece, silver and turquoise. I wanted to make a good impression. But what makes a good impression on a cop named Sonny Gandolfo or a dick named Duke DeNobili?

At which point I realized that I didn't have subway fare, let alone cab fare. Plus I had to have something to eat or I was going to faint. The adzuki beans and rice were gone.

"Ralph," I said, "please, please, please can you loan me ten dollars so I can get to work, I'll pay you as soon as I get paid."

"You really have this," he said, cautiously, "it's not just a call-back or something?"

"It's a job, Ralph, and I'm just asking for ten dollars."

"I only have five," he said, "but it's yours."

So I got a slice of pizza, just like Gene Hackman, took a bus, and had $2.50 left over.

Duke was right. Sonny looked so exactly like an ex-cop that I did recognize him instantly.

I said, "Are you Sonny?" I was trying to figure out

what the elements were that made his identity so clear. It's details like that that make good acting. He was big, but that wasn't it. He wore a lot of heavy jewelry, rings, bracelet, watch, gold chain. Great character lines in his face. Actually great character lines come from cigarettes. That's an important beauty tip—not smoking, over the course of a lifetime, is worth at least fifty facials and five lifts. But none of that was it.

"Yes," he said, looking me over. He looked a little doubtful. "You the actress?" What a voice! Bass rolling with the gravel of 21,900 packs of Marlboro and double shots of whiskey, beer chasers.

"Annie McGrogan," I said and held out my hand for a handshake. He enveloped it in a large, heavy paw.

"You carryin'?" he asked.

"Nah," I said, "the Duke didn't say I should be carryin'."

"No problem," he said. "Let's get going." He turned around into the lobby of 1191 Lex. I followed him. There are two classes of luxury buildings in New York, prewar and postwar. The war referred to is WW II. Before it, they built places like the Dakota, the famous bastion on Central Park West at Seventy-second Street where Yoko Ono and Lauren Bacall live. Those buildings have large rooms, high ceilings, big windows, eat-in kitchens, thick walls and floors, wood trim. They at least resemble the apartments in old movies about swank New York. After the war they lowered the ceilings, thinned the walls, made the kitchens strictly utilitarian, and eliminated the maid's room. The ultimate result is something like Trump Tower, in which you can buy a multimillion dollar apartment and still hear your neighbors' private functions. Most of the "new" luxury apartment buildings are on the East Side of Manhattan. This one was typical. It had a doorman and a deskman in a lobby with marble paneling on the walls and a copper sculpture oxidizing artistically green. It had one couch and two armchairs in a pit, where people you were willing to go out with but you wouldn't let in your apartment could wait. Sonny strolled in like he belonged there, like he belonged anywhere. I followed him. The doorman and the deskman, they got it too.

"Detective Gandolfo, to see Mrs. Hoffman," he said.

The deskman called upstairs. Sonny looked at him like he knew the guy was running some kind of racket. Making book or selling reefer. "Go right up," the deskman said, "It's twenty-eight B. Top floor."

In the elevator Sonny said to me: "We're just baby-sitting."

"OK," I said, like I knew what he was talking about.

There were only four apartments on 28. The walls around the elevator were paneled and there were two oil paintings hanging. They looked like originals. Old, but not very good. Fifty dollars apiece at auction in Saugerties. Not very much for a painting, but a lot for something that you hang where it could be stolen. One was a fox-hunting scene, the other was an old woman at an old window.

Sonny rang the bell. The door opened instantly. A black woman stood there.

"Detective Gandolfo and Detective McGrogan," Sonny said. Detective McGrogan! I had just been introduced as *Detective* McGrogan. If I treated it as an improv I could pull it off. Jeff Corey always said, "Be intuitive. There are no rules outside the artist. Freely associate."

"Very good," she said. "I'll tell Ms. Hoffman you're here." She showed us in. The apartment looked like it had been done by a set designer doing "a rich woman's apartment" on a soap opera. A moment later the lady of the house arrived.

"I'm so glad you got here," she said. But it wasn't Ms. Hoffman. It was Lucinda Merrill, better known as Shanna McWarren, star of "Forever and Ever." As big as Susan Lucci (Erica) on "All My Children," Marcie Walker on "Santa Barbara," or Conan Geary on "General Hospital." She had a look, and it was unmistakable, a daytime Veronica Lake, straight blond hair down over one eye, a slinky body with poses lifted from early Lauren Bacall. What saved the persona from being a flat and obvious bit was that her features projected a sort of sweetness, even innocence underneath, like a grade-school girl playing vamp. She could pass for thirty in full sunlight but real time gave her at least another ten years. The best that money could buy kept her young.

"Seven o'clock," Sonny said, looking at his thick gold watch.

"Oh, but I worry so." She spoke in character. Shanna McWarren was the (aging) kittenish vixen who always desperately wanted some man, did whatever it took to get him, always got him, then got rid of him. But that wasn't her fault, a contented couple is the end of a story line. Consummation in a soap opera is the start of divorce. No one wants to watch happiness.

"Can I go now, Ms. Hoffman?" the black woman said.

The mistress of the house said: "Yes, Sheila. Thank you for waiting. I hope your little boy won't mind."

"No, ma'am, that's all right," Sheila said. Impenetrable tones, sincere or obedient, I couldn't say. She picked up a rather drab cloth coat and made her way out behind us. The coat looked vaguely familiar. I searched my memory. I was with a gaggle of girls in a road company of *Idiot's Delight* for three weeks. There was not very much to do in the afternoon and four out of seven of them were fans of "Forever and Ever" so whoever's room you went into, that was what seemed to be on, and they gossiped more about the video sex lives than their own. At that time there was an extended sequence in which Shanna McWarren lost her wallet, her wardrobe, and her mind, one of those amnesia stories in which the character takes up a blue-collar life that is beneath her and has to dress down. That was the source of the coat.

Lucinda "Shanna McWarren" Merrill Hoffman turned her gaze on me. I gazed back. I did not humiliate myself, as so many others of my profession might, by announcing that I too was in the profession and instantly trying to ingratiate myself in hopes of getting a role. I already had a role and I was playing it. I took my cue from Sonny, who stood there like he just didn't give a damn. "Oh, you look very young," our client said.

"She knows what she's doing," Sonny said. He said that about me! I was thrilled. In my entire life, no man had ever lied for me so soon after meeting me.

"I didn't mean to imply that she didn't," Ms. Hoffman-Merrill-McWarren said. "It's just that, just that I do take these threats seriously."

"Yes, ma'am," Sonny said.

"And you will be here all night?"

"Yes, ma'am."

"Someone must be watching the door at all times." She pointed to the door we had come in by. "No one is to go in or out."

"Out, ma'am?"

"You know what I mean, I'm a little frantic. I'm sorry. There's plenty of coffee in the kitchen. Sheila already made you a pot. There's also sandwiches. The guest bathroom is there," she pointed. "I shall be in my rooms. If you need me."

"Mrs. Hoffman," Sonny said, "is there a Mr. Hoffman who might come home?"

"Yes, there is a Mr. Hoffman. And he might come home." She said it sadly. "If he does, you may let him enter."

"Got it."

"But make him show his driver's license or his passport first." She delivered the line like it was the zinger—a hurt that could not be repressed—and Sonny was Camera One.

"Is there any other way in," Sonny said, "besides this door?"

"No," Ms. Hoffman said. "Unless someone comes down from the roof on a rope."

"Yes, ma'am," Sonny said. "The only way up there, it's locked and padlocked."

"You checked that?"

"Duke did."

"I guess everything's all right then. You will be careful won't you?"

"Yes, we will," Sonny said.

"I hope you're comfortable, and if there is anything . . ." She brushed her hair away from her face and looked lonely. "Good night."

"Good night," Sonny said.

That's how I spent my first night as a detective. Sitting in a luxury apartment on the East Side, eating sandwiches, drinking coffee and San Pellegrino, shooting the breeze with Sonny Gandolfo, and watching a door that never once opened.

CHAPTER THREE

S o you're an actress, huh?" Duke said, looking me over. "What've I seen you in?" I hate that question. Fortunately, he didn't seem to expect an answer. "You know, you don't look like an actress. I mean you don't look like I expect an actress to look."

I suspected that what he expected an actress to look like was my friend Willie doing her Marilyn Monroe thing. "I can change my look, change my voice, that's why I think I could be a good detective. I bet I could make myself so different you could pass me on the street in five minutes and you wouldn't recognize me. Without makeup or anything. I read in the article that you did that."

"Yeah, when I was a detective, did that all the time. So, whaddaya think, you think I'd make a good actor? If they made a movie of me, you think I could play myself?"

"Clearly, there's no one like you," I said.

"Yeah, you think so?" he said, taking it as a powerful compliment. "The Duke thinks so too. You want to know why they call me the Duke?"

Yes, I did, in a rather general, it-can-wait kind of way. What I really wanted to know was how soon he would pay me and whether he wanted me to work again.

"What happened was this," he said, his pinkie ring flashing. His suit cost over a thousand dollars. More to the point, it *looked* like it cost over a thousand dollars. His style sense was the same as that of John Gotti, the current godfather, known in the press as "the dapper don." "When I was in anticrime, that's plainclothes but not yet detective, it's like them having you doing detective work but you don't get the title or the extra pay grade. We get a call on this shooting, up 113th Street, in the Two-Five, that's Spanish Harlem, mostly. Once it was all Italian, you know that? There's only two blocks still Italian, up by Rao's, you ever eat in Rao's?"

The phone rang. The bartender answered it. It was for the Duke.

"Stay right there, the Duke'll be right witcha," Duke said to me. He took his drink with him. If it wasn't Scotch it was the color of Scotch, in a short thick glass. "Thanks, Tommy," he said to the bartender. "Give her something to drink, whatcha drinking, doll?"

"Just a Perrier," I said.

"You don' want a real drink? Go ahead, it's on me," Duke said.

"I don't drink," I said.

"Whaddaya mean you don't drink? I don't trust people who don't drink."

"I don't drink often," I said. If I say I don't drink at all people assume I have a problem.

"Get yourself something to eat. . . . Tommy, give her a menu and make sure she orders something," which meant, I decided, that he liked me and was willing for it to be all right that I didn't drink, so long as we could bond by him buying me something. He took the phone and wrapped himself away from us.

Although he had an office—I could tell from the 718 area code and the accent of his secretary that it was in

Queens—the Duke ran his business and his life out of
the Stuyvesant Room, a bar and restaurant in the Hotel
Renssalaer on Forty-fourth Street, between Fifth and
Sixth avenues, near the Algonquin. It was a colorful
joint. He looked at his watch. I couldn't make out the
brand name but it was very thin and very gold, while
the band was very thick and very gold. Guido Pellegra
had portrayed him as double tough, tougher than
leather, Rambo in the raw. He was skinnier than I
expected. Younger and more mercurial too. Where
Sonny had lines and shadows and time etched all over
him, Duke's face was smooth, almost bland, except for
a Roman nose and an air of good cheer about him,
which didn't fit the tough-cop reputation and saved him
from being homely.

"How about a burger?" Tommy said to me, "or a
steak?"

"Something a little lighter," I said.

"Get the chicken-salad platter," Tommy said, "very
nutritious, but light on the calories and your polyun-
saturated fats. I can see that you're a health-conscious
person, I'm that way myself." He drank vodka and
cranberry juice, nursing it very slowly.

"How'd you like Sonny," Duke said when he came
back to the table.

"I liked Sonny," I said, and I had, more than anyone
I'd met in a long time.

"All the women like Sonny, he's got something, just
don't do your liking on the job."

"I don't like him that way," I said. I didn't think I
did. I certainly thought that if we were working together
it would be much better if I did not. Though I could see
how another woman might. I could definitely see that.

"He's a good guy. He was up the Two-Five."

"Uh-huh," I said, like I knew what a Two-Five was.

"It's funny, once you been in the same precinct with a guy, it's like you know him for the rest of your life. . . ."

That's what a Two-Five was. Cop talk for the Twenty-fifth precinct. I carefully stashed that information in my male-bonding file.

"So we were out on this man with a gun call when suddenly this naked woman comes running out in front of the car. Her . . ." He tried to think of a polite word. ". . . she's big and everything is bouncin' around. She's also bleeding. She's bleeding so much she's leaving footprints. So I slam on the brakes and I jump out of the car and go to help her. My partner starts to call it in then he suddenly yells, 'Watch your back!' I'm going after this big bouncin' bleedin' woman and he's yelling 'Watch your back!' So I turn around and there is this big, big colored guy. Six two, six three, maybe two-hunnert-fifty-sixty pounds. Barefoot. This's February. I didn't tell you this's February. So I know the guy, he's flying on something. His feet, they're not touchin' the ground, 'cause if they're touchin' the ground, he's got frostbite and he's gonna stop and say 'Oh bay-bee, i's col' outside, Ize goin' home.' But this is not what he's sayin'. He's wavin' a chopping knife, like from a kitchen, chop vegetables, about this long, and he's sayin' 'Get outs mah way, white meat, or I cuts you to the bone!' The woman's screamin' 'He mean it, he mean it. He mean. He crazy, Lord Jesus he'p me!'

" 'Get the woman,' I say to my partner. My partner screams, 'I'll take him out, get out of the way,' he's got his thirty-eight out and he's in the stance like they teach at the academy.

" 'You can't touch me,' this guy screams, 'cause I'm the King. De King of 111th Street!' And he roars. I swear to God, this guy he roars, like he's a fuckin' lion.

" 'Now, let's be calm,' I tell him, like he's gonna

listen, which he's not but I gotta try, 'cause I'm a cop and that's my job, to keep the peace not to blow people away, which is still what my partner wants to do. 'Everybody calm down,' I say and I say 'Put down the knife, just put down the knife.' And I start to walk toward him, slow, like I'm not afraid of nothin'. I'm wearing a vest 'cause we were goin' to a shooting. But I don't have no idea if a vest is any good against a knife. I hope it is, but I don't know.

" 'You can't touch me,' he says, but I got him mesmerized. 'I'm the King of 111th Street. You can't touch the King.'

" 'Yes, I can,' I say, moving closer, watching that big, big knife. 'I'm the only one allowed to touch the King.'

" 'How's that, you 'llowed to touch the King.'

" 'I'm allowed 'cause I'm'—and now I'm right up close to him—' 'cause I'm the Duke of Earl.' Believe it or not, he starts to think about that. When they're on drugs all kinds of weirdness happens in the brain. Boom, I pop him one." He flexed and pointed at his arm. When I touched it I realized that there was a tree inside his thousand-dollar Mafioso suit. "I put everything I had into it. He just stood there like it hadn't happened. So I did it again. He looked at me. 'The Duke of Earl, huh,' he says. And then he falls over. Straight down, like inna cartoon.

"So after that, any time I wanted to do something, my partner, he says, 'He's allowed, 'cause he's the Duke of Earl.' You know what precincts are like, pretty soon everybody, they call me Duke of Earl, then just the Duke."

A waiter in a hotel uniform appeared from somewhere far away with my chicken salad platter and a steak platter for Duke. Both dishes were plentiful. Duke's steak was thick, the sort that Dr. Hubert used to

make on his backyard barbecue when I was a little girl.
The Huberts were the richest family around, which in
the time and place I came from meant that they drove
a Buick, had enough bedrooms for each of three children, and got sirloin from the butcher instead of ground
chuck from the A&P. Duke's plate had a slice of purple
onion, a slice of tomato, lettuce, and ketchup. There
was a pile of french fries and a pickle on the side. He ate
very fastidiously, cutting off small pieces with a knife
and fork. I tasted my chicken salad and was pleased to
find that it seemed very recent, the celery still crisp and
the mayonnaise not yet congealed. It too had a full
garnishment of vegetables. I'm normally rather indiffer-
ent to food. But I was still in this so-poor-I-was-going-
hungry phase, and the sights and scents of nourishment
were making a much more vivid impression than they
usually did.

"McGrogan?" he said. "That's what, an Irish
name?"

"Yes," I said.

"Lots of cops are Irish, you got any cops in your
family?"

"I have a cousin of my mother's who was with the
state police," I said, wondering if having blood relations
with law enforcement was a qualification. "Up in Mas-
sachusetts."

"So you ain't from here?" Duke said.

"Actually I was born in New York."

"Uh-huh."

"But I grew up in New England."

"I been up in New England," he said. "Nice there in
the autumn, the trees and everything, up in Vermont. I
been up to Maine, too, moose hunting," I must have let
something show on my face. "But don't worry, I didn't
kill nothing. I don't even kill people."

"Oh, that's good to hear," I said. "So I grew up in a small town, it was mostly Irish and Slavic. I went to Catholic school."

"Yeah, me too."

"You're Catholic?"

"Nuns and everything. You have nuns and everything?"

"Yes," I said expressively. I felt we were bonding.

"Nuns! I'd rather be out in the street, rousting crack dealers. Nuns are tough."

"And mean," I said.

"Yeah," he said. "But that discipline, I guess it's good for kids. A kid, he's been to nun school, he's gonna make something of himself. He's gonna get in the department, get a job, something. Even if he becomes a criminal, he's more likely to become like organized crime, not just street trash."

"You could say that," I said.

Two young women dressed in a provocative manner entered the bar. They looked to Tommy. Tommy gave them a look that sent them over to a corner table where two businessmen sat drinking. One of the women recognized Duke and waved to him. He waved back.

"Ya see what's going on?" Duke asked me.

"Yes, I think so," I said. "They work through Tommy."

"They're very high-class girls," Duke said. "They're hookers, but high-class. You got an astute eye."

The Duke got another call at the bar. I knew one of the girls, not even her name, just to say "hi" to if we sat down next to each other at an audition. Or maybe she just looked like the one I knew. The man she was sitting next to was squeezing her knee. Actually his hand was way above her knee. I turned my attention back to my chicken salad platter.

"You ever serve a subpoena?" Duke said to me when he got back to the table.

"No," I said.

"It's easy," he said. "Here's the thing, legally, what you got to do, you gotta say their name and then you gotta touch the person with the subpoena. You go up to the guy, you say something, 'Mr. Joe Loser, this is for you,' something like that. Maybe they don't want to take it. Your job is you got to touch them with it, then it don't matter it drops on the ground, it gets swept away in a tornado, nothing.

"We don't do no sewer service, you gotta really serve the person. Then you write it up in your report, when, where, how you made the identification, any special circumstances. I don't want it to come out sometime later they can prove they were in Cleveland when you say you were serving them on Twen'y-eighth Street. It doesn't matter how long it takes. You get paid by the hour, I get paid by the hour, I tell the lawyer, the lawyer gets it from the client, *capisce?*"

"I understand," I said, deducing that that was what *capisce* meant.

"I gotta stay here and meet some people. But I got a subpoena needs service. Jump in a cab, you go up to Steely, Birnbaum, Needham and Dan, two forty-seven Madison Avenue, twenty-second floor, you see Nancy Binken, she's a lady lawyer, you tell her you're my operative, you get all the details and the paper from her. You got any problems, you call me here, on my beeper, or on the car phone."

"Wait a second while I write this down," I said, scratching in my bag for a pen and paper.

"Another thing, you get a notebook, you write everything down, what you do, where you go, so you can always refer to it later. You get up on the stand, nobody

remembers what the . . ."—he deleted the f-word—
"what they was doing on April twenty-second, 1986, so
they look at the book. Don't forget the date and all other
salient information. You can use the same book, keep
track of your expenses."

"Uh, about expenses . . ."

"You short? You need some money?"

"Well, maybe if, for last night . . ."

"That was what, seven in the P.M. to eight in the A.M.,
that's thirteen hours at fifteen, that $195. Any ex-
penses?"

"Not really, just one subway fare. Sonny gave me a
ride home."

He took a big roll out of his pocket. He peeled off two
$100 bills. "Normally you send me a bill, I mail you a
check."

"I'll get change," I said. I owed him $3.75.

"Get outta here," he said, incredulous, but pleased,
I think, that I'd at least suggested it.

I had two hundred dollars in my pocket where minutes ago I had none. Where the day before I hadn't even
had prospects. With the promise of more to come. This
was rent. This was food. I was ecstatic. Of course I
didn't let it show.

CHAPTER FOUR

After I introduced myself to the receptionist at Steely, Birnbaum, Needham & Dan I expected someone to yell "cut." Time to get out of there and move to the next camera setup. Why film the ten minutes I spent sitting in the waiting room?

After my meeting with Nancy Binken I expected an overweight woman with pinched eyes to say "thank you very much, next" and to discover that it was only an audition and the part had been cast on the coast with Whoopi Goldberg.

The subpoena was addressed to a lawyer, who I shall call Syd Shyster, in the financial district. Ms. Binken, an obviously intelligent type, and very pleasant for an attorney, warned me that Shyster was a very elusive person well practiced in the avoidance of paper.

Downstairs I called information from a pay phone, then called for Mr. Shyster. His secretary wanted to know what it was about. I said that my aunt was dying and had requested that a will be drawn. Naturally the secretary wanted to schedule me for some time in the succeeding year. But I said "You don't understand, when I say she's dying I mean she's at it right now. Knowing my aunt, she won't rush things, but I don't think it can take much longer than two or three days. The estate, I'm told, is very considerable and I must get back to her side and if Mr. Shyster can't do it today then I simply must find someone else." The receptionist put me through to Mr. Shyster. I repeated it all over again, just as one must in reality, and he told me to come right over in a very kindly greedy manner. I did a less than honest thing. I estimated what a cab would cost, wrote that down in my book, and took a subway.

I arrived very close to my appointment time and Mr. Shyster saw me right away. I acted quite distressed, though businesslike. "You are Sydney Shyster," I said when we got into his office.

"Yes, yes, I am," he said.

"Here are the papers," I said, holding out the subpoena and additional documents. When he put his hand on them I said, "These are for you."

"Huh?" he said as I got up to leave.

"You have been served," I said, fumbling to open his door, afraid he would get really, really angry and even violent. He had what is called a choleric complexion.

"You mean it was all a ruse?"

"Yes," I said.

Then I expected Uta Hagen, waving her cigarette around, smoke curling up, its odor infecting everything, to step out and say "not a bad improvisation, but . . ." with a list of things I had done less creatively than she would have done.

None of that happened. No "cut," no curtain call, no "don't call us, we'll call you," no critique. It was all real. No one even suggested that I was acting. Such was the quality of my performance that I easily passed for real in the real world. That's what acting is supposed to be about, exactly the quality that casting directors didn't seem to understand.

What I didn't know was that much drama had already happened and more was to come. Almost immediately.

I called Ms. Binken at Steely, Birnbaum, Needham & Dan to tell her that her papers had been served. "So quickly," she said, and sounded pleasantly surprised. "There is a message here for you," she added, "to call Mr. DeNobili. I don't normally handle messages but he said this was particularly urgent. He said he would be at one of these numbers," and she really did begrudge giving out four of them—his office, car phone, the Stuyvesant Room, and one I didn't know at all—as if she really were a secretary, not someone who had been in the 99th percentile in all her tests all her life and had put in many hours to take advantage of her gifts rather than indulge herself in mere clothes, boys, and cosmetic surgery.

I found Duke at the fourth number. Another law firm, Zimmerman, Robert and Petty. He was in with Mr. Petty and I was, he said, to rush right over. So much employment, so quickly. I felt like a taxi with its meter clicking.

Duke was with senior partner Petty, an otherwise lean and cadaverous man who had jowly cheeks, and a Detective Witte, a wide man of middle age who wore off-the-rack suits from Bonds that failed to conceal his shoulder holster and who was dying for a smoke.

Sonny was also there. He was the only one who looked relaxed. So far, I had never seen him look or sound otherwise.

"I wanna talk to her alone," Witte said. I suspected that I was the object of the pronoun since I was the only female in the room.

"You got an attitude," Duke said to Witte.

"Youse ain't a cop no more, DeNobili," Witte said. "So youse should be buttin' out. This is department business now."

"I'm more a cop off the force than you are on it," Duke said.

"Youse was a grandstanding asshole when youse was in de department and youse is an even bigger one now."

"Hey, there's a lady present," the Duke said.

"Oh, excuse me," Witte said. He faced me with a mocking bow. "A princess who has never hoid that woid."

"I certainly wouldn't use it in public," I said.

Sonny broke out in a smirk. He popped a True out of his pack.

"Oh no, not here, you mustn't," Mr. Petty said.

"That's a stupid fuckin' rule," Sonny said, and got up and started to leave.

"Wait a damn minute," Witte said, "I ain't tru wid you."

Sonny ignored him and kept walking. The testosterone level rose all around the room. These cops, ex or not, were very masculine animals, eager for an excuse to butt horns and lock antlers, snort and stomp. Mr. Petty, a lawyer, a man of rules and reason, spoke up. "We have a smoking lounge," he said. "Past the receptionist and turn left. It used to be a storage closet, but we expanded it and added an exhaust fan." It was an effective intrusion and once he saw how much control he could exercise, he went on. "I think it would be perfectly proper for Detective Witte to interview . . . Ms. McGrogan is it?" I nodded yes. "Ms. McGrogan alone, provided we tape-record the interview and I am present."

"That OK with you, McGrogan?" Duke said.

"Whatever you say, Duke," I said, acting cool but

assuming the end had finally come, I was about to be unmasked and the show would fold.

"OK," he said and left the room.

My stomach turned over. Had I ever faced a tougher audience? One less willing to suspend disbelief? One more eager to find fault? Yes, and yes again, I told myself.

"Sit right here, Ms. McGrogan," Mr. Petty said.

"Thank you, Mr. Petty."

"No smokin', stupid-ass rule," Witte mumbled to himself, his fingers twitching to the pocket where he had his pack. "Awright, McGrogan," he growled, "let's talk about . . ."

"Shouldn't we start and date the tape before we begin," Mr. Petty said.

"Sure, sure," Witte said.

Someone once said that "theater is life with the dull parts left out." Legal proceedings are the parts of life that are left over when the good stuff gets taken out for the theater. Soap opera is the only form of drama that moves slower than real time, and even soaps move quicker than depositions. We recorded the time, date, address, full names and titles of those present, and, once we began, we did the same for anything else under discussion.

He asked how I had spent the previous night.

"On an assignment from Duke DeNobili," I said. I figured that the less I said the less likely I was to unmask myself.

"What was that assignment?"

"To meet Detective Gandolfo and do what he told me to."

"To meet him where?"

"At 1191 Lexington Avenue."

"What's that? A store, an apartment house, a what?"

"An apartment house."

"At what time were you supposed to meet him?"

"At seven P.M."

"At what time did you meet him?"

"At seven P.M."

"Very prompt, aren't you?"

"Yes," I said.

And so it went. In the door, announced by the concierge, to the elevator, push the button, in the elevator, push the button, up the elevator, ringing the doorbell, admitted by a woman later referred to as Sheila who appeared to be a housekeeper. Why did she appear to be a housekeeper? Clothing, general style, manner of address between her and the apartment's occupant. She left shortly thereafter.

"Who else was in the house?"

"Lucinda Merrill," I said.

"Lucinda Merrill Hoffman," Mr. Petty said.

"Is this person personally known to you?" Witte asked.

"No."

"How did you identify this person?"

"She is known to me as an actress who plays a character on an ongoing television series which I have seen."

"Which television series?"

" 'Forever and Ever'," I said.

"That's what's referred to as a soap opera?"

"Yes."

"You feel you could identify this person with certainty?"

"Yes."

"You could not be mistaken?"

"I don't think so."

"You don't think so, or you could not?"

"I think what Ms. McGrogan means," Mr. Petty said, coming to my rescue, "is that she could identify Mrs. Hoffman with a reasonable degree of certainty."

"Exactly."

"But not total absolute certainty," Witte said.

"Is there such a thing?" Mr. Petty said.

Witte grunted. He thought. "How long did you have to observe her? The alleged Mrs. Hoffman?"

"Several minutes," I said.

"At what distance?"

"At about the same distance that I am from you."

"That's about three feet," Mr. Petty said.

"Did you converse with Mrs. Hoffman?"

"Yes," I said.

"For how long?"

"A few minutes."

"Did this help in your identification of Mrs. Hoffman?" Mr. Petty asked.

"Yes."

"Very much?" Mr. Petty asked. Lucinda Merrill Hoffman has a very distinctive voice. It's one of the things that has made her a star in a theatrical form that is populated largely by generics whose looks, accents, voices, and wardrobes are largely interchangeable.

"Yes."

"Do you feel you could have identified her by voice alone?"

"Yes," I said.

Mr. Petty gave Witte a look that was both smug and prim. Witte gave him a look back that said 'youse ain't fazed me yet' and resumed control over the questioning. Now he wanted to know if I was there all night. I said I was. Did I leave at any time? No. Not for this, not for that, not for the other. Did I fall asleep? Did Mr. Gandolfo fall asleep? Did we leave the room? Did we engage in any other activity that might have distracted us?

"No," I said.

"A man and a woman alone, all night, everything they want right there, a fully stocked bar . . ."

I said nothing.

"Well, what about it," Witte said.

"What about what?"

"You and Gandolfo alone," he sneered.

"I beg your pardon, is that a question?" Wow, I was cool.

"No. It didn't seem to be a question," Mr. Petty said.

"All right, I'll ask a question," Witte said. "Was youse and Gandolfo messin' around?"

"What do you mean by messin' around?" Mr. Petty said, getting into the swing of things and showing more spirit, in a very dry and sly way, than I would have credited him with. "Do you mean finger painting?"

"Was youse playing sex games or havin' sexual intercourse?" Witte said. Having been forced to be explicit he seemed doubly offensive.

"I am offended," I said.

"So you should be, and so am I," Mr. Petty said. "This is what I would call sexual harassment."

"I'm just tryin' to find out if the bimbo was payin' attention to her job."

"Let me ask you this," the gallant Mr. Petty said, leaping to my defense in his lawyerly way. "Would you have asked the question of Mr. DeNobili had he been on duty with Mr. Gandolfo?"

"No, but . . ."

"Or of myself," Mr. Petty said.

"No."

"I think you owe Ms. McGrogan an apology . . ." A

beat, a beat, none forthcoming. ". . . rather than force me to file a complaint."

A beat. A swallow. A twitch. A wish for a cigarette—Detective Witte made his feelings utterly obvious even in silence. A great quality in an actor. Probably not in a cop. "I coulda I guess . . ." A furrowing of brows—oh I had to remember all of this. ". . . I coulda been overstepping the bounds."

"Very good. I think that's acceptable, don't you, Ms. McGrogan?" Mr. Petty said.

"Adequate," I said, dry and terse.

"Continue," Mr. Petty said.

"What I was getting at, did you ever have such a distraction that someone coulda left the apartment wid out youse knowin'?"

"No."

"Absolutely positive?"

"Yes."

"You never left the room?"

"I did leave the room," I said.

"Hah!" he said. "How often?"

"Once," I said.

"For how long?"

"About three minutes," I said.

"Where did you go?"

"To the bathroom."

"What did you do there?"

"Oh, come on," Mr. Petty said. "What does one do in the bathroom that takes about three minutes?"

"That," I said, "and freshened my lipstick."

"What did Mr. Gandolfo do when you were out of the room?"

"I don't know," I said.

"Did he ever leave the room?"

"Three times," I said.

"Where did he go?"

"Twice to the bathroom, once to the kitchen."

"Did you ever leave the room when Mr. Gandolfo was gone?"

"No," I said.

"Anything else?" Mr. Petty said. Witte paused. He did the series of twitches and furrows that signified thought, then set his face in a way that showed determination and decisiveness. Here it comes, I thought. He's going to ask me how long I've been a detective. How much experience did I have? Where did I train? Did I have references?

"Make sure you're available," he said. "I might want to talk to you again."

"What was that about?" I asked Mr. Petty when Witte was gone.

Duke burst in. Sonny ambled in. "How'd it go?" Duke asked.

"Ms. McGrogan was an excellent witness," the lawyer said. Witness? "She testifies very well."

"I told ya," Duke said. "When you get Duke Investigations you get only the best. Well-trained professionals, every one."

"Yeah," Sonny said.

"Her testimony matches with yours," Mr. Petty said to Sonny.

"That's what happens when you tell the truth," Sonny said. If what he had told me during the night we spent at Lucinda Merrill's about his relationships with women was any guide, Sonny and veracity were strangers to each other. Still, the way he chimed in had a comradely ring to it.

Whatever it was, everyone seemed pleased and satisfied. I was dying to ask Duke if I could bill for this testimony, though I was sure I could, which meant I could start acting classes again. There was a teacher named Ellie Renfield who I'd heard wonderful things about.

"Alas, poor Artie," Mr. Petty said, "I knew him well."

Mr. Petty, who seemed such a pedantic person, had misquoted. It was a famous speech and I knew it well. It's from *Hamlet*. Most people don't know that for years it was a favorite part for famous female performers. Sarah Siddons. Ellen Terry. I longed to do it. On a major stage. *'Alas, poor Yorick!'* Hamlet says, holding up the skull of his late court jester, having stumbled upon it while in search of morbid sentiments in a cemetery. *'I knew him, Horatio. A fellow of infinite jest, of most excellent fancy; he hath borne me on his back a thousand times; and now, how abhorred in my imagination it is! My gorge rises at it. Here hung those lips that I have kissed'*—not a homosexual reference but one of affection from an earthier, more physical age—*'I know not how oft. Where be your gibes now? your gambols? your songs? your flashes of merriment, that were wont to set the table on a roar? Not one now, to mock your own grinning? Quite chap-fallen? Now get you to my lady's chamber, and tell her, let her paint an inch thick, to this favour she must come; make her laugh at that.'* I did not correct Mr. Petty.

"Yeah, tough break," Duke said.

"Will you need me anymore?" I asked. I wondered who had died.

"Mrs. Hoffman is particularly concerned with her security," Mr. Petty said, "now that Mr. Hoffman is dead. We should definitely continue."

"It's her husband who's 'poor Artie?' Who's dead?" I blurted out.

"Yeah," Sonny said, "he got whacked last night."

"Oh," I said.

"We're her alibi," Sonny said.

"Not that she needs one," Mr. Petty said. "Although criminal law is far from my field, I understand that in murders the spouse is rather automatically considered a suspect. Am I not correct, Mr. DeNobili?"

"Absolutely," he said. "It's dope, money, or love. In all my years on the force, I tell you one thing, I never heard of no hit where the butler done it."

CHAPTER FIVE

I barely had time to go home, eat a light dinner of salad and chocolate, spend an hour in the bath—bath time is very important, it's where I read scripts and make my best phone calls—before I had to hop back out, select a wardrobe, dress and do my makeup, run downstairs, and catch a cab back to the East Side. I picked up all the papers, the *Post* and the *News* and the *Times*, and browsed through them while the driver crossed Central Park.

Mr. Hoffman's death had made no impression on the media. No one had put it together that he was Mr. Lucinda Merrill, husband of famed soap star. In and of itself there was nothing else in the manner of his passing, as it was initially observed, that made it newsworthy in a year of New York violence. Ordinary murders did not get tabloid space or tape at eleven. That was reserved for children shot by accident, interracial assaults, murder that included child abuse, or body segments found in separate boroughs. When the press did get one of those, they dwelt on it, lived in it, lavished us with details, reflected on it, doted on it so long as it might be worth a single ratings point. That was one of the reasons that when the nine-inch black-and-white television that came with my apartment, abandoned by the previous tenant, sputtered, crackled, then whimpered its long life away, I did not replace it.

The bereaved and fearful widow, Lucinda Merrill Hoffman, wore black.

And looked good in it. There's nothing wrong with a woman looking her best on all occasions. I would want to do as well if I had a husband who died.

"I can't tell you how glad I am that you are here," she said to the two of us. "I don't want to be alone. Frankly, I'm frightened. I love my fans. I adore my fans, it is our fans, after all who make us what we are, but sometimes they are . . . obsessive. Obsessive . . ." She dwelt on the word, savoring its flavoring, then gave a little shiver. I had seen her do the same sound and gesture—I don't remember if the actual word was the same or different—when she was Shanna McWarren swearing undying desire to Drake or Deke or Donald, someone, at any rate, with hard, masculine consonants in his soap opera name. There is nothing wrong with using the same expression for disparate circumstances. The genius Russian director and film theoretician Eisenstein had a classic experiment that he presented to his film students to explain his Theory of Montage—the idea that when the filmmaker puts two images next to each other the audience fills in the relationship between them. He used footage of a great actor responding to the sight of a mother playing with a young baby, then he showed the actor responding to the murder of a child on the Odessa steps, one of the classic scenes in cinema history. The students responded, always, by raving about the brilliance and range of the performer who could bring such depth of response to such different events. Eisenstein then revealed that the actor's two different "responses" were the same piece of film. The audience filled in the space—invented the relationship—between the two, and it was the audience who imparted meaning to the actor's expression. This helps to explain why some of our biggest stars have been created out of our blankest faces.

". . . Obsessive," she said. "I get letters, you know. Of course it's good to get letters. They tell us how we are doing. It's a sincere measure of our popularity. In daytime television the audience is involved. They live our lives with us. They thrill with us, cry with us, laugh with us, hurt with us. And they tell us about it. We, in turn, respond to them.

"But it can reach extremes, excesses. As you know."

"Yeah, sure," Sonny said.

"As we know?" I queried.

"Yes. The letters. Surely you saw the letters: 'If you seduce Jason, there will be a price to pay!' Well, I can't help it if I seduce Jason. That's the story line. That's the writers' decision. Of course he can't help but respond to me. Men do. It's not beauty alone. The pretty young thing who plays his pure little bride, Jennifer McGuffin, she certainly can be beautiful, when she works on it. But she doesn't have anything more than that going for her. Look at her name. A name to whimper with. It's not nice to criticize someone for their name, if it's their given name, but our names are something we choose, like our hair color, so we had better be prepared to stand by them! I think her real name is Quatroccochi. That would be more interesting. Of course no one can spell it."

"Q-U-A-T-R-O . . ." Sonny proceeded to spell it. Apparently correctly. Both Lucinda Merrill Hoffman and I watched in awe.

"My," the widow Hoffman said.

"There was some Quatroccochi brothers up in the Two-Three . . ."

A blank look passed across Lucinda's face.

"Twenty-third precinct," I said knowledgeably.

". . . three of them, if I remember. They cut up a guy. They were loan sharks, and some guy was coming into what they thought was their territory. A Rican, you know, the neighborhood was changing."

"East Harlem," I said, with just a hint of New York streetwise inflection.

"They cut 'im up, you know," Sonny said, "and put his head on a post. Somebody had a wrought-iron fence kind of thing, front of a brownstone, where the end part, it was just right for putting somebody's head. One of them had read a book or seen something like it in the movies, nah, it musta been a movie, I can't see no Quatroccochi reading a book. We busted all three of them for it anyways. So I spent a year it seemed like writing Quatroccochi on arrest reports."

"I see," Lucinda said. "How . . . exotic."

"Nah, it was messy. Stinking too. They didn't put that head up there fresh, it was ripe."

I would have gagged, but as a fellow detective I was used to that sort of thing. Lucinda seemed charmed by it. "As police officers you must see such terrible, terrible things," she said.

"That's the job," Sonny said casually. Oh, when machismo was called for, these guys strutted sitting down, John Wayne and Clint Eastwood barely had a clue. I mentally recorded his gravelly nonchalance and stored it for future reference. "You handle what you gotta handle, even spelling."

"I haven't seen the letters," I said.

"Oh, they are dreadful," Lucinda said. "Some fan out there is in love with Blair Cambridge. That's who the McGuffin girl plays. Do you watch daytime?" she asked Sonny.

"I go to the track," Sonny said.

"There is usually an ingenue. Someone very young, very blond, very blank. We replace them every twelve to eighteen months. Interchangeable actresses with little character and little ability except being able to read a teleprompter without the camera catching the movement of their eyeballs. Our current one is the McGuffin girl." Although she was putting down another actor from her show, it wasn't offensive, it was simply vivid. Because of her animal vitality, which may have been the quality that made her different from her younger competitor. It was like watching Maggie the cat from Tennessee Williams's *Cat on a Hot Tin Roof*. "She is to be married to Jason. We have a big wedding planned. I am helping. I love weddings. The ritual, the ceremony, the sheer celebration of life."

"On the show?" Sonny asked.

"Weddings are great for ratings. I am rattling on. Excuse me for rattling on. It helps if I talk about something." She took a breath. "Jason has been eyeing me. Covert glances. An unreciprocated but understandable fascination. Someone mentions it to McGuffin, who replies, not realizing that I can overhear her, 'Oh no, Jason could never be interested in someone that old!'

"Well! No one hands a challenge like that to Shanna McWarren and lives to tell the tale. . . ." Lucinda's character, if I remember correctly, had arrived some ten or fifteen years before as a wild young femme fatale, home wrecker extraordinaire. She'd come from the wrong side of the tracks. But soaps do, in their own peculiar way, provide for upward mobility. There are two ways a girl can rise in the world of Daytime; discover she is the daughter of someone better born or lift herself up by her own bra straps. Shanna had been permitted both—she married up, to Euclid's second-richest man, and then it was discovered that she was actually his unknown daughter. Lucinda had had several other husbands, several almost husbands, a multitude of affairs, loves, crushes, and flirtations. "I am going to have that young man before wedding bells ring. Though knowing what a mad, passionate, romantic creature I am, I may just fall in love with him and have to steal him away totally, completely. And make him mine."

"I know exactly what you mean," Sonny said.

"It has generated a lot of mail," Lucinda/Shanna said.

"I can see where it would," Sonny said.

"My affairs always generate more mail than others. But this time there is someone out there who is taking things too seriously. An anonymous creature who wants Blair and Jason to succeed at all costs. In the letters 'all costs' is written in all capitals. Do you think . . . do you think . . ." Overcome, she sat, she sighed, she gathered her strength and her courage. "Do you think they could have struck at Arthur, poor Arthur, poor dear Arthur, as a way of striking at Shanna? Could it be that when they saw that I was safe behind the wall of your protection, and security at the studio, that they struck instead at my beloved, at my cherished husband?"

"You never know," Sonny said.

Lucinda/Shanna sat very still. Moisture welled in her eyes. A single tear formed in her right eye. When it fell it sort of banked off her nose before finding a path down her cheek. I suspected she was wearing Ernst Lazlo's No Tears mascara. That's what I use when I want to cry without my makeup running.

"What should I do?" she said to Sonny. "What should I do?"

"About the letters?"

"About . . ." She took a very significant pause, big enough to contain 'dying hand' gesture number four. ". . . everything."

"The police should have the letters," Sonny said.

"They do. My lawyer, Lester Petty, has seen to it. Also security at the studio has copies."

"That's good," Sonny said.

"I thought you had seen them."

"Can I get you something to drink," Sonny said.

"Yes, thank you. He will be missed. Oh how I will miss him. Whatever will I do without him?"

"Gin and tonic?" Sonny said.

"Vodka tonic," she said.

"Perrier with a twist," I said.

He made Lucinda's drink and forgot mine. I didn't mind. She took it and looked up at him through thick Max Factor real-mink #7 eyelashes. "We loved each other. Oh, of course we had our problems. My incredible success, the excitement generated by stardom, not to mention the financial rewards, all that put a stress on our togetherness. But still."

"You should get some rest," Sonny said.

"Yes, I guess I should. I'll try to sleep. I don't know if I can. The shock."

"Yeah, it's tough," Sonny said.

"You know what I would like to do," she said, "is go away somewhere and just break down and cry. Not worry about how bloodshot my eyes get, not care about how I dress . . ." She played all this just as she would have if it had been the scene for Tuesday's episode. That included sending a message that what this crying bit really needed was a man's shoulder, that not caring about how she dressed meant something close to un-dressed, and that the real cure for grief was consum-mation. Was it conscious? Was it a tease? Was it habit?

Was it real? I didn't know, but it certainly was obvious, and Sonny ate it up. ". . . That's what I feel like and that's what Arthur deserves. But that's the one luxury I can't afford."

She took her drink and, elegant in black, slid off to her bedroom, from where, I was certain, she could look out at the cold but glamorous glitter of the city lights spread as far as the eye could see, below her.

Alone with me, Sonny sipped his drink, a big hand with two big rings on it around the glass. "Whaddaya think? You think she's comin' on to me?"

"I don't know," I said. "I know so little about that. I'm realizing it now. I was never part of the dating scene. Or even the coming-on scene. I was with the same guy for fifteen years."

"Jesus Christ, my life is already too damn complicated. Caren is talking about coming up this weekend." That was his girlfriend in Miami. She was Lithuanian and a psychiatrist. "But it's Mercedes's birthday Saturday." That was his girlfriend in Jersey City. She was Puerto Rican. A social worker. "Maybe I'll say the hell with all of them and go out and spend the weekend with Sonny Jay." That was Sonny Jr., his son. Sonny had two children. The other was a girl. They lived with their mother on Staten Island. She and Sonny were not divorced. Nor were they married, in any real sense, except in the eyes of the Church. And of any of the other women who might be thinking of marrying him.

"How do you feel about all that?" I asked him. I too was an Adulterer. But when I did it, it tore me all to pieces. I felt like I had a scarlet A imprinted front and back, like a sandwich board, a badge of shame for all the world to see. A sort of beacon that would draw nuns from all over who would then surround and scold me. That never actually happened, but I was sure it would.

"How do I feel about it? Well, I think I should go see the kid. Throw a football around. Get outside, fresh air and sunshine, you know. That would be a good thing. If I'm with one of the girls, we'll spend the whole time indoors."

"Yeah," I said. "That's a consideration."

"The truth is," Sonny said, philosophically, "is that I'm not a real ambitious-type person, not like the Duke. When I was in the department, I did my job, but I didn't have to be no sergeant or lieutenant or put in for a citation every time I popped a hype with a nickel bag. I was just a cop. Now that I'm a private eye, I don't take that so serious either. You do your job, you watch out for your friends, you collect your check." He was very thoughtful. And serious. "But everybody's got to have something they're really about, you know what I mean? You know what it is I am, Annie—I'm a Lover."

Andrew got the part on "Forever and Ever."

His character called himself Jim, short for James Allan Earl. But that was a lie, a cover, a deception. He was really an Arab fanatic, agent of the mad dictator Mommar Hareem. Andrew had guessed wrong about the name. It was not Rasheed Rashad Abdullah, but Ali Abdul Mohammed. In one story line, rumor had it, Mommar not only tortured clean-cut Westerners from Euclid, he did it in drag. But on the set of a soap that struck too close to home, and Mommar was to be portrayed merely as a mad-dog raving loon. Jim's immediate aim was to ingratiate himself with oil millionaire Beaumont Ridley, earning a position of trust so that he could steal his money, ruin his reputation, seduce his daughter, sell his wife into white slavery, and turn his dogs in to the ASPCA for violations of the leash law.

For anyone unfamiliar with daytime television, this last, in particular, might sound apocryphal, but "Forever and Ever" prided itself on being the soap with real children and real animals. Both of which constantly upstaged the adult humans. They were notorious throughout the acting community for it. Beaumont, for example, had a matched pair of Chesapeake Bay retriev-

ers, large, beige, obnoxious dogs. As with Lassies and
Rin Tin Tins, there were actually many dogs who played
the parts through the years. One of them, a neutered
male named Chester, now thankfully retired, regularly
received more fan mail than any single two-legger on
the show. Neither the infants or the animals could read
teleprompters and they both caused delays, the 'real'
children more than the canines, which put the adult
humans under additional pressure to make up for the
downtime.

Beaumont loved his retrievers. Andrew, as Jim aka
Ali Abdul, was planning to remove their tags and then
have them sent to the pound. There would be a long and
tension-filled search—would BR find his beloved pets
before they were put to sleep? This would drive Beaumont to the edge of madness and distract him from
Jim/Ali Abdul's other plot to steal back his inheritance.

Willie decided to throw a party for Andrew. I said
that a good party required a theme. She agreed and we
decided to rent burnooses for everyone. The question
was what time? I wanted to do it early so that I could
come. She wanted to do it late so that actor friends
appearing onstage could drop in after the final curtain.
As all our friends are in the theatrical community, this
sounded like a good idea. But when we went through
the list we discovered that we didn't know a single
person who was actually working in a show in New York
City. There were people in commercials, on soaps, on
stages out of town, in industrial shows, in movies,
made-for-TV movies, on sitcoms, kid shows, prime time,
HBO, cable, and public access, but not *treading the
boards* in the Big Apple. I didn't know how to take that:
should I hope that it said more about the state of theater
in New York these days than it did about our friends, or
did I prefer to think that it was just our circle that

couldn't cut it and there still was a theater, alive and well, capable of providing employment?

So the party started after lunch, around three, and ran, officially, until Willie's on Tenth started serving dinner at five. Willie provided food and a keg of beer. I thought that was very, very generous. She claimed that the party people would end up staying and spending far more than she was investing. I think she said that because she was a woman and had to prove she was doing things out of a sound business sense rather than sentiment and caring.

The talk was all of acting, agents, and auditions. Of parts to be had, almost had, had until the show-film-pilot got canceled. I ran into Irene. She'd had a call-back for Zest-Time Cola.

"Great, congratulations," I said. I don't have a dog-in-the-manger attitude about parts I don't really want. If I'm going to be envious of another actor I'll save it for Glenda Jackson doing Lady Macbeth on Broadway.

"Yeah, right," she said with a twist to her lip and a bitter tone.

"Well, call-backs are always encouraging," I said, trying to make her feel good. "Even if you don't ultimately get the part. It says something. That you're at least standing out from the crowd. It means they're paying attention and they'll think of you next time."

"You're such a goddamn goody-two-shoes," Irene said.

"What does that mean?"

"You know what I was called back for?"

"What?"

She shoved her breasts together in a very crude and angry gesture, doing what the shoulder pads in her bikini had done at the audition. "One of the client guys wanted to put his face in them."

"Oh," I said.

"So the call-back was a crock. So I went out with him."

"Did he take you anywhere expensive?"

"He feeds me the usual line. They have a bunch more spots coming down the pipe. That's the way he talks, I swear to God. 'We got a bunch more of these here com-mer-ci-als a-comin' down the pipe!'" She switched to a high-pitched voice. "Oh golly gee Mr. Zesty-Time, this little girl is so impressed! Would you like me to play with your pipe! Would that help my chances?" She switched back to a semibass and the client's hoo-ray hick talk. "'Well hey hey, honey, if you think you're woman enough for Big Jim. That's what my wife calls it, Biiiggg Jim.'"

"Isn't it great," I said. "About Andrew. And 'Forever and Ever.'" I didn't want to hear her story.

"Well, you know what . . ."

"Some people look down on soaps," I said. "But for Andrew, it's perfect."

". . . Big Jim turned out to be li'l dickie-wickie and he di'n't wanna come out and play. Oh-noey-noey. So Mr. Zesty-Time, he blames-wamesy you know who! So instead of being *on track* for all the commercials coming *down the pipe*, Irene baby won't even get called to the *starting gate*. . . . Why do we do it?"

I don't! is what my brain said. If they want me as an actor to act, that's fine. But that's all. Fortunately, all that my mouth said was, "I'm sorry."

"What the hell," Irene said. "It's great about Andrew."

"Isn't it," I said, relieved that she had finally changed subjects along with me.

"Seven hundred dollars per show. To start. You appear three times a week. Twenty-one hundred a week!

That's a hundred thousand a year! Imagine making that much money and you only have to deal with men's fictional dysfunctions, instead of their real ones."

"Are you taking any classes?" I asked.

"Just aerobics," she said, not realizing she was pushing one of my very few buttons.

"I meant acting," I said.

"Keeping the old bod in shape. Younger ones are coming up every year. Thank God it's not L.A. at least. Out there they think you're over the hill when you reach puberty."

"There's Andrew," I said. "I have to go say a few words to him."

"You know, I know someone on that show," Irene said.

"That's nice," I said. "Excuse me."

"Actually I know the *husband* of someone on that show." She made the word husband a double entendre. "Lucinda Merrill's husband."

"Oh really." I stopped in my tracks.

"What a kinky little soap that is."

"Oh really," I said, for the first time anxious to hear about Irene's personal life.

"Ex-cuse me," she said, "there is Dominick Griff." Irene straightened up, readjusted her cleavage, and went straight for him. Dominick was Andrew's agent. Not a great agent, a little fluttery and given to hysteria, but not bad either. Although Andrew got the part through his own talent, hard work, good luck—with perhaps a gentle helping hand from myself—it was assumed that the Power of the Agent had scored for him.

Dudley Craig, a tall and gangling actor I knew from L.A., greeted me fulsomely. His real name was Craig Dudley but a Craig Dudley was already registered with Equity—the union tracks stage names and there is only one of anything allowed, no matter how real your real name is, you can't have it if someone else signed up for it first—so he reversed it. The truth was he was more a Dudley than a Craig anyway. His problem was that he had not yet acknowledged that and always saw himself as a romantic lead when he was more castable as a comic sidekick.

"Annie, darling," he cried, and embraced me. "You look younger than ever. So slender. So girlish."

"Dudley, when did you get to New York?" I gushed. I wondered how Irene knew the late Arthur Hoffman.

"Just this week, just this week! It's so vigorous! And . . ." (sotto voce) ". . . so filthy."

"The air is better than L.A.," I said. Since I'd been here longer, it was up to me to defend the city. What did Irene mean, 'kinky'?

"The streets are garbage heaps," he said.

"In L.A. you never see the streets, you'd have to get out of your car first."

"Oh guess what?!"

"What?"

"Rowdy is coming to New York," Dudley announced.

"Oh," I said. Rowdy Randolph was the event, if not the reason, that caused me to leave my husband. The pain and the confusion of what followed certainly had a lot to do with my move from the West Coast to the East Coast. It was not just a search for Theater and Art. Even I knew that.

"He's doing an MOW."

He does a lot of movies of the week. Right after I left my husband to go to Rowdy, Rowdy left me to do an MOW. In Minnesota.

"Won't it be great to see him again," Dudley said.

Now there was an interesting question.

I'd done that before. Seen him again, that is. After

that Minnesota business, I left. For a long time. To clear my head. Then I decided to give it, him, a chance to redeem himself.

The idea that everyone in a profession is the same is as narrow-minded as saying that race determines character. I'm sure that there are women of taste and intelligence who want to spend their lives watching themselves doing disco calisthenics in front of wall mirrors. It's possible to have a mental age of over fourteen and really like neon colors that clash. And not every female who wears Lycra for pleasure is a bimbo.

But opening the door of the cute little house in the canyon that was supposed to be our love nest and seeing Tanya with the tawny hair working on her routine for the class she taught at Voigt's on La Cienega has left me with a serious distaste for any form of organized exercise that includes loud music. "It's a cop picture, Rowdy plays a New York City detective. One of those real tough streetwise types."

"Oh yeah," I said.

"He's so good at that," Dudley said, a little enviously.

"It's great to see you in New York," I said. I was watching Dominick and Irene. Dominick was flushed and sweating. Not in a way that had anything to do with Irene. Some sort of fever perhaps, and I had a very sad thought. He excused himself from her and I excused myself from Dudley. Irene headed for the bar so I went there too. My path crossed Andrew's.

"If this thing . . ." Andrew crossed his fingers and knocked on wood. ". . . lasts more than two weeks, I am going to put some money down on an old heap and we will go to the country to look at trees and grass and other genuine nature things."

"I'd love it," I said.

"What a great party. I love Willie for it. It almost makes it worth it being her *slave* all these months. These dreadful months."

"She's great," I said.

"Yeah, she is," he said. "You are too. I bet the burnooses were your idea. God, we all look silly in them."

"Not you," I said. "You look like Peter O'Toole in *Lawrence of Arabia*."

"Epic? Or like I enjoy flagellation?"

"Positively epic," I said.

He kissed me on the cheek and I gave his hand a squeeze, then I finally got past him and to Irene. Some of Willie's real customers had started to come in. Mostly men, some of them construction workers from the Javits Center. Four guys were hitting on Irene and two more turned to me when I arrived.

"What'll you have, sweetheart?" a beefy guy with beer breath said to me. He flexed and sucked in his gut, but it still hung over his belt. Nonetheless, it was a polite enough offer.

"Perrier," I said.

"Have a real drink," he said.

"With a twist," I said, and moved passed him to Irene.

"Hi, Annie," Irene said. "Guys, this is my friend Annie. Her red hair is real . . ."—big pause, comic timing—". . . I'm told." It got some hearty male chuckles and a few looks of prurient interest.

"How well do you know Artie?" I asked her.

"Oh, well enough."

"Irene, baby, here's your drink," one of the guys said. "You had dinner yet? I'm gonna sit down, have-a-bite, whyn't you join me?"

"Maybe," Irene said. "If I don't get a better offer."

His friends all laughed at that.

"You'll have to tell me about it some time," I said.

"Huh?"

"About Artie, Artie Hoffman."

"Oh, Annie, you didn't go out with him, not with Artie Hoffman?"

The real Annie was aghast at the thought. Would have been aghast at the thought even if I hadn't known he was dead. He was married and I have never ever done that. And somehow the picture I had in my head of him was not a very appealing one. But Annie McGrogan, girl detective, said, "Well . . ."

"Here's your Perrier with a twist," beer gut said.

"Oh, thank you," I said.

"I can't see you and him . . ." Irene said to me.

"Why not?" I asked her.

"I thought you were Saint Joan, right? Aren't you the one that thinks acting is Art? Real capital A stuff."

"Hey, there's a table free," the guy said to Irene. She looked him over. He had very dated sideburns, a clean, pressed shirt, a tolerable tie, clean fingernails. "How about it?"

"Yeah," Irene said, "I'll be with you in a minute."

"How about you and me make it a double date," beer gut who'd bought me the Perrier said.

"No, thanks," I said.

"What're you, too good for me?" he said.

"Irene," I said, "what's with Artie?"

She leaned over to me and spoke to me like a sister out of a bad dream, "Hey, everyone is entitled to a little kink. Everyone's a little bent, right? But some people it gets out of hand. You know what I mean?"

"No," I said. I didn't.

"You are *such* a goddamn goody-two-shoes," she laughed.

"Am I really?" I asked her. "And is that bad?"

"What's the matter? I asked you . . ." beer gut said, shoving his way between us, ". . . are you too good for me?"

"Guido," Willie said, with a voice as stern as professional dominatrix, "leave my friend alone."

"I was on'y talking to her."

"Don't be obnoxious," Willie said.

"Aww, Willie," he said, "why you call me Guido? My name's Frances."

"Have another beer and be good," she said.

"Thanks, Willie," I said. Irene was heading for a table with the guy who had dated sideburns. The clock over the bar said six-thirty, and I was due on the Upper East Side by seven. To baby-sit the widow Hoffman whose husband had been too kinky.

CHAPTER SEVEN

I t was bound to happen.

Someone connected the otherwise obscure killing to the celebrity wife.

Once the story hit, it appeared everywhere. The *Post*, the *Daily News*, the *New York Times*, the "Six O'Clock Report," "Action News," "Live at Five," and the rest.

REAL-LIFE DRAMA FOR SOAP STAR!

FOREVER AND EVER, DEATH OFF CAMERA

WHO KILLED MISTER LUCINDA MERRILL?

The only odd thing about it was where the story broke.

It broke in *Soap Opera Digest*. This is a magazine that calls an actor "daring" if he moves from "One Life to Live" to "Days of Our Lives." This is a magazine that knows that the characters the actors play are more significant than anything that could happen in reality. Finding actual news in *Soap Opera Digest* is like looking for truth in campaign commercials. In fact, they stopped the presses and reprinted the cover to get it.

This at least raised the suspicion that the story was

deliberately leaked in the hope of raising the ratings. Which it did. Immediately and dramatically.

Before the story broke:	After:
1. The Young and the Restless	1. The Young and the Restless
2. General Hospital	2. General Hospital
3. As the World Turns	3. As the World Turns
4. Days of Our Lives	4. Days of Our Lives
5. All My Children	5. All My Children
6. Bold and Beautiful	6. *Forever and Ever*
7. One Life to Live	7. Bold and Beautiful
8. Guiding Light	8. One Life to Live
9. *Forever and Ever*	9. Guiding Light
10. Another World	10. Another World
11. Loving	11. Loving

I learned more from the papers than I had on the job.

I found out that Mr. Hoffman had been shot twice. Once through the heart and once through the head. None of the neighbors had heard a shot. This led to speculation that a silencer was used, inferring that it was "a pro job," "a mob hit," "a contract whack," "a rubout." On the other hand, it might have meant that the neighbors did not want to get involved and only *said* they heard nothing.

Mr. Hoffman had died in his *other* apartment. It was, depending on who one read, a pied-à-terre, his private digs, that special flat for entertaining, charming, a luxury one-bedroom, rundown, a walk-up, a rent-controlled dive, an East Side love nest in the Seventies.

In spite of the way the apartment was characterized, there was no specific woman or women mentioned in the story. Or man. Nor did the media talk about a woman who was not there who was wanted by the police. Maybe Arthur Hoffman just needed a place to read or cook things that were off his wife's diet. Things are seldom what they seem.

In the meantime: we were off the case.

I've seen the scene a hundred times. The police detective tells Rockford: "You're off the case!" The Captain tells Starsky and Hutch: "Orders from the top— you're off the case!" The Chief tells Baretta: "You're off the case!" The wimpy guys tells Kojak: "You're not just off the case, there is no case, now stay away from it!" The Deputy Chief tells Clint Eastwood: "Harry, you're off this case, if I see you near this case, I'll have your badge!" Cybill Shepherd tells Bruce Willis: "We're off this case!"

And it always means the same thing! They're on the case. And getting close!

It wasn't like that. Nobody said a word. One day we were protecting this woman who wore widow's weeds so well. The next day we weren't.

Did I know why? No. Did anyone discuss it with me? No. Did anyone warn me not to pursue it on my own, not to stick my nose in other people's business, did they ask, 'Stay out, peeper, this is police business now?'" No. Once again, I was struck by the reality of it all. Speaking as an actor, I would say that in real life the dialogue is generally better, but plotting and story line are nonexistent.

I wasn't fired. I knew that, because Duke used me on other jobs. I did a couple more subpoenas, then he called me to do a surveillance.

"Is it with Sonny?" I asked.

"Nah, goddamn Sonny, I made a big mistake with Sonny."

"What was that?"

"I paid 'im everything I owed him," Duke said.

"Oh," I said.

"You give Sonny too much money, he goes to the track and I lose him."

"How much time can he spend at the track?"

"You don't go to the track?" Duke asked me.

"No," I said.

"Well, this time of the year, you go to the track, you go to Hialeah. That's in Miami," Duke said. "So you'll work wid Dominic, that's Dom Mazzelli. Meet him at Fifty-five East Eighty-third Street. He'll probably be in his car. It's a Chrysler Imperial, black, two years old, plate number FSX 283. You'll recognize him, he don't dress too good, looks like a cop."

The Chrysler was parked at a hydrant, three doors down from the address.

"Duke says you're new at this," he said.

"Yes," I said.

"He says you did OK on a job with Sonny."

"Yes."

"I'm diff'ent 'an Sonny."

"OK."

"Sonny takes things a little bit easy. I don't take things so easy. I was in homicide."

"OK."

"Now this ain't homicide, this is bull, this is a marital. Who's shtupping who. That's Yiddish, you *capisce* Yiddish?"

"I understand what you mean," I said.

"Awright. You see that door?" he pointed.

"Yes."

"Don't take your eyes offa that door. You see a white female Caucasian come out that door, five-six, a hundred and eighteen pounds, blond hair, no distinguishing marks visible if she's dressed, does have a scar on her left thigh but I don't expect we'll see that, what with its being practically winter, this weather we're having.

Here's a picture, you look at it, remember it so you can ID her. Age sixty-eight." I looked at the picture. "Keep your eyes on the doorway," he said. "She could come out in a blinkin' of an eye"—he snapped his fingers—"and you've lost 'er."

I did. I stared at the door as hard as I could. I think I looked like one of those dogs tied up by their leash outside a shop with their owner inside whose eyes are locked in perpetual despair on the spot where their master last disappeared. Dom opened the *New York Times* and began to read. About a half hour later he said, "Also you should tell me if you see anyone pull outta a parkin' space. If we gotta follow the suspect I don't leave the car in a tow zone. That's another rule. You can leave the car where you get a ticket, put it on expenses, client'll pop for your ticket. But they tow your car and they damage it, you unnerstand?"

"Yes," I said. Without taking my eyes off the door, I tried to sense any cars pulling out of a more legal spot.

An hour later someone got into a blue Lincoln with MD plates across the street. I thought they might be leaving.

"There! There!" I cried, tearing Dom away from news of the Middle East.

"What's it?"

"Parking space."

"You done good," he said gravely, switching on the ignition. He whipped the car out, just in case someone else might be trying for the spot. He was right. Someone else had spotted the action. But Dom beat them to it and then glared them down. I kept my eyes on the doorway.

Awhile later he asked, "You keep a notebook?"

"I have one," I said.

"Lemme see," he said. "But you, you keep **your** eyes

on the door." I fumbled blind in my pocketbook, staring fiercely at the door, found my book by feel, and handed it over. He thumbed through it. "What you do, at the start of the day you put the date down. You got an assignment, you write that down. You arrive, you write that down. Your partner is there you write that down. That's four entries, already, you shoulda had. You don't play makeup later, 'cause people forget. Or you get shot on the job, whoever's picking you up, they should be able to look in your book, see what you were doing, where, when, and why. You unnerstand?"

"Yes. Should I do that now?"

"OK," he said. "I'll watch the door."

"Thank you," I said, and carefully filled in a new page.

"What you do, each time you're on a job, you continue straight ahead, one day after the other, you don't try to organize it by job or nothing fancy like that. You got files for that, or somebody does anyway."

When I was done, he checked my work. It seemed satisfactory.

"OK, now we'se been here two hours. So we check in. I'll go to the phone booth over there and call the Duke. You, you keep your eyes on the door."

I kept my eyes on the door.

It finally opened. It was our quarry in all her sixty-eight-year-old furry glory. Hat and coat were fox. Even from this distance I could tell it was the real thing. She wore designer boots. Not the sort of designer who puts his name on mass-market merchandise. The sort who sells through four select outlets, New York, Paris, Milan, Tokyo. Very busy. Full of things. Her gloves matched her boots. Her hair was as worked over as her coat and had only slightly more life in it.

"It's her, it's her," I yelped.

"Awright," Dom said. "Let's go."

We got out of the car and locked it behind us. "Best way to follow," Dom said, "is to heel from across the street."

"Heel?"

"The position a dog is supposed to be in when he's walking with ya. At her heel. But we do it from across the street." Which was what we were doing. She turned down Madison. As we went around the corner the wind hit us. It was damp and chill and I realized I had underdressed. The woman in furs was unperturbed. She took her time, she was window shopping. She had a unique walk. She floated. Her feet never touched the ground. I don't know how she did it, but I filed it in my acting file in case I played someone old and very rich. "What ya gotta watch out for," Dom said, "is trucks and especially buses. A bus goes by, wipes you out visually, the subject they could go in a building, get on the bus, jump in a cab, get whacked for all you know, and they're gone. Careful with buses."

"She got a name?" I asked, the way one of the guys would have.

"Call her the billionairess," Dom said.

"She's got a billion dollars?"

"Her old man, he's got a billion fuckin' bucks. Oh, excuse me.

"That's OK."

"He owns half of Manhattan."

"It's cold," I said. The wind was cutting through my jeans and my jacket both.

"Half of Manhattan, he's seventy-eight, he's hooked to a dialysis machine, and he wants to know if his wife is screwing around. If she's screwing around, I say more power to her. Ahh, rich people." The billionairess stopped at a shop. We stopped. She went in. "OK," Dom said. "You stay on this side the street, I cross over. I wait right at the entrance. You don't go nowhere till you see me movin'."

"Got it."

The billionairess came out. She walked half a block. Then she went into Argentos. I stood still and did toe curls and yoga breathing to fight the chill. I made a note of both stops in my notebook. She came out in fifteen minutes. Dominic came back to my side of the street. Then she floated on down Madison with us heeling behind her. If it were an animated film we would have been an old bloodhound and . . . what would I be were I a canine? I wouldn't be a canine. . . . A bloodhound and a Burmese cat, purrrrr. Our quarry went into Chez Maison D'Arte. Where they sold art. We watched through the window. She was shown small sculptures. I couldn't make out the details from across the street, but the overall quality the pieces conveyed was lumpy. She came out. Dom crossed back. She floated on downtown another block or two into Fausto Santini—shoes. Traffic held Dom up from crossing and a bus passed. We were reasonably sure we hadn't lost her. But time passed, and with the least little kernel of uncertainty its passing takes on a greater intensity. Ten minutes of nervousness is an hour of certitude. Dom signaled me over. Dodging traffic, grateful to move that quickly since it got my blood circulating, I crossed Madison.

"Go in, take a look-see, see if she's there."

I did as I was told and she wasn't. We'd blown it. Now the director would yell cut, and, worse than never getting cast at all, I would be *replaced*.

"Well, whaddaya know," Dom said when I reported.

"Whaddaya think?" I said.

"I don' know," he said.

"Oh," I said.

"Yeah," he said thoughtfully.

Then the billionairess walked out of the dress shop next door.

We fell into step about a foot behind her. A dog length more than proper heeling. So close that I was certain she would hear Dom when he said, "We'll follow her more close."

"This close?" I said.

"Why not," he said.

As he said so, she turned around and came almost straight at us. My heart dropped. She stepped right past us and out onto the street to flag down a cab.

Dom was waving one down right after her. We were lucky that there was another one cruising right after.

"Where to?" the cabbie said.

"Follow that cab," Dom said.

"Oh verry, verry good, yes. What arre you saying?" the driver said in an Indian accent.

"Follow that cab," Dom said slowly and carefully.

"Oh, after it!" the driver said. "Are we in a moving picture?"

"Yes," Dom said.

"Oh, verry, verry good."

The billionairess pulled up in front of Bergdorf Goodman, on Fifth between Fifty-seventh and Fifty-eighth streets. We got out. We followed her around Bergdorf's until we felt she would have to spot us. So we went outside. Where I became cold, hungry, and colder still. Dom got us some pizza. It got cold. I was finally playing Gene Hackman in the female *French Connection*. Except my suspect was not a heroin peddler, she was a shopper. She stayed in Bergdorf's for three hours. Three cold hours. Then she came out. She went home. We got to sit in Dom's car and warm up.

That was good. Then she went out. What did she do? She shopped. She bought some baby things and a sweater. I wrote all this down in my notebook.

We were set to do it the next day again. But I had an audition.

Now I knew that if I were with Sonny, I could cut out. What would Dom, who was so much stricter and by the book, say about taking personal time? I needed the work, but I needed the job to be subordinate to acting.

"Sure," Dom said. "I cover for you, you cover for me. That's what partners are for."

I was ecstatic. I kissed him on the cheek.

"Whaddaya think?" he said, "you think I could get some acting work. If it was something I knew, like playing a cop?"

I barely gave a thought to Lucinda Merrill, except insofar as it had been my first detective job. There were other things far more important. Geraldine Page had called to tell me she was starting a new acting class. I was in discussions with a personal manager who seemed very interested in taking me on. And Rowdy Randolph was coming to town. That sort of loomed over everything like low-lying clouds or high-flying fog. I prefer rainy days and misty nights to sunshine. But I don't know if that explains how I felt about Rowdy at all. I was certainly eager to see how he behaved. Hopefully, he would fall to his knees to perform an act of contrition, he would humble himself, apologize, and beg forgiveness. Would I allow him to sweep me off my feet, or would I tell him to say three Hail Marys, four Our Fathers, and if he must sin some more, do it somewhere else, in someone else's city?

Andrew kept track of the "soap opera killing," as it

had come to be called. He noticed that they altered the story line slightly to give Shanna McWarren as played by Lucinda Merrill more airtime. Soap fans everywhere watched to see if they could discern the grief, the pain, the loss—or the relief—of the widow beneath the character. They watched like drivers rubbernecking a wreck. This delayed Andrew's entry into the series. After a week of that, however, the ratings went

from:	down to:
1. The Young and the Restless	1. The Young and the Restless
2. General Hospital	2. General Hospital
3. As the World Turns	3. As the World Turns
4. Days of Our Lives	4. Days of Our Lives
5. All My Children	5. All My Children
6. *Forever and Ever*	6. Bold and Beautiful
7. Bold and Beautiful	7. One Life to Live
8. One Life to Live	8. *Forever and Ever*
9. Guiding Light	9. Guiding Light
10. Another World	10. Another World
11. Loving	11. Loving

Then the new headlines came out:

SOAP STAR SEEN AT MURDER SITE

SECRET WITNESS SEES SOAPER

ACTRESS SUSPECT IN HUBBIE HIT

FACT FOLLOWS FICTION—SOAP OPERA MURDER

The ratings jumped

from:	to:
1. The Young and the Restless	1. The Young and the Restless
2. General Hospital	2. General Hospital
3. As the World Turns	3. As the World Turns

The case of Lucinda Merrill was open again. There was a big meeting.

It was held at the offices of United Broadcasting Systems on Sixth Avenue. It was almost like an advertising agency casting—everyone was there. I could only imagine the tiny turf battles that would mean jobs kept or lost, income staying in six figures or crashing down to none.

Samantha Trent, Vice President for Daytime Programming, a woman who wore expensive feminized suits and ties, seemed to be in charge. Not that I was introduced. She was flanked on either side by Her People: Garth Wimphle, Assistant to the VP-DTP; Effie Norfron, Head Writer; Stan Ruddiman, Producer; Vickie Lazlo, Publicity.

Mr. Petty and his associate Joshua Silverman were on either side of Lucinda Merrill. She was dressed to the nines and wore too much makeup for anything but a camera. Whoever had done it, probably the show's makeup artist, had used his trowel artfully. Backing them up, like a little gang, were the Duke and his boys: Sonny, back from Miami with a tan and a new gold watch that his Miami girlfriend had given him, Dom, Bobby Callahan, and me. I hadn't met Bobby before. Detective Witte had a space all to himself. He was aligned with no one and against all.

"It's in everyone's best interest that this case be investigated," Ms. Trent said.

"I'll tell you what's in everyone's best interests," Witte said, "is that you let the police do their job and keep amateurs and has-beens out of it."

"This is one has-been that'll break your face," Duke said, ready to rumble.

Mr. Petty raised a frosty eyebrow.

"It'd be my pleasure," Witte said, "and on top of being out of commission you'll be in the slam."

Lucinda Merrill, Effie Norfron, and Garth Wimphle were all the sort of people who enjoyed it when two snorting bulls pawed the ground and challenged each other. Part of their pleasure was that they knew that in that sort of confrontation both bulls would be losers.

"Gentlemen, please, save your petty squabbles for the playground," Ms. Trent said.

Mr. Petty said, "I think we have a publicity problem here. Negative publicity."

"It hasn't hurt the show any," Garth, the Assistant to the VP-DTP, said. "I have the Nielsens right here."

"You should see the letters," Stan, the Producer, said.

"I have," Lucinda said, a touch of frost in her famous voice.

"Come, come, darling," Stan said, "they are largely sympathetic. Your fans adore you and are sure you're being framed."

"Framed? I'm not even considered a suspect," Lucinda snapped. "Am I Detective Witte? Am I?"

"It's a open case, open case," Witte said with a certain satisfaction. "Anybody could be a suspect."

"These rumors are totally unfounded and we want them squelched," Petty said.

"That's not really under anyone's control, is it?"

Samantha Trent said with the sort of smooth, waffling disavowal that one expects in a network executive.

"Samantha," Lucinda said. "Pardon me for being frank. You like the situation. It raises the ratings. Your writers like the situation, it raises the ratings even with the tripe they hack out. It is only I who do not like the situation, since it is I who am being slandered. If I find out that these hideous stories were leaked from this office, I will sue!"

"Believe me, dear," Samantha said, "I am sympathetic." Anyone who has watched daytime, or nighttime, soaps, knows exactly the tones these two venom-dripping felines used with each other. "And that is why we are willing to support your attempt to clear yourself."

"Clear myself! Clear myself—" Lucinda sputtered.

"Ms. Merrill hardly has to clear herself," Petty said. "Ms. Merrill was with two detectives the night her husband so unfortunately died."

"Humph," Witte snorted. I was insulted. Sonny just smiled. Duke flexed his mighty biceps and flared his football-thick neck. "Speaking on behalf of the department, we don't like ama-two-ers messing around with capital cases. For those of you who don't know, a capital case is like murder."

Duke's ears turned red and he rumbled in his throat.

"Detective Witte," Mr. Petty said, "is there any substance to these rumors? Is there a cause for these headlines—" he held them up:

SOAP STAR SEEN AT MURDER SITE

SECRET WITNESS SEES SOAPER

ACTRESS SUSPECT IN HUBBY HIT

FACT FOLLOWS FICTION—SOAP OPERA MURDER

"Is there a 'secret witness' who claims to have seen my client at the scene?"

"Counselor, I gotta give you a no comment on that, a neither confirm nor deny along with departmental guidelines, you understand what I'm saying."

"Do you have any idea who might have leaked the story?" Mr. Petty said.

"Absolutely none," Witte said.

Mr. Petty shifted his gaze to the network people. They put on their best blank faces. Not believable for a second. "Nonetheless," Mr. Petty said, "Ms. Merrill's name, profession, and livelihood must be safeguarded. We intend to do that with all the means at our disposal."

"Absolutely," Samantha said. "And you have our support."

Lucinda gave her an icy stare. I have excellent hearing. I thought I was the only one in the room who heard her whisper, "You dyke bitch, you'd have shot him yourself for two ratings points."

"Don't worry, we're gonna solve this case for you," Duke said, rising to go.

"Ah, DeNobili," Witte said, "you're a bull in a china shop. Always have been. You mess around in this, someone's gonna get hurt."

As we exited the meeting Samantha cozied up to Lucinda. "Two ratings points," she said, "is a lot."

CHAPTER EIGHT

The ideal thing for Mr. Petty and Duke DeNobili to do," I said, "would be to send me in, undercover, as an actor on 'Forever and Ever.' Once there I could ferret out whatever was amiss." It's what Nancy Drew would have said. And done. She would have ended up hiding on the catwalks, peering down, overhearing a criminal conversation. Then the doors would close and the lights go out. "Though soap opera acting is not what I would want to spend my life doing."

"If I got a soap," Ralph said, fervently, "I would know that I had made it."

That was probably true, I realized. He was a male version of Blair, the ingenue described by Lucinda Merrill as played by Jennifer McGuffin née Quatroccochi. He was large and handsome and could conceive of only one emotion at a time. He lived alone in a single, tiny room.

Our brownstone is a picturesque relic, and it is owned by one. She is Lidie Murphy of Mississippi. Among the hundreds of pictures on her walls is a larger-than-lifesize portrait of the infant Elvis. Beside it is a moody sepia nude. It looks like an old Storyville photo. It's Lidie herself and was probably taken about the same year that the Elvis was. She is an actress, chorus girl, hoofer, and nightclub entertainer. She played Tehran and the Shah of Iran adored her. She's a dynamic dame with great legs, somewhere between "fifty and death," given to stalking the halls in see-through gowns.

All the halls and stairs, from the basement to the fifth floor, are lined with her playbills, her pictures, her reviews, her mementos. Like a boardinghouse set from an all-singing, all-dancing, all-color musical about Broadway babes, the two top floors are single-room occupancy, with shared baths. Ralph's room is the most cell-like of them all, a square in the center of the building, without windows, just a skylight, with space for only a monkish bed and a seaman's chest.

He had left a seminary to pursue an acting career, and perhaps Lidie Murphy's is his personal halfway house, a place to make the transition to whatever his reality will be.

"It would be exciting," I said, thinking about soap opera acting, "to be a ham. Forget about all the subtlety and realism and Chekovian Moscow Art Theater stuff and be a real ham."

"I would watch you every day," Ralph said.

"It could be great fun if it were the right part," I said.

"A villainess," Ralph said.

"Yes," I said.

"Psychopathic," he said.

"Deceitful," I said.

"A compulsive liar," he said.

"And manipulator," I said.

"With a certain charm," he said.

"Capable of great evil and yet redeemable," I said.

"Just like," we spoke in chorus, "Shanna McWarren."

The phone rang. As if on cue. It was Duke DeNobili.

"You wanna work?" he said.

I knew how eager he was to crack the Lucinda Merrill case. I smiled at Ralph, indicated at the phone, mouthed Duke's name. It was falling into place faster than I could possibly imagine. My detecting was about to give my acting exactly the boost it needed. "Yes," I said. "I want to work."

"Hook up with Sonny," he said. "You got his number, right?"

"Right, Duke," I said. "What's the case?" I winked at Ralph.

"That woman youse was following, with Dominic, we're still on it."

"But she doesn't do anything," I said. "All she does is shop."

"Ours is not to reason why, ours it to do what the client pays for. Even if they don't need it. And call in every two hours."

"What about Lucinda Merrill?" I said, but he'd already hung up.

I don't know why Dom was off it and Sonny on it, but Sonny and I followed the billionairess for the next three days. Her life was two blocks wide, from Fifth to Madison to Park, and twenty-two blocks long, from Seventy-ninth to Fifty-seventh Street. Sonny was much more casual than Dom, and we did a lot of our following in his car, the Silver Bullet, a ten-year-old Cadillac, immaculate except for the dense, ineradicable aroma of ashtray. It was wide and warm and soft and comfortable, like a port-a-couch with a little living room attached.

We talked. A lot. Sonny was the kind of guy who could have done a lot of things. He was talented, tough, athletic, attractive, smarter than he ever admitted to himself—he cruised through the *Times* crossword puzzle every day, never stuck for very long, filling in every word. He called it, at forty cents, the best entertainment value in town.

What he had been was a cop. The old-style New York cop that they made movies and books about. Quick with his fists: "On my beat we used to give out beatin's. Nobody ever complained, because we never beat on anybody didn't know they deserved it." He acted like he could, almost as easily, have been a mobster. "I mean if you ever wanna buy a car, cheap, you talk to my cousin, Frankie the Thief." He never said as much directly, but I think that he was proud of having chosen the right side and of being one of the good guys. He told me about the first time he'd been shot at. And the first time he'd been shot. In the shoulder, nicked the lung, four hours in intensive care. "But I was young then, Annie. Healed fast. Outta the hospital in a week. Which was just when racing season began, so I did my convalescence up at Saratoga." He proceeded to tell me about the girl that he met up there. He still saw her occasionally, though it was twenty years later. She was married now, as was he then and now.

"You don't see your wife much," I said.

"Nah, just when I pick up the kids."

"Are you getting a divorce?"

He looked at me like it was an idea he'd never heard of. He didn't disapprove of it, but neither did he consider it.

When you sit in a car all day to watch someone else doing nothing important, you talk about a lot of things. We had decided right at the beginning that we weren't going to do a man-woman thing. Believe me, I don't know how, if I did know the secret I would pass it on. So Sonny talked to me like I was one of the guys. Which meant, among other things, referencing women on a physiological basis and referring to sexual behavior in more specific detail than I had heard even in my psychology courses in college. Even if they had not been told to me in confidence, I would never repeat them. He had a very different moral perspective than I did—or should I call it amoral. Had I never met a man like Sonny before? Or was this the perspective that all men had and the vocabulary that they really used when we weren't around to hear them?

Sonny called us the SAD Squad, Special Antiadultery Division.

The irony of Sonny as the watchdog of infidelity was too heavy-handed for either of us to comment on. I had no right to throw stones at glass houses either.

"What would I have to do to be an actor?" Sonny asked me.

I had to make a decision whether to humor him or tell him what it's really about. "It's not what it appears to be," I said. "It's a way of life, a way through life. Yeah, some people get an agent, get a job, get on TV and they're actors, for a moment. But other people work for years, studying, learning about life, about the business, being in plays, all to do some sitcom that you yourself wouldn't watch . . ." I laughed ruefully, because it would take exactly that—a boffo bit on "Who's the Boss" or a feature as the adopted white daughter of the Cosbys— before my mother would ever admit that I had a profession. ". . . so that you'll finally be acknowledged as a real actor."

"I could play a cop, you know, or a mobster. Look at me. I been with some girls, said I should be in the movies, I'm a natural."

"Maybe you should take a couple of acting classes," I said.

"I think they said it because I lie so easily," he said. "And they could never tell."

Then I was back on the Lucinda Merrill job. Nobody told me why. Just as nobody had explained why it was that after the meeting in which Duke had been so gung ho to solve the thing we had done nothing.

"What we wanna do," Duke said, "is find this witness that we keep hearing about that places Lucinda Merrill at the scene of the crime. Anybody want a drink?"

"Scotch rocks," Sonny said, gravel grinding in his throat. He lit a filter-tip cigarette with a gold Zippo.

"Pellegrino," I said. Somehow the guys found that less disturbing than Perrier. Maybe because it was Italian water. Maybe it was the name of somebody they'd arrested back in the Two-Five and it brought fond memories.

"Nice lighter," Duke said, waving to the bartender.

"Mercedes," Sonny said, meaning that it was a gift from that girlfriend. These guys had a knack for finding girls that liked to give them gold. Duke had a bracelet from Sandy, his regular girlfriend. Dom, who was much more staid than the others, had a gaudy wristwatch from his wife. Even Bobby Callahan, who was Irish not Italian, got gifts of jewelry. Was this some deep mystery of man-woman relating that I had yet to understand? Certainly men like these, faithless and lying as they might be, had certain essences that would act very powerfully with many women. Would I someday find a man that I would buy chunky gold bracelets for? And stay with however brazenly he cheated on me?

"I like Puerto Rican girls," Duke said. "They're hot." He looked at me. "You know what I mean. You're not offended. That's life, right."

"Nah, she's not offended," Sonny said.

"Scotch rocks, Pellegrino," Duke called to the bar, "and . . ." he pointed to himself.

"She's all right, you can talk to her. You know, Annie," Sonny said to me, "you're the first friend I ever had that was a female that I wasn't, you know, doing it with."

"Tell that to Mercedes," Duke said.

"Yeah," Sonny said, with that warm gravelly laugh. Mercedes would not know of my existence until some accident revealed it. Sonny was certain that she could never believe that he and I could spend the night on a stakeout together and not be physically intimate. She had, he said, a very suspicious nature.

"I went out with a Rican the other night," Duke said. He had a wife, Anita, and three kids out in Howard Beach. Unlike Sonny, he still, in his own way, lived with his family. Sandy, his regular girlfriend, lived on Twelfth Street, near University Place, in Greenwich Village.

"Oh yeah?" Sonny said as the drinks arrived.

"The one that was in *Penthouse* last month," Duke said, and shot his cuffs. He was wearing one of those shirts where collar and cuffs were a different color than the shirt itself, in this case something between silver and blue, and starched as stiff as a nun's wimple. "I bought her an ankle bracelet—her birthstone encrusted with diamond chips. Whaddaya think, Annie, think she'll like that?"

Tommy arrived with the drinks and a bowl of salted nuts.

"Jewelry is always good," I said.

"I bought it at Fortunoff's," he said.

"Fortunoff's is always good," I said.

"Fourteen hundred bucks, she better like it," Duke

said. He took a sip of his scotch. "The cops ain't giving us nothing about this secret witness."

"It's in all the papers," Sonny said.

"It's Witte," Duke said. "He's got something to prove."

"Plus he don't like you," Sonny said.

"That's because I don't got nothing to prove. What I want you to do is go talk to the neighbors. Slow and methodical. Like the city was still paying your salary. You got a tape recorder?" he said to me.

"What kind of tape recorder?"

"You get one of these little ones. These here ones that play microcassettes. Now I don't know what you think you know from the movies and such, but in this here state, New York, it is legal to tape-record any conversation you are part of, in person or on the telephone or whatever. So you get a small tape recorder, it's easy for a broad, you carry a pocketbook, you wear certain kind of clothes, you got a place to put it. So if you're doing witness interviews, this isn't suspect interviews anyway, just witness interviews, you record it. You get everything exact and perfect that way. Plus don't forget the notes too."

"What kind of tape recorder should I get?" I asked. "Any particular brand? How much are they?"

"Also, I got you pictures of both Mr. and Mrs. Hoffman," Duke said. "It was tough getting anything of Mrs. Hoffman that wasn't an eight-by-ten glossy with her hair all done and the light on it. Actress pictures. You know what I mean."

"When you're going to go record someone," Sonny said, "you talk to the tape first, put the date, and time, and who you're going to talk to, and the location and any other salient fact you got at hand."

"You should talk to Bobby Callahan," Duke said,

"about which brand. He's into that electronic stuff. It's nothing real complicated. But you should practice with it a couple times before you go out, so you're used to it."

"When do we start?" I asked.

"Now," Duke said, as if that were self-explanatory.

We couldn't start right now. I didn't have the tape recorder and I wasn't dressed for it.

It was a frantic afternoon. First I found a mini-recorder to borrow. I got it from a girlfriend who had been leaving it on in her apartment to hear who her boyfriend called when she was out. It was voice activated, it worked, she'd thrown him out and didn't need it anymore.

I put on the muted green raw silk jumpsuit, dark brown suede boots with a low heel, dark brown gloves (naturally), a camelhair coat, a brown beret, and an over-the-shoulder bag that went reasonably well with the boots and gloves. I put the tape recorder in the bag. Comfortable, yet appropriate for the East Side.

Arthur Hoffman's address had been 422 East Seventy-ninth Street, apartment 3R, that is, on the south side of Seventy-ninth Street between First and Second avenues, on the third floor, and, since most brownstones have two apartments per floor, the R meant rear.

Sonny met me out front.

The building, reasonably well kept, had a lock and intercom system to control access. We weren't trying to gain access where we weren't wanted so we didn't need any tricks to get in. We simply buzzed the apartments, starting with 1F, until someone answered, which turned out to be the woman in 2R. According to the directory her name was L. Goldberg. She asked who was there.

Sonny said "Detective Gandolfo," which was not a lie.

"What do you want?" she said.

"We're canvassing the neighborhood for witnesses. I just need a couple of minutes of your time."

"Why me?" she said.

"You're the first one answered her bell," he said.

"Oh," she said, and buzzed us in.

We entered and walked upstairs. Sonny knocked, she looked out her peephole at him and opened the door. If I'd had to guess, I would have said she was a "professional" woman, that is she worked at something white collar, above the level of secretary, but she wasn't a doctor or lawyer. She was in her late thirties. She wasn't born to be beautiful, but she worked at all the things that we do to make ourselves pretty. Her hair, makeup, and clothes were all flattering to her. She probably went to the gym. It helped, but nature was going to win. It was clear that she was home alone for the evening. She examined Sonny. The suspicion with which she had answered the intercom was gone. She was, at least, intrigued. She smiled.

"Hi there," Detective Gandolfo said in that super-macho voice, and smiled back. "What's the L stand for, Ms. Goldberg?"

"Lenore," she said.

"Call me Sonny," he said. Even bigger smile.

Then she looked at me.

"Who's she?" she said, annoyed.

"That's my partner, Detective McGrogan," he said.

"Oh," she said.

It was a lesson in expression, subtext, and body language. Rarely had I seen two people go so far, so fast, with words that meant so little.

"You might as well come in," she said.

Sonny followed her in. I followed Sonny. I thought she was a little wide in the hips. Sonny thought she was available. That made her lovely and appealing. I could see that happening in him. It was a chemical thing, or an animal thing, a male thing. It almost had an odor.

"Can I get you something to drink?" Lenore said.

"Scotch for me," Sonny said, smoky voice, his favorite music was Sinatra.

"Nothing for me," I said.

"Do you mind if I smoke?" Sonny said.

"No," she said, "do you need a light?"

"Sure," he said, the lighter from Mercedes resting comfortably in his pocket.

She had a glass bowl of souvenir matchbooks on the shelf. She reached in and picked one. "This was one of my favorite places," she said. It had the name of a bar on the cover. "I had some good times there." She split a match off from the rest and looked at Sonny. He took a cigarette out of the box, paused, and put it between his lips.

This was who Stacey Keach was trying to be when he played Mike Hammer on television. A guy so tough that every (you should pardon the expression) broad in town flashed her cleavage for him and turned "good morning" into a double entendre.

She lit his cigarette for him.

Then she went to get his drink. She brought it back straight up. "Do you want anything in it?" she said.

"Nah," Sonny said.

"I figured you for the kind of guy who took it straight."

Sonny nodded. She handed him the glass and watched him hold it.

"Thanks," he said.

"You have really big hands," she said.

"I gotta ask you a couple of questions," he said.

"Go right ahead," she said.

It was so thick that if it were not for the fact that I was supposed to learn how it was done from Sonny, I would have left the two of them alone with their subtext-laden inanities.

"The guy in three R? No I didn't know him. . . . Well sure, I guess I've seen him. Going in, going out. . . . Not very loquacious. At least not with me. . . . I don't know if I ever saw him with a girl. . . . But, hey, I know he had some girlfriends. I mean this building is old and you don't hear too much, but I know women went up there. . . . Hey, I'm not a nosy neighbor. Their business is their business and my business is my own. I didn't move from Lake Ronkonkoma, Long Island, to Manhattan and pay Manhattan rents so that my neighbors could make my business their business. . . . Look, I wouldn't say this, except that he's dead. I think he was into drugs. . . . What makes me think that? I'm not a clinician in a drug clinic, but you notice little things, maybe it's just an attitude, like a person being too hyper. Did you ever notice those Partnership for a Drug-Free America ads? If you have an employee on drugs: Fire him! It's for their own good? Who do you think is behind those ads?

". . . Yes, I mean coke when I say drugs. Maybe there were other things, but if you told me the guy was doing crack I wouldn't be surprised. . . .

"The night he was killed? . . . No, you don't have to tell me the date, I remember from when it was in the papers a week later, I said: 'Hey! That's my address! That's the guy from upstairs. What night was that?' And I counted backward and I said: 'Wow. Lucky I was out that night!' I was on a date. Guy took me to see *Cats*. I'm not seeing that guy anymore. I'm not seeing anybody special at the moment.

"No . . ." she said when Sonny showed her a photo of Mrs. Hoffman. "I've never seen her here. I know who Lucinda Merrill is. I mean, who doesn't. But I've never seen her here."

"Thanks," Sonny said.

"Thanks," I said.

"If I think of something, shouldn't I call you?" she said, having seen more TV shows than we had and knowing the routine better.

"Oh yeah, definitely, if you have any thoughts at all," Sonny said. He took out a Duke Investigations business card that had his name on it. "You call me at this number. And you should give me yours. In case I need to get in touch with you."

She recited her number and watched carefully while he wrote it in his notebook.

"I really like your hands," she said.

We went downstairs. One F and 1R were both duplexes that included the half-basement space. They were both lived in by couples, straight in front, gay in back.

One of the gay men in back was a model who appeared in print advertisements for Obsession perfume. There was a big blowup of him in one of the ads on the wall. He claimed he'd seen Hoffman one day in front of the building arguing with a man. Not the night of the murder. A few days, even a week or more, before. He thought it was about money, probably drug money. Sonny asked him what made him say that.

"I'm pretty sure I heard the guy say 'You owe me.' "

" 'You owe me' or 'You owe me money?' " Sonny asked him.

"I don't know if he said the word money, but I thought it was about money. Maybe he said 'You better pay me what you owe me.' Or 'Get me what you owe me, fast.' Whatever the exact words were, that was what I got out of it."

"And drugs?"

"What else does anyone owe money for anymore?"

The couple in front had a lot of things. New, expensive things. Video things, computer things, audio things, and special shelf things to hold the things. He was a lawyer. She was a broker. They hadn't known their neighbor.

"I hate to say it," the lawyer said, "but it's probably best that it ended this way."

"What do you mean?" Sonny said.

"Well, if it was about drugs . . ."

"Why do you say it was about drugs?"

"Isn't all this killing today about drugs?" the lawyer said.

"It's our parents' fault," the broker said. "If it weren't for the hippie sixties promoting all that excess behavior we wouldn't have all these drugs and the killings and the AIDS. We would be a much more productive society." Her manner was low-key but adamant, as if her opinions had been approved by the FDA after passing all federally mandated laboratory tests.

"Do you know something specific, that you witnessed personally, that involved Arthur Hoffman and drugs?"

"Would I have to testify?" the broker said.

"Nah," Sonny said, genial as can be, "it's just background."

The lawyer shook his head at the broker. It was a tight, tense little shake.

"No," she said. "It was just something I assumed."

"Why did you say it was best that it ended that way?"

"We have friends," the broker said, "who have had people in their buildings start to use drugs. One addict can poison an entire building. They sink lower and lower. They bring in other users and pushers and prostitutes. We own this apartment, we don't rent. This is a quick, clean ending to what otherwise could have been a long-drawn-out tragedy for all of us."

"The papers, they say someone saw his wife here that night, implying that she might have killed him."

"It wasn't in the paper, I read the paper every day," the broker said.

"It was in the *Post*, the *News*, on the nightly news."

"Was it in the *Wall Street Journal?*"

"Maybe not," Sonny said.

"You see," the broker said.

"That's all we have to say," the lawyer said. He looked at his watch as if they were late for an appointment. It was about a quarter after nine. I didn't think they were going out, but I didn't doubt that their nights at home had schedules that had to be kept.

We went upstairs. Arthur Hoffman's apartment still had the police seal on it. I thought the lights were on in the apartment opposite, 3F, but no one answered when we knocked.

There was no one home in 4F, but the girl who lived in apartment 4R, directly over Artie's, was home. She was suspicious. She asked to see a badge. Sonny held his ID up to the eyehole. She opened the door a crack but kept the chain on.

"I've already spoken to the cops," she said.

"Yeah, I know," Sonny said, "but this'll only take two minutes. Five at the most."

"Fine," she said and looked at her watch. "You got two minutes."

The radio was on inside and the sweet aroma of marijuana drifted out.

"The night the man downstairs from you was murdered, were you home?"

"Yes."

"Did you hear anything?"

"No."

"Nothing at all?"

"Had the radio on."

"No shots?"

"What's a shot sound like? Like on TV? Like a truck backfiring? I didn't hear no shots."

"Screaming? Yelling?"

"No."

"You ever hear any screaming or yelling from downstairs?"

"Everybody screams sometimes," she said.

"Even the lawyer and the broker who live in one F?" I said.

"Except them," she said.

"Tell me about the screaming and yelling downstairs," Sonny said.

"Sometimes I heard yelling."

"One person?" Sonny said.

"What are you, stupid? What kind of person yells at themselves."

"Two people?"

"Your time is up."

"Give me a break," Sonny said. "Two people?"

"Give *me* a break," she said.

"Man and a woman?" Sonny said.

"That's who screams at each other, a man and a woman," she said. "You wonder what they get together for. Stupid, isn't."

"Same woman all the time?"

"I don't know," she said. "I don't pay much attention to women who go out with men."

"What did they yell about?"

"I'm not a stenographer. I didn't take notes."

"Was it people fighting about money?"

"I told you what they were fighting about."

"Sorry, I musta missed it," Sonny said.

"They were fighting about being a man and a woman," she said and closed the door.

Sonny turned to me. "You hungry?" he asked.

"Yes," I said.

"There's a joint on the corner. We're on expense account. Let's get a burger."

W e went back the next day and tried the apartments we'd missed. Four F turned out to be a
waiter, actually an actor. Although he had yet
to work professionally he was studying with an acting
teacher who taught his students to say "I *am* an actor,
I'm *going* to be a star." He didn't know much about his
recently deceased neighbor. He was out at the time of
the murder, waiting tables at Navaho, a Native American restaurant serving authentic southwestern cuisine
including snake steak, armadillo cutlets, and blue-corn
tortillas. It was, he said, a *performance*, since he was
supposed to be an actual Native American. Tough for a
blond boy named Dennis from St. Paul with a distinctly
bovine face. "It's all in the attitude," he said. "I think
stoic. I feel close to the earth. I meditate before I serve
on being one with the sky and wind. Of course I wear a
black wig."

Three F wasn't home. Or didn't answer the door. I
suspected the latter.

So we went to the house next door. Two of the eight
residents were home. One wouldn't talk to us at all. The
other said she had no knowledge of Arthur Hoffman or
Lucinda Merrill/Hoffman even after we showed her photos of the couple.

Duke drove up at noon to check on us. He drove a gold Cadillac Seville. I should have been able to predict that. With real leather seats. The outside was freshly polished, the inside was immaculate and sprayed with "NewKar" aroma.

We gathered in the car. He asked how it was going. Sonny gave him a brief summary.

"You tape-recording everything?" Duke asked.

I took my recorder out of my over-the-shoulder bag, wound it back a short way, and let it play. After three seconds he nodded. I realized that he was checking up on us, suspicious that instead of working Sonny was taking off to the track or me to an audition while we were on his time.

"Yeah. Fine," he said, and I shut it off. "Listen to me, you doin' real good. I think you should go talk to the stores, too. A person lives someplace, even if only part-time, they gotta go to the liquor store, the deli, the drugstore. I been thinkin' about it."

"Sure," Sonny said. "We'll do that."

"How's she doin'?" Duke said, about me. "Doin' good?"

"Real good," Sonny said.

"OK," Duke said, "I gotta run. You need to get holda me, you call the beeper. Keep checkin' in."

We got out of the car. He drove away.

"You got an audition?" Sonny said.

"Yes," I said. It was even something I wanted to do. At last. It wasn't a sitcom that was an imitation of a movie that had not been very good in the first place. It wasn't a commercial for some substance that I wouldn't touch and didn't really think anyone else should use either. Not if they cared for their well-being. It was a Play. Written by Alisha Thornton-Fishbein, whose work had been staged at Theater in the Square, at Yale, and at the Performance Market and who had been nominated for two OBIE awards. At the Theater for a New America, a dedicated (I had heard), nonprofit theater company committed to the art of acting and to new writers. It sounded a lot like my beloved Company of Angels in Los Angeles, of which I had been a member and which gave me tremendous artistic sustenance. It sounded like what I had come to New York looking for.

"You go," Sonny said, very nonchalant. "I'll cover for you."

"Are you sure," I said.

He took out a cigarette, lit it with Mercedes's gold Zippo, inhaled with pre–Surgeon General's Report relish, cool as Bogie, big as John Wayne. "That's what partners are for," he said.

"Thanks, Sonny," I said.

"Hey, if you see a part that would be good for me, bring back a copy of the script."

The theater was on Forty-second Street.

Times Square and the blocks west had degenerated quite badly and become a mecca for drugs and pornography, crime and violence. In an effort to revitalize the area, subsidized housing for artists was built on the north side of Forty-second Street between Ninth and Tenth avenues and a group of small theaters were developed on the south side.

Theater for a New America was one of those, with a stage on the ground floor and three floors of rehearsal hall and office space above. It had that gritty but uplifting backstage artists-at-work feeling.

The receptionist was very busy with things that were very important so that it was ten minutes before she looked up, handed me the audition scenes, waved her hand, and said "Wait over there." I took the five pages with me and found a seat among the other waiting actors.

WANDA: I told you to cut his balls off.
MAUREEN (my part): I did what you told me.
WANDA: You didn't.
MAUREEN: I did.
WANDA: Good for you.
MAUREEN: Ground 'em up into burger meat.
WANDA: How did it taste?
MAUREEN: I didn't eat it.
WANDA: Who did?
MAUREEN: He wants to leave me.
WANDA: Be strong. I'm glad you cut his balls off.
MAUREEN: I am too. I celebrated.
WANDA: If men were more androgynous there would be no war.
MAUREEN: I hate war. Football too. I spit on his balls after I cut them off.
WANDA: You're better off without him. He was a closet queen anyway.
MAUREEN: Are you sure?
WANDA: Didn't you see him with Donald. They hugged.
MAUREEN: Cut 'em all off!
WANDA: They fix dogs, don't they! [the title line]

Midtown traffic was noisy and jammed so I took a subway back. As I walked from the station I passed the store on Arthur Hoffman's corner that sold cigarettes, candy, an eclectic assortment of small but useful things—like ibuprofin and ballpoint pens—newspapers and two hundred different magazines, many of which had extremely suggestive covers. It was the sort of place that everyone in the neighborhood drops in on some-time for something.

There were two men in conversation behind the counter. There was a small black-and-white television on behind them. They ignored it. I said, "Good after-noon." The older one, a dark Pakistani with kindly eyes and a bald spot, moved forward to help me.

"What can I do for you, miss?"

"I'm Detective McGrogan," I said. "There was a murder a couple of weeks ago, down the block."

"On this block here?" he said, as if the information surprised him.

"Down that way, on Seventy-ninth," I said. "You must have seen it in the papers."

"Oh yes. Terrible and shocking, isn't it, in such a very nice neighborhood."

"A lot of the people in the neighborhood must stop in here," I said. "You must know a lot of people."

"I know nothing about this murder," he said. "Oh, nothing at all."

"I can tell that you are a very astute man."

"Thank you, very, very much."

"And a good businessman."

"Well . . ."

"You know that a good businessman knows his cus-tomers, right?"

"Of course this is important," he admitted.

The other man behind the counter said something to him in Hindi. Or Pushtu. Or maybe it was Urdu. I only have high-school French.

A customer appeared at the front window. The other man behind the counter, without a word being ex-changed beyond "Good afternoon," pulled down a pack-age of Captain Black pipe tobacco and some gum. He didn't need to look at the paper the customer had selected from the outside rack to know that it was the *New York Times* and to charge him 40¢ for it.

"Look at that, that's nice," I went on, with my best smile and friendly female manner. "When somebody comes in, you know what they want, a pack of Camels or the *Daily News* or a Hershey bar."

"Well, not always."

Another customer came in to buy a lottery ticket.

"The reason you are making a success here"—I virtually fluttered my eyelashes—"is because you are thoughtful and attentive. So would you do me a favor and look at a couple of pictures for me? Just to see if they came in here? It would help me out." I put the picture of Arthur Hoffman on the counter.

"Oh yes, certainly, anything to be helpful." He took the picture, looked at it, said, "Oh no, I don't know this man," and handed it back.

I didn't believe him.

I took out the photo of Lucinda Merrill/Hoffman. "How about her?" I said.

He smiled cheerfully, ready to do me any service. He looked at the picture. I thought I saw something pass over his face but once again he said, "Oh no, I don't think I have ever seen this lady." That was pretty difficult to believe. She'd been all over the *Post* and the *News*. Both of which he handled every day. The current issue of *Soap Opera Digest* was hanging from a clip four inches from his nose every time he sold a Lotto ticket; just a week ago Lucinda had been its reluctant cover girl.

"Look," I said, "you could really help me out. I'm new at this. This poor guy got killed . . ."

Another customer came in. A well-dressed woman of forty-five or so. She bought a pack of Juicy Fruit. While he made change she slipped a York Peppermint Patty in her pocket.

"Excuse me, miss," the younger man said. "I am sure you are wanting to pay for your York Peppermint Patty, it's so refreshing."

"Oh, yes, silly me. What could I have been thinking of?" She put some change on the counter. "I get to thinking. Absentminded. Sorry, sorry," she said, backing out of the store. "Sorry."

"Did you want to buy something?" the balding man said to me.

"No, never mind," I said.

I found Sonny sitting in the Silver Bullet smoking a cigarette and finishing up the crossword puzzle. I told him about the newsstand at the end of the block and said, "I think I blew it, I think they knew something."

"Nah, you didn't blow it. Sometimes you gotta go back, two, three times. Let's go over there and see."

Most of Manhattan's streets are one-way. This means that to get half a block by car in the wrong direction you may have to drive eight blocks. We drove. Sonny pulled up in front of the little store and double-parked as if it were the right and natural thing to do.

"How you doing, pal," he said, smiling when he entered.

"Can I be of assistance," the man with kindly eyes said.

Sonny bought a pack of Trues. Lit one. Then he commented on the television. Asked the guy what he watched. Found out that there was an Indian program on cable, if you could get cable, which they couldn't out in Queens where they lived. Then he bought a Lotto ticket and discussed how much the prize was and whether they had any winners at their shop and if the winners tipped. Sonny thought they should. So did both Pakistanis. But it had never happened. The older man was the proprieter. The younger, a cousin. Sonny offered each of them a cigarette. The cousin accepted. Sonny lit it for him.

"You gotta help me out here," Sonny said. "This guy got killed, down the block. I mean he hadda come in here to get his papers, his butts. It's the closest place." He slipped the picture onto the counter. They both looked. "I don't know what you think will happen if you say you've seen him, but believe me, you got nothing to worry about. I been up the block there, to the Greek joint, the morning guy told me this man used to have breakfast there. Kinda late breakfast, even told me what he ate . . ." None of that was true but it seemed to relax them. ". . . and that he always had a paper. And cigarettes. So, uh, did he buy his paper here?"

"Oh yes sir," the older man said, "this is where he bought them."

"And cigarettes?"

"He is a smoker of Camel Lights."

"Ever buy anything else here?"

"He is liking the magazines," the proprieter said, and gestured with his head toward the end racks where the magazines went from soft core to hard and then to homoerotic.

"Which ones," Sonny said, "the boys or the girls?"

"Oh, the girls, always. But very hard core."

"All right," Sonny said. "That's as much as I need to know about him. Thanks."

"Oh, I am happy to be of assistance."

"Oh yeah, yeah," Sonny said, as if it was an afterthought. "Did you see this woman?"

Sonny put the photo of Lucinda Merrill, so recently

Mrs. Hoffman, on the counter. Again there was an odd hesitation.

"This is just background stuff. You know, nobody's taking official statements. I don't need the aggravation. You don't need the aggravation. I just need to know if she was ever in the neighborhood."

The older man spoke to his younger cousin in their native tongue. Then he turned back to Sonny and spoke in English. "I have maybe seen this woman once. She is come in here, and I say to my cousin, Hari," he pointed at the younger man, "this is a familiar woman face, but I cannot place it. Did I not say that, Hari. Then when this woman's picture becomes the face on the front cover of *Soap Opera Digest* I say to Hari, that is the woman that came into our shop the night I said to you this is a familiar woman's face. Yes I would have recognized her sooner but for that I have never watched 'Forever and Ever' for we are big fans of 'All My Children' which is its rival and on at the same time."

"You only saw her once?"

"Oh yes, only that once."

"When was that?" Sonny said.

"The night this other man was killed. When I am reading about it in the newspapers, I say to myself, why this is the very same night that I have seen her."

"What did she do when she came in here?"

"She bought a pack of cigarettes . . . Camel Lights. Also lighters."

"How come you remember?"

"She bought four of them."

"Never saw her before that?"

"No sir, never not once."

"Or after?"

"Never, not once."

"OK, fine," Sonny said. "By the way, did anyone take a statement from you before this?"

"You said this was not official."

"No, it's not," Sonny said.

"We have not talked to anyone about this."

He thanked them both. As we stepped outside Sonny said to me, "You did good, Annie."

"No I didn't, I blew it."

"Nah, you spotted it. And we came back and got it. But he's still not the eyewitness we're hearing about."

"Sonny," I said, "is this guy wrong, or did Lucinda Merrill somehow get past us?"

CHAPTER TEN

The next day, late in the afternoon, we found another witness, probably *the* witness who had talked to the police, whose existence had been leaked to the media in a way that had put Lucinda Merrill on the cover of *Soap Opera Digest*.

Her name was Anne Lynn Murphy, a widowed nurse in her late fifties. Her apartment was across the street from Arthur Hoffman's. She'd been there for thirty years. She had a Palm Sunday cross woven out of fronds hanging above a twenty-seven-inch remote-control television and her mother's rosary beads on the wall over a picture of Jesus whose eyes followed us around the room no matter where we stood, in fact he was able to watch both Sonny and me simultaneously. It reminded me of the home I'd grown up in. I felt painfully claustrophobic.

"Oh sure, I saw her," Anne Lynn said. "The very night her poor dead husband was so brutally murdered. What is this city coming to? The killing, the drugs, distributing condoms in the public schools. The shame and disgrace of it all."

"What time did you see her?"

"It was three o'clock in the morning. I'm a little insomniac. My husband, Kevin, God rest his soul, used to take a drop of whiskey for sleeping. But I disapproved and since he passed, it's fifteen years now, sixteen next July Fourth, I haven't let a drop pass my lips. Though I consider it now and then as a soporific. Some people say that exercise will do the trick, but aren't I on my feet all day, fetching and carrying and lifting and tending to the sick and helpless, doing whatever the doctor orders without complaint, isn't that exercise, and still I have trouble sleeping. Well, we each of us have our cross to bear and so be it."

"When do you usually work?"

"I'm day shift," she said. "You would think for an insomniac working the night shift would be just the thing. But it doesn't work, not at all, because I can't sleep during the day. Not a wink. From five A.M. to seven A.M., those are my best hours. I think it was working nights, which I did for many a year, that first destroyed my ability for sleeping. And I work five days a week, taking Sunday off of course and also one weekday, which varies according to them that sets the schedules. You happened to catch me on my at-home day."

"So what did you see?"

"It was full of drama. Just like a scene from late-night television. Here comes Shanna McWarren, and don't I know her as well as my own relations, flying out of the brownstone across the street, she comes stumbling on the front stoop, tripping on her own high heels. Personally I can't wear 'em. Sensible shoes, that's the thing, with nice cushiony soles, for any decent woman who works. Who would want to come home every night with pinched toes and sore back? Well, let me tell you, she almost falls down the steps tripping on her own shoes. So she takes them off, cold as it is, and runs out into the street.

"There's a cab cruisin'—it is the city that never

sleeps—and she waves it down, jumps in, and it takes off."

"Are you really sure it was Lucinda Merrill?"

"Lucinda Merrill?"

"The actress who plays Shanna McWarren."

"Of course I'm sure. Haven't I seen her every day for nine years now?"

"But don't you work all day, when 'Forever and Ever' is on?"

"Have you never been in a hospital, then?"

"Well yes, I have."

"Have you ever seen a nurses' station without a little television, just so those poor girls who work so hard can keep up on things, and isn't there a TV set in almost every room, so even if you have to be watching over someone from one to two, you can keep an eye on the doings of Shanna McWarren, the Ridley clan, and all the rest?"

What a great witness. I could understand why Detective Witte had been skeptical of my testimony. And angry about it.

"It's a terrible thing she's doing," Anne Lynn Murphy said.

"What?"

"Using her enticements with that nice young Jason just when's he's finally about to marry Blair, after all their troubles. A nicer girl you never met. I wouldn't be surprised if whatever happened in the house across the street that night had something to do with their illicit feelings for one another."

That night, after we had reported to Duke, I found a message from Rowdy Randolph on my answering machine. He was here. In Manhattan, in the same city that I was in, once again. I was angry. This was my town. I'd left Los Angeles to him, why couldn't he stay there. He was at the Hotel Warwick. My machine said I could reach him there or through the production office of Galtwick's Galaxie Pictures, the company making the MOW, which, if successful, would be the pilot for a series called "Streetwise," the story of the cops who work the mean streets. Oh God, did the world need another one of those? Kojak was bald, Baretta had a parrot, what great insights were left?

Was I going to call him back?

I was determined that I wouldn't call. But that night I dreamed about him. I had several dreams, actually, one right after another, like a series of story conferences, each trying to work out a watchable plot for the same tired setup. At the beginning of each dream-conference everyone understood that the climax was to be a climax, with the hero and heroine clinching and thrashing in intolerable passion. But, as in most of my sex fantasies, I always got stuck trying to decide what to wear for the affair.

When I woke up I was still thinking about him. That made me mad and I willed him out of my mind. I did my yoga exercises and my yoga breathing and emptied my mind. Nothing but the rhythm of my breath. In and out. A soft sigh, like the ocean, waves rolling in, rolling out, pacific. The Pacific. The beach, near Malibu, where, walking, he first kissed me. Shocked me, though I wanted him to, because I was a married woman at the time. I got lost in his arms. The delirium from some silly old song. Which is what I thought it was supposed to be and wasn't with Patrick. Had it ever been? Back when I was fifteen years old?

I called Duke and I asked him if we should go back and look for more witnesses. Duke said to hold off. He was conferencing with Mr. Petty and the network. Besides, finding witnesses didn't seem to be doing our client much good. They'd found one witness to put her at the scene—we'd found two.

"I swear to you," I said, "she did not leave the apartment."

I decided to go down to Willie's on Tenth and have a long girl-to-girl talk about what was wrong with men and with women for loving them and whether or not I should see Rowdy and if I decided not to, how to stop thinking about it. Besides, I'd been paid by Duke and had enough money to buy my own lunch.

I didn't see a bus coming so I decided to stroll downtown from bus stop to bus stop until one came or I got tired of walking. I passed a newsstand and there was a hot-off-the-press afternoon *New York Post* with the headline:

FAN NAILS SOAP STAR

I bought a copy.

The *Post* had also found Anne Lynn Murphy, insomniac nurse and fan of "Forever and Ever." Of course the *Post*—home of Hero Cops, Love Nests, and Mob Rubouts—dressed it up some. Anne Lynn, was a "dedicated" nurse who had been "tragically" widowed, was "stunned!" and "shocked!" to see her "favorite star in all the world," the "glamorous siren of the daytime screen whose steamy acting style" had made her "notorious for her heated love triangles" (as Shanna McWarren, that is) come running out into the "rain-slicked street" (that was new) in a "clinging sexy satin outfit" that displayed "every detail of her ample figure and left little to the imagination" (had the *Post* reporter gotten more than us or was it a flair for tabloid embellishment?) and driven off in a cab while her husband, "shot three times through the heart" (a different story than I'd heard), lay bleeding to death upstairs.

There were two sidebars, one detailing Lucinda Merrill's career, the other about her husband, a show-business accountant who had been credited with helping 'create' the Shanna McWarren persona that had made his wife one of the queens of daytime. He had, "friends revealed," subsumed himself in her business to the detriment of his own. He'd been "a caring, thoughtful accountant," "a good, but conservative dresser" "who really loved animals, but tragically, couldn't have any pets due to allergies," but most of all he was "the kind of guy you want on your side in an audit."

When I got to Willie's on Tenth I was shocked to find Andrew there, working.

"Aren't you an Arab by now?"

"Do you believe it," he said. "You scrape and claw, you beg and plead, you do any number of things that a normal person would be ashamed of, you live on callbacks and scraps of hope while your family is begging you to come home and work at dad's furniture showroom and all your school friends snicker at you behind your back after they ask 'what've you been in lately? . . . The dishwasher? Hah, hah hah!'

"Then at long last, you finally get a part. A part that pays, a part that your family and those stupid snickering friends will watch and admire you for, and what happens?"

"What?" I asked. "Did they cancel 'Forever and Ever'?"

"Not even that good," Andrew said. "I have been written out."

"No!"

"Yes."

"I'm so sorry," I said.

"Do you want to know the new plot? My agent forced it out of them. He said that he had to tell me *something* when he was going to inform me that my life was going down the toilet. The new plot will feature Shanna McWarren. Beaumont Ridley calls Shanna to force her not to ruin the life of Jason—who unknown to Jason is Beaumont's illegitimate child. Jason thinks that Shanna is going to resume her relationship with Beaumont, who is one of Shanna's four or five ex-husbands. So Jason goes to stop them. But Blair, that's the wimp ingenue who is Jason's intended, already thinks that *she* is the illegitimate child of Beaumont Ridley. She thinks Jason is rendezvousing with Shanna at Beaumont's, so she goes to stop Jason. And to stop Beaumont from telling Jason that he is his illegitimate son because that would make them, she thinks, step-siblings and getting married would be a Big No-No. So everybody goes to Beaumont's. Beaumont gets murdered. Along with, thank God, those two dreadful dogs. All the evidence points to everybody and there will be a long 'who-killed-Beaumont Ridley' thing. Then they will do a murder trial."

"I don't think I followed that," I said. "But I am sorry, Andrew."

"Do you think that witch killed her husband just to build her part?"

He was being facetious, but I felt a need to defend my client and myself. "She couldn't have done it," I said. "I was with her that night."

"Really?"

"When did you find this out, Andrew?"

"Today. At noon. I was, they claimed, the first to be told. Out of concern for me."

That gave me a pretty good idea of who had turned the *Post* on to Anne Lynn Murphy. Each time Arthur

Hoffman's murder made headlines "Forever and Ever" shot up in the ratings. If they could keep the reports featuring Lucinda Merrill as a real suspect alive in the media while they ran a story line in which Shanna McWarren was a fictional suspect, they might move up as far as the number two-spot, fighting it out with "General Hospital." If Lucinda was indicted and put on trial for the murder of Artie while the Shanna story line put her on trial for the murder of Ridley, "Forever and Ever" might even surpass "The Young and the Restless" to become number one. I didn't doubt for a minute that a producer would be willing to destroy an actor for a rating point.

Then a really wild idea came to me. Was it possible that one of the producers of "Forever and Ever" had killed Arthur Hoffman specifically to frame Lucinda Merrill with the intention of raising the ratings? Did such things happen only in fiction? Or were producers evil as well as merely tasteless, puerile, and abusive?

"Annie," Willie cried. "I'm so glad you're here. Did you hear about poor Andrew? Isn't it tragic? Gettin' written out. It's tough to be a woman, but being an actor is a bitch."

"Rowdy is in town," I said. "He called me."

"Have a Bloody Mary," Willie said. "On the house."

"I have money," I said. "From my work as a detective."

"That is so thrilling. Do you carry a gun?"

"What would I do with a gun? I can't stand hearing insects die in bug zappers."

"But isn't it dangerous?"

"I always have one of the guys with me, as backup," I said. "And they carry guns." I returned to what was important: "Should I see him?"

"Did he beg and plead?"

"No."

"Not until he does," she said. Not that Willie had either great luck or good sense about men, a thought we both had at the same time, and she sighed "Oh Annie," and I sighed "Connie Jean," her real name, and we hugged each other. "Come on, sit here with me," she said. We sat at a table and she waved Andrew over. "Two Bloody Marys," she said.

"Not for me."

"Have *some*thing," Willie said.

"All right. White wine," I said to Andrew.

"What's the matter?"

"She's got man problems," Willie said.

"Don't we all," Andrew said.

When I went home I hennaed my hair. I took a long bath. I read a detective novel that a friend had recommended. It was about a female detective and he was sure I would just love it because, after all, wasn't that just like me. It wasn't like me at all. She was a tough guy. She carried a gun, got shot at, and shot at other people. She got beat up and beat up other people. In fact she wasn't like any woman that I knew at all. It seemed to me to be a man pretending to be a woman, as if wearing panty hose with a brand-name .45 automatic was all it took.

I didn't think the author got the detective part right either. This detective worked directly for the client—we always worked for a lawyer—knew what was going on—we just knew what we were assigned to do—and did not care about money, just about justice, and worked really hard for nothing. We took it easy and enjoyed getting paid. Duke marked up our wages at least 100 percent, which was why he was able to hang out at the Stuyvesant Room, drive a Seville, buy his suits where John

Gotti shopped, and maintain so many relationships. The lawyers certainly marked up what he charged them, though I don't know how much, and the client paid for all of it or none of it happened.

In my judgment the author had never been either a detective or a woman and, if called upon, would not do either very well.

There was a miserable romance thing going on at the same time—not in the book, in the reader—and to make a torturously long story with many petty twists and turns, inconsequential details, fits and starts, into a short clear tale, I did not telephone Rowdy Randolph that night.

CHAPTER ELEVEN

I was taking another class from Geraldine Page. If I was in Geraldine's class, that's where Ralph wanted to be. The only problem was that he would need to audition. I promised to help him.

I finally found a monologue that suited his heroic looks and one-dimensional style, Henry V's patriotic exhortation at the gates of Harfleur: "*Once more into the breach, dear friends, once more; or close the wall up with our English dead . . .*" all the way to "*. . . The game's afoot! Follow your spirit and upon this charge Cry, God for Harry! England and Saint George!*" It shows at least that an actor can cut loose with full patriotic fervor and not a shred of embarrassment, or as my first Shakespearean acting teacher, Deveron Bookwalter, would have said: "Hit the high C." So, with my coaching, he too auditioned and was accepted.

To my surprise, Andrew was also in the class.

"I wasn't going to take it," he said, sounding sad and drained, "but I need to be doing *something* actorish."

"Don't be so down about it," I said.

"I heard," Ralph said. "A tragedy."

"Be quiet, Ralph," I said.

"My whole life is acting," Andrew said. "And I'm good. I know I'm good. Aren't I good?"

"You're very good," I said.

"Thanks, Annie," Andrew said.

"You *are* good," I said.

"So why am I a waiter?"

"Your turn will come," I said.

"Your turn did come," Ralph said, supportively, he thought. "You were cast in a to-be-featured role in 'Forever and Ever.' That's great!" He really was impressed at meeting a man who had been cast-but-written-out.

"Look at us," Andrew said. "We auditioned, we competed, for the opportunity to pay money to do what we do. How perverse can it get?"

"Well, it's like going to college," Ralph said.

"What was it for you, Annie?" Andrew said, a little campy. "Did a traveling troupe of players come through your town. And you saw them up there on stage and got star dust in your eyes. Or did you want to be Garbo! Personally, I always wanted to be Gary Cooper. Or Judy Garland."

"I'll tell you the truth," I said, knowing it was quaint. "It was a road-show production of *Oliver* . . ."

Andrew and I looked at each other and burst into song. "Food, glorious food," rhyming "mustard" with "custard," dreaming of peaches and cream and ending with that plaintive refrain "Please, sir, I want some more."

Andrew sat down and there were tears in his eyes. "Where did it go?" he said. "*Broadway*. Whatever it was supposed to be. Or was it always this way? Two hundred thousand of us and only five parts actually cast on any given day, and four of those go to whoever did them before."

"Or to someone whose parents are in the business."

"It's not really that hard, is it?" Ralph said.

"I don't know," I said. "There was a time when I went from part to part, in L.A. Plays, movies, television. I never auditioned. Well I did audition, but I never got anything from that. I got my parts from people who knew me and knew my work."

"I hate casting directors," Andrew said. "A bunch of jealous queens."

"Most of the casting directors I've met have been women," Ralph said.

"They're all of them wannabees. Who know they're not good enough to be actors. So they hate us. That's why they treat us with such rudeness and contempt."

"The last casting I went on . . ." Ralph said.

"What?" Andrew asked him.

". . . the casting director wanted to have dinner with me."

"Even that doesn't work," Andrew said. "None of it works. Did you ever fuck for a part?" It was a bitter and out-of-character question. We both were taken aback.

"No," I said. I hadn't and I wouldn't.

Ralph blushed.

"Yeah, well, that doesn't work either. All it'll get you is sick."

"Oh no," I said. Not that. Not Andrew.

"Oh," he said, realizing what I thought he meant. "Not that. *This* comedy had not turned *that* tragic, yet."

Then class started. I liked Geraldine. She didn't prance in surrounded by spear carriers, announcing with every ounce of her being "I am a Star!" as several acting teachers do. She looked older than her years, she looked blue collar, she had a round face with no makeup, a smile that was adorable and sinister, almost, but not, simultaneously. She wore sweats and sneakers and her hair hung down in need of a brushing. Class began. Andrew mastered his despair and showed me once again how very good he was. Ms. Page said so too. Ralph was wooden but earnest. By the time class was over at least one guy and one girl had crushes on him and were trying to make time with him. But he reacted as if the attention confused him and he ran after Andrew and me.

"I want to work with you," he said to us.

"We're doing a scene together," I said. "Already."

"There must be scenes for three," Ralph said, quite logically.

"Why not," Andrew said.

They both looked at me. I said, "Fine." And we went out for coffee, arm in arm in arm, me in the middle, all actors together, living on hope, chitchat, acting classes, go-sees, call-backs, looking for monologues and audition pieces, wanting no more than to spend our entire lives learning lines and making art out of our being.

I checked my answering machine when we were done. Martha Fiel, my agent, was on the tape: "A call-back. They said you were a new Spacek with a strong Streep streak but utterly and completely yourself. To-morrow! Theater for a New America. *They Fix Dogs, Don't They?* Wanda." I called her back immediately.

"I auditioned for Maureen the last time," I said. "Do you have any instructions about Wanda?"

"Let me look at the sheet," she said. I was put on hold. There is no silence so long or so deep as on hold. She came back brightly. "Maureen was twenty to twenty-five, slender but energetic, intelligent but not bookish, serious with a playful side, tormented by her life but resilient. Wanda, on the other hand, is older . . ."

"How much older?"

"Older. She's willowy but athletic. With a quixotic quality. Serious but with a sensuous side underneath. She's lived in the country and owned dogs before."

"Thanks, Martha," I said, "that's a real help."

I felt so good about myself, called for a call-back and starting a new class, that I decided it would be all right to call Rowdy back. In the evening when I was at home alone.

The other call was from Duke. There was a big meeting. My presence was requested at Zimmerman, Robert and Petty. I looked at my watch and I was due there now. I flagged down a cab. I would get a receipt and mark it in my notebook to expense-account it to, I assumed, Lucinda Merrill.

Everyone else was already there. Mr. Petty in his usual somber legal garb; Duke in one of his pin-striped Mafia banker suits with a particularly elegant silk tie; Sonny with his best pressed jeans, a shirt with a collar, a leather jacket, and gold hung on various parts of his person; Lucinda Merrill in a hugely shoulder-padded businesswoman creation by Lorelei that she had certainly worn on the show, it was much too elegant for the brutality of real life in the city; Samatha Trent, VP for DTP, in an off-the-rack version of what an actress playing the part of a Network vice president would have worn; Stan Ruddiman doing an L.A. look, those unpleasant colors that never quite got fashionable in New York, pleats on his pants and a shirt that buttoned at the neck without a tie; and Detective Witte with a suit that told us he couldn't possibly be on the take, rumpled, weary, and blue. There were two people I didn't know, but if I had to guess, one was the network's attorney—he sat next to Samantha Trent, had a yellow pad and sharpened pencil in front of him, and wore a gray Brooks Brothers suit and a muted red power tie. The other was a small, jovial, older man with white hair, pursed lips, and a professional twinkle in his eye.

I took him to be Lucinda Merrill's agent, the almost legendary Bobby Motzkin.

"I'm so glad you could come, Ms. McGrogan," Mr. Petty said.

"So where we are is back at the same old bull," Witte said.

"I'm sorry I'm late," I said.

"No problem at all," Mr. Petty said.

"Which is that your people are lying hoo-ers," Witte said, meaning me and Sonny.

"Detective Witte, this isn't necessary," Mr. Petty said.

"With your jaw broke you wouldn't talk so much fuckin'—excuse me—crap," Duke said.

"I didn't come here to listen to this," Lucinda Merrill said.

"It's almost entertaining, maybe I should take notes and use it," Stan Ruddiman said, supposedly sotto voce to Samantha Trent, but really clearly enough for us all to hear.

"What I did come here for," Lucinda said, "is to have Mr. Petty tell you that I will sue you, Samantha, and you, Witte, for slander, defamation of character . . ."

"Please, let's not bring that up again," the Brooks Bros. suit with muted-red power tie said. "It won't wash."

"I know damn well how this piece of trash"—Lucinda held up the Post—"got hold of this piece of trash." She displayed the Anne Lynn Murphy story.

"Calm down," Samantha said. "It's the best publicity you'll have in your lifetime. Even if it's true . . ."

"You bitch," Lucinda cried. "You slut. I'm going to make you eat this." She ripped the Post into pieces and balled up a piece in each fist as she stood up and began to go after Samantha.

"No, no," the Brooks Bros. suit cried, "this is assault." He would have risen and gotten between the two women but he wasn't courageous enough.

"I'm in charge here," Witte yelled, but no one listened to him.

"Vell now," the agent said in an oily Viennese accent, "I'm sure we can find a vay to cooperate. Everyone can make money."

But by then Lucinda was standing over Samantha trying to shove the *New York Post* down her throat. Samantha was holding Lucinda by the wrists, digging her short, painted-natural-at-the-Korean-nail-parlor nails into Lucinda's skin. "Help me, help me," Samantha cried.

"What should I do?" Stan Ruddiman asked her.

"Hey, now," Sonny said, kind of getting between the two women and easing them apart.

"I don't have to take this," Samantha said. "I wouldn't even put up with this from Susan Lucci."

"Our ratings have never been higher," Stan said to her.

"Well, I don't know what to say," the Brooks Bros. suit said.

"I'm gonna solve this case," Duke said to Lucinda, "don't you worry."

"This isn't gonna help," Sonny said to Lucinda, "we should relax here."

"Let's take a moment and regroup," Mr. Petty said.

"As you say," Bobby Motzkin, Lucinda's agent, said, "the ratings have never been higher. And as you are exploiting my client to make them so . . ." He held up his hand to show he thought that was all right, just part of the way the game is played.

"Damn right," Lucinda cried, "they're destroying me. For their goddamn ratings points."

"Now, now, Lucinda," the agent said, "let us not complain of ratings points, they are, after all, what pays for *everything*."

"You got a light," Sonny said to Lucinda, taking out his Trues.

"This is not a designated smoking area," Mr. Petty said.

"Ah, screw that, that's a stupid rule," Sonny said.

Mr. Petty smiled at him pleasantly, pushed the intercom button, and asked for ashtrays to be sent in.

"I don't normally smoke," Lucinda said, but she accepted the cigarette Sonny offered her, put it in her mouth, tilted her head, bent down and held the hand with which he held his lighter, just as it is always done in B movies.

"It was Witte leaked it," Duke said. "It's the kind of scuzzy cop he is."

"As I was saying," said the agent, "since it is my client who is raising the ratings points, she too should profit. Don't you agree?"

"It's impossible to say what makes viewers tune in," Samantha snapped. "Right, Stan?"

Stan sat up and barked on cue. "Absolutely, Samantha. An impossible task. If we knew that kind of answer, we'd all be rich."

"Ve all are," said the agent, smiling with deep pleasure. "The point is for us all to get richer."

"I'm gonna charge your client," Witte said, pointing a finger and stamping a foot. "Enough of this bull! Take her away in handcuffs like the common riffraff she is."

That just united everyone against him.

"Let's go slowly here," Mr. Petty said.

"Blow you outta court in a minute," Duke snapped.

"Let's not be hasty," Samantha Trent said.

"Yes, we don't think you should be hasty," Brooks Bros. said. "And the network is pledged to stand behind Ms. Merrill."

"Let's not rush this thing," Stan said. "Let's milk the sugar tit as long as it lasts."

"You bastard," Lucinda said.

A secretary came in with ashtrays. She looked at Sonny and Lucinda smoking and exhaling. She disapproved.

"Can we discuss this, please, like adults, who have attorneys," Mr. Petty said.

Everyone made a sound, from a sigh to a grunt, of assent. Except Witte, who fumed.

"What I would like at this time," the lawyer went on, "is cooperation. I would like my investigators to have access to Mr. Hoffman's apartment. It is, after all, now my client's premises, even if the will has not yet been probated. And access to any other information pertinent to the matter."

"Fo'get about it," Witte said.

"We go along with that," the network attorney said, agreeing with the Petty plan as if Witte were not present. "We've already been in touch with the mayor's office and the chief."

"What chief?" Witte whined.

"Chief of detectives," the network attorney said.

Witte wore the look that Custer must have worn when he finally figured out he was in a losing battle.

"We think that an independent investigator is appropriate," the network attorney said. "We think that is so important that the network will pay the tab for that investigation. Of course we expect to share the information, for our own protection, naturally . . ."

"Out of the question," Mr. Petty said. "The conflict of interest is so clear . . ."

"Let's talk real world a minute," Samantha Trent said. "If Lucinda Merrill wants to go it alone, that's fine. She can go. But I mean alone. Off the show. Bye-bye. If we're going to gamble by keeping her, the network needs to be protected."

"You mean turn my trouble to your profit," Lucinda said.

"Ve are so emotional," the agent said. His voice had a rising, falling, enveloping sound on the word *emotional*. "No need," he said to Lucinda. "Let us talk contract," he said to Samantha.

"Come on, Bobby," Stan said, "your client is under contract, it runs for another three months. With a built-in option to renew."

"Ve are haffing stress, duress, a lot of problems," Bobby the agent said. "I think that in view of her problems my client is simply too exhausted, in her emotions—the emotions of an actor are so delicate—that her verk schedule must be reduced sharply. That is the medical advice ve are haffing."

"Don't pull that crap!" Stan cried.

"I'm talkin' murder. Murder with malice afore-thought!" Witte slammed his hand on the table. "And you people are negotiating contracts."

"Poor, poor Arthur," Lucinda sniffled. She held a handkerchief to her eyes. "I loved him and he is dead. Does no one care? No one?" The sniffles turned to tears. Were they tears of mourning, or was she one of those performers who can cry on cue—many of us can—or did the handkerchief conceal an onion? "I can't go on. Alone. I'm alone." She rose. She drifted toward the door—we all watched—she heaved one sob and she Made an Exit.

Sonny, ever gallant, went after her. He couldn't bear the thought of a woman alone in her misery. Unless he was married to her, of course.

"Ve vere talking contract," the agent said, and one could see him rubbing his hands together, even though he didn't.

"No negotiations," Stan said, sounding as if he'd been watching old John Wayne pictures or George Bush videos.

"You haff been at number four on the daytime Nielsens," Bobby said. "For the first time effer in history. A history of number eight, number nine, down there with 'Loving.'"

"We've never been below 'Loving'! Never!" Stan said.

"How much are we talking about?" Samantha asked.

"My dear, you are so sensible, that is vhy I loff dealing with you so much."

"Cut the caca, Bobby," she said fondly. "Name the number."

He wrote a number on a piece of paper and slid it along the table toward her. We all watched, totally silent, fascinated by and respectful of money.

Stan looked over Samantha's shoulder. "My God," he blurted, "that's a million dollars a year!"

"And she is verth it," Bobby the agent said with conviction, with joy.

"No," Samantha said.

"Just to move 'Forever and Ever' from ninth place to eighth place is verth ten times that. This is something you haff not been able to do with all of the doggies and real little babies."

"It's a temporary phenomenon, Bobby," Samantha said.

"Yeah, Bobby, your babe is gonna end in the slam," Witte said.

The agent ignored him and spoke to Samantha. "Vhut is the hardest thing in the entire show bizziness vorld to do? I vill tell you—to get soap opera vatchers to change shows. They are addicts. So, my client has moved you all the vay up to number four. Incredible. Unbelievable. They are deserting 'All My Children' and 'Days of our Lives' to see her. No matter vhut happens, some of them vill become addicts of *your* show, with the silly doggies and the little babies, and you will keep them."

"Don't disparage dogs just because you don't represent any," Stan said. It was well known in the industry that the animals were his pet idea. Of such things are careers made.

"Half," Samantha said.

"A new three-year, no-cut contract," Bobby said.

"We don't do no-cut contracts," Samantha said. "This isn't baseball."

"Walk away from it, Sam," Stan said, "let her twist slowly in the wind. She'll come crawling back. Don't give in to this shyster extortionist."

"Vhut a shame. I haff an offer from ABC. Lucinda Merrill, Susan Lucci on the same show they are thinking they can knock off 'The Young and the Restless'. I haff an offer to go prime time."

"Yeah, what," Stan scoffed.

" 'Dark Shadows,' " Bobby said. "It is perfect."

"I think we can agree in principle," Samantha said.

What a performance. An extra half million dollars a year on top of whatever her contract already was. Lucinda Merrill had just popped to the top spot in soap salaries. And it was guaranteed for three years, even if she were sick, drunk, or in prison.

I wanted that man to be my agent.

I went home and made myself dinner. Then I took a short bath. Then I called Rowdy Randolph.

He had checked out of the hotel and returned to Los Angeles.

CHAPTER TWELVE

Duke had Sonny and me meet him at the Stuyvesant Room the next day at 10:00 A.M. A guy named Paulie joined us.

"Paulie here is gonna be our forensics guy," Duke said. "And photographer. Also anything special anybody needs in the way of a wire, you should talk to Paulie. You start by going over Hoffman's apartment. Here's the keys. You can cut the tape. Paulie photographs everything, let him get it before you screw it up."

"Sure, before we screw it up," Sonny said.

"Me and Dom are gonna go over to Hoffman's office and start from there. End of the day, we meet back here, see who's got what. What we're looking for is somebody else had a reason to waste this guy. Means, motive, opportunity. What else we're looking for is bad stuff about Hoffman. You know, Petty, he doesn't say stuff like that out front, but I gotta figure the fall-back position is the 'the sonuvabitch deserved to die' defense."

"What do you think?" I said, outraged. "That she got by me and Sonny?"

"Things is always possible, all kindsa things."

"If," I said, "Lucinda Merrill could have gotten past us, I would have told you so."

"Nobody's sayin' you're a liar. Siddown, relax."

"I'm not standing," I said.

"Yeah, that's true, lemme buy you a drink."

"Sonny and I did not let Lucinda Merrill get past us."

"Nobody said you did," Duke said.

"OK," I said.

"All I'm saying is that Witte likes her for it, he's got witnesses that put her there"—he held up his hand to me in a keep-the-peace gesture—"and motive . . ."

"What?" Sonny said.

"They were married to each other, best fuckin' motive for murder in the world," Duke said. Everybody laughed. Except me. Even if it was true, it wasn't funny. "So what we're looking for is enemies, friends, family . . . anybody ready to slander the guy."

A woman of about thirty stalked over to our table. She was dressed to kill: short, tight skirt, mesh stockings, high heels, and a lavender blouse that showed her ample breasts. She said: "You sonuvabitch, you two-timin' slime!"

"What'sa matta, honey?" Duke said plaintively.

"Your wife just called me!"

"Don't pay no 'ttention to her," Duke said.

"No, no, I want you to hear what she said to me."

"C'mon, honey, there are people here."

"Your wife has a nasty mouth. She said: 'You whore, it's one thing that you're gettin' on your knees in front of my husband, you cheap slut, but when you start taking the bread outta my children's mouths, you're going too goddamn far. If I ever hear of you coming near my Kenny again . . .'"

I had no idea that the Duke was really named Kenny. It was cute. And this had to be the famous Sandy. She was really angry.

" '. . . I'm gonna cut your tits off.' Your wife really, really has a foul mouth on her. So I said: 'What's your beef lady, if you could take care of your man, he wouldn't be bothering me.' She says: 'I don't want to take care of him but I sure as hell am not going to allow him to buy no low-life home-wreckin' whore no god-damn fourteen-hundred-dollar ankle bracelet from Fortunoff's.' I said to her: 'What are you talking about, fourteen-hundred-dollar ankle bracelet from Fortunoff's?' You know what she said, Kenny, she said: 'I'm looking at his American Express bill, it's right in front of me, and I sure didn't get it.' And she hangs up.

"Well, Kenny," Sandy said with a low, ugly snarl, "I didn't get it either."

It was a studio apartment, one large room plus a hallway converted to a kitchen and a bathroom with a shower, no bath.

If old despair had a smell, this had to be it. It was a mixture of dried bodily fluids, take-out foods, dust and cockroaches. I wanted desperately either to leave or to clean.

The outline of the body was still on the floor. So were the blood and urine stains. The police had dusted for fingerprints and those marks were still there.

Paulie lit a cigar. Sonny lit a cigarette and offered me one. I took it and let the smoke wreath my face and fill my nostrils. Paulie had two equipment cases. He opened them on a clear spot on the floor. One held camera gear. The other held a collection of forensic equipment. He took out three pairs of surgical gloves, one size fits all, gave them to each of us, and made a safe-sex joke. Then he went back to the first case and took out a camera with a strobe. We waited while he methodically photographed the room.

The bed was rumpled, the sheets were stained. I noticed several filled ashtrays. Paulie looked at them too, poked at them with the tip of his pen, and said "cops." He didn't take a picture. "You see anything interesting, tell me, I'll shoot. Don't touch it, it probably doesn't matter, the cops left this worthless as a crime scene. Probably."

I instinctively went to the closet. Paulie hadn't shot it yet. As I opened it he said, "Oh yeah, lemme get that." Even as the strobe went off I saw that the closet was half-full of women's clothes.

"Can I look at these?" I said.

"Yeah, go ahead," Paulie said.

"Can I take them out?"

"Yeah, lemme examine the bed, then you can lay 'em out there. Let's do it methodically, you know. I'll shoot them."

While Paulie shook out the blankets and sheets and looked inside the pillow cases, Sonny looked through the kitchen drawers. "We got some paraphernalia," Sonny said.

"Whaddaya got?" Paulie said.

"Baking soda, Clorox, razor blade stuck in back, glass stirrer . . . hey, hey, natural coffee filters. Funniest thing in the world, health-conscious dope fiends."

"I heard o' that," Paulie said. "It's not a health-conscious thing. You use the filters to make sure you get all the dope out of the solution. Problem with coffee filter or tea bags, it's white on white, your natural coffee filter, it's brown, so you get white on brown. Get every little bit o' your dope."

"Here's an empty gas canister, back of the cabinet."

"Bag it," Paulie said. "We gonna get an inventory of what the cops took outta here?"

"Beats me, talk to the Duke," Sonny said.

I carried a group of dresses out of the closet and put them on the bed.

"Whaddawe got?" Sonny said. "Cross dresser?"

"Not unless he was slender," I said.

"Slender?"

I held one up. It was one or two sizes too big for me. And I'm a size five. These fit someone with a twenty-five-inch waist, at the most. I'd never met a man who could've gotten into these.

"Girlfriend," Sonny said.

"I think they belong to Lucinda Merrill," I said.

"What makes you think that?"

"They're her style. Actually, they're Shanna Mc-Warren's style."

"How do you know?" Paulie asked me.

"I don't know exactly," I had to admit. "I just recognize it."

"She's sharp, Paulie, you should listen to her."

"Yeah, but how does she know?" Paulie said.

"You see a guy, he's not wearing blue, how do you know he's a cop? You see a skell on the street, how do you know he's street scum? You see a guy he's connected, you know. When it's your business you know things. Annie, her business is being a woman."

Boy, who wrote these guys' dialogue, I thought.

"It was my understanding," Paulie said, "that this was his home away from home, you unnerstand. I mean, this was supposed to be his place for strange, not to bring what he had at home. Or does everybody have it all wrong?"

"You know what it is," Sonny said. "It's a mystery, is what it is."

There were more women's clothes in the closet. We cataloged and photographed them all. There were also three hat boxes with hats, a wig stand, and several strands of blond hair on the shelf above the hanger rack. Paulie put them in ziplock bags and carefully labeled them. I looked through the men's clothing as well. The police had done that before me, looking for notes, I suppose, leaving the pockets turned out. I looked at the labels, the cut, the fabrics. Arthur Hoffman had been a generally conservative dresser, though not so much as a corporate lawyer or banker, who bought from 'better men's stores,' but he hadn't been looking after his things too well.

On the closet floor there were a pair of men's running shoes and slippers and four pairs of women's stiletto "fuck me" heels in different colors. Three of the four, in my opinion, went with specific dresses.

Sonny opened the dresser drawers. We found more men's things—underwear, socks, T-shirts, sweat shirts and pants, a couple of sweaters—and women's lingerie and underwear. Sonny and Paulie liked the pieces but I didn't. They may have looked like silks and satins but they were polyester. They wouldn't feel good against the skin and they wouldn't stand up to wear or washing. It makes so much more sense to spend a few dollars more to get natural fibers—if indeed it costs more—because you get so much more value for your money. It's also healthier.

There was nothing unusual in the narrow linen closet. Sonny found a stack of magazines under the bed, the kind that Hoffman used to buy from the Pakistani. I didn't look at them, but I was aware that they were more extreme than *Playboy*. The bathroom had a collection of patent remedies—for headache, for backache, gas, indigestion, diarrhea, sore and irritated eyes. Several soaps, shampoo, conditioners, disposable razors, shaving cream, after-shave. There was an old-fashioned clothes hamper. It was full, mostly with men's things, but with two pieces of soiled women's underwear.

It felt strange and terribly intrusive going through someone's home this way. I told myself it was an acting exercise. One of the things one learns to do is to create biographies of the characters one plays. The author may not supply any scenes in the bedroom or bath, say nothing about the character's childhood or parents or job or school or state of health, but we, as actors, should know, as we walk onstage, where we are traveling from and what baggage we carry with us. So when we imagine the part, we should imagine the indigestion as well as the glamour, what's in the medicine chest and what's in the closet.

"Hey, Annie," Paulie said, "Sonny tells me you're actually an actress?"

"Yes," I said, "I'm an actor."

"How come you say actor?"

"Yeah, how come you say actor?" Sonny said.

"Because if you're an actor you at least stand a chance of being respected for what you do; if you say actress, people expect you to jiggle for Zest-Time Cola."

When I got home there were two messages on my machine. One was from my agent, my call-back for *They Fix Dogs, Don't They* had been rescheduled. She reminded me that Theater for a New America was *highly regarded* and that this piece was written by an *important* playwright.

The second was from Rowdy Randolph. He was sorry that he had missed me. He had to go back to the Coast— where he was speaking from—but would return to New York. Shortly. And hoped to see me then. This was an awful lot of effort for Rowdy considering that I was someone with whom he had already scored, whose marriage he'd already destroyed. What was in it for him? I thought, thinking like Sonny or Duke. Perhaps my absence had lead him to a perception of my finer qualities. Or was there really some sort of caring there?

CHAPTER THIRTEEN

got up early to make sure that I was prepared for my audition. I looked over the character description. I did my yoga so that I would be *willowy but athletic*—rather than *slender but energetic*. In my meditation I thought about being *serious but with a suppressed sensuous streak*, as opposed to someone *tormented by life but resilient*. Then I went over the script.

MAUREEN: I've decided to produce for the cinema.
WANDA (my part, this time): Yes, the cinema needs you.
MAUREEN: Too long have I toiled as a housekeeper.
DEREK (wearing a truss): Who will care for me?
MAUREEN: If my husband, who is an idiot, can be a lawyer, I can direct films.
WANDA: Make it a statement. Make it mean something.
MAUREEN: Do you know what I do all day? I compiled a list. I awake and see to it that my husband squeezes enough oranges for the entire family.
WANDA: It is so important to do that.
MAUREEN: I make breakfast of course.
WANDA: Nutrition starts a day.

DEREK: (pawing at his truss): Is there anything under here?

MAUREEN: I give each person their portion of cereal, then allow them to pour their own milk. Shall I go through the entire list or just hit the hight points.

WANDA: I want it all. All. All.

MAUREEN: I'll just hit the high points.

DEREK: Is there some way to get this off?

MAUREEN: Dressing is probably the first big thing. You know, I almost wish he could grow his nuts back so we could fix him again.

WANDA: Great idea. For a film.

MAUREEN: Yes, that's it (she rises). That's what my first film will be about.

Music, swelling, upbeat, New Age, as Maureen looks off toward the horizon.

Perhaps, I thought, Theater for a New America would have a brilliant director who would illuminate this for me. Maybe it was good and I just couldn't grasp it. Perhaps it meant something and I just didn't understand it. The possibility that it was as bad and devoid of meaning as I thought was too depressing to contemplate.

I was on time. I waited an hour. There was a short, wide girl with a yellow fifties angora sweater who appeared to be running things.

I said: "How much longer do you think I'll have to wait.

She said: "I dunno."

I said: "Could you find out, please."

She said: "How?"

Sometime later I was called into the inner sanctum. Four people were waiting to watch me. There were no introductions. I guessed them to be the Director, the Writer, the Assistant, the Other Assistant.

"I'll read with you," the Other Assistant said.

"I've been waiting an hour and a quarter," I said, not unpleasantly.

"No, no, don't start yet," the Director said.

"I think that's really rude," I said.

"I can't find that line," the Other Assistant said, frantically turning pages for a spot where Wanda talked about waiting.

"What do you think actors are?" I said.

"What page are you on?" the Other Assistant said.

"How much abuse should we take? How much disrespect?"

"Would you tell me what page you're on," the Other Assistant said.

"Is someone going to acknowledge the things I'm talking about?"

"I'm sorry, I'm lost here, let's take it from the top," the Other Assistant said.

"Those aren't lines," the Writer said. "At least not my lines."

"You're here for Maureen," The Assistant said.

"No. Wanda," I said.

"No. No. No, can't be," The Director said. "You're a Maureen."

"I don't understand the play at all," I said. "I shouldn't admit that I guess. But I don't and I don't think I relate to it," I said.

"That's not my line either," the Writer said. "I thought they all had to read my lines."

"She's talking," the Other Assistant said. It was a realization.

"What is it you want?" the Assistant said.

"Several things," I said. "An apology for keeping me

waiting this long would be nice. Then, some insight into the play, if you don't mind."

"You really mean that you don't *get it?*" the Writer said.

"Just read it," the Director said.

"She doesn't get it," the Writer said.

"OK," the Assistant said, "you *are* here for Wanda."

"I found the page," the Other Assistant said. "Are you ready to start?"

"We sent out character descriptions," the Director said.

"Wanda is older," the Assistant read. "Willowy but athletic—not slender but energetic! With a quixotic streak. She's lived in the country and *owned dogs!*"

"Does that say anything to you," I said. "It doesn't say anything to me."

"Oh God, oh God, how can anyone be so dumb, they don't *get it,*" the Writer said. "My work is very, very deep, but very, very accessible."

"That's why we're doing it," the Director said. "It's intense but lightened with levity, very contemporary yet timeless, it's antisexist yet not male hating."

"I'll pass," I said, shocking them, yet shocking myself more. It felt like I was doing something daring yet comfortable, bold but correct in the circumstances, losing an opportunity but gaining . . . what?

Lucinda Merrill had a private dressing room. It was functional and windowless, rather than glamorous, but it was hers and enough so that she had covered one wall with photos. They were mostly of herself, head shots, publicity stills, mementos of moments with other celebrities, winning her Emmy, and there was one of her husband, Arthur. There was a stack of fan mail on her make-up table. Even with the door closed we could feel the bustle of controlled hysteria out in the studio. The scene coming up was one of those that would lead to Shanna McWarren's appointment with Beaumont Ridley when Ridley would be murdered. She was in costume and finishing her makeup. "You will help me, won't you," she said. She played the line as an appeal from the heart.

"We'll do our best," Sonny said.

"How does it look?" she said. "So far?"

"Can I ask you a question?" I said.

"Certainly, anything."

I spread out the photographs of the shoes and dresses we had found in her husband's apartment. "Are these familiar?"

The recognition was instant—in my opinion—but she looked them over carefully before she answered. "They look like mine. From the show. Of course they're all old. I mean you can see that they're hardly this year's look. They're mine."

Lucinda looked at me to tell her what that meant. I looked to Sonny. Sonny doesn't like to tell people what they might not want to hear. He looked back at me.

"This apartment that your husband was killed in, did you go there often?"

"I was never there," she said.

"These clothes," I said, "and shoes to match. They're from that apartment."

"I don't understand," she said.

"Neither do we," I said.

"We're working for you," Sonny said.

"I'm sorry, Ms. Merrill," I said, trying and failing to find a delicate way to put it, "but we keep finding things that place you in the apartment."

"Why do I have you working for me?" she said with

a bitter bewilderment that would have played perfectly in one of the great black-and-white films of the forties.

"See, we just go out and ask questions and look around and we can't help what we find," Sonny said.

"What is it that you have found that is so terrible?" she said. Bravely.

Sonny looked over to me. "Here's what we've come across so far," I said. "The man at the corner newsstand, he says you came into his place the night your husband was killed. He doesn't remember the time, but it was probably close to the time the medical examiner says your husband died."

"Do the police know about him?" she said.

"We don't think so," Sonny said. "And we work for you so we're not about to tell them. We give our reports to Duke, who talks to Mr. Petty, your lawyer, that's all."

"Won't he tell the police?"

"Mr. Petty wouldn't do that, ma'am. He works for you," Sonny said.

"We all sat there, you and you and me," Lucinda said, "while Petty and that awful man Witte and that bitch, Samantha Trent, agreed to share all information. That was the agreement at the meeting."

"Sure," Sonny said. "But you're talking about a lawyer, a cop, and a television executive, you can't worry about someone like that living up to an agreement. For example, your husband's phone book, which would be helpful to us. The police took it from your husband's apartment. When Petty asked Witte for it, Witte says he can't release it without a court order. Now that is a crock, you understand. That's purely his own discretion, there's no rule about that."

"Are you going to be able to get it?"

"Yeah, sure," Sonny said. "Lester Petty's a smart lawyer. He'll see the judge, he'll say you have to continue your husband's business affairs, you need the phone numbers, give us the book or a copy of it. It'll take all of a day or two. Duke and Petty, they'll play their games with Witte."

"But what about the network? The network is paying for your investigation. And they'll get their pound of flesh," Lucinda said. "I know them. That woman, that Samantha Trent. That's not her real name. She's really Sophie Schmerdlinch. She hates me, she really does. Because I'm more beautiful than she is. I don't mean to be vain, but it's true. Because I make more money than she does. Because I had Arthur."

"Really," Sonny said.

"Yes, really," Lucinda said. "Arthur was an accountant and the cliché is that accountants are like nerds but not as smart. Arthur was, what? . . . reasonably good-looking, but he had something special. An assurance, a quality, he made a woman feel safe. You have that too, but in a more physical way," she said to Sonny. Sonny nodded, he knew that. "And oh my God, I loved him." She brushed the famous forward-falling locks back from her face and blinked the tears out of her eyes. She turned abruptly from us and dabbed her eyes with a tissue. "Save the makeup," she said.

"We'd like to talk to some people who knew him," I said.

"Of course, yes, you have my permission. I'll tell them so. I am sure that you will hear that Arthur and I . . . well, that we fought a lot. Lately, we did. Big ugly fights. Nobody can get you as crazy as someone you're close to." She gave an "ironic" laugh. "I guess that's what soap operas are all about, right. Anyway. I won't deny that we had our troubles. But he was a wonderful man and *I knew it.*"

"The clothes," I said. "Why were they in Arthur's apartment?"

"But the biggest reason that Samantha Trent hates me," she said, "is because I'm the actress."

"That I understand," I said.

"Yes, they told me you were an actress, too," she said, and reached over and touched my hand. "The real magic is getting out there, on the stage or in front of the camera, and *doing it*. Everything else is support services. They would like to make us into just product. But they can't.

"People like Samantha Trent hate us for that. Because she realizes that we are indispensable and she is not. When an actor leaves a show—people care. They cry. They call their friends to share the pain. They write letters to the network. When a producer goes, nobody, but nobody, gives a tinker's damn. Nobody even knows the goddamn difference."

Right on! my heart cried.

An assistant director knocked on the door, stuck his head in, and said, "Ready to roll?"

"When do they want me?"

"Now," he said.

"I have to go," she said to us. "Thank you for caring."

"Just doing our job," Sonny said.

"And if there's anything I can do for you," she said.

"No, that's fine," I said.

"Who's your agent?" she asked.

"Martha Fiel," I said.

"Oh, you poor dear," she said. "Annie McGrogan, you have a quality. You do. I'm going to speak to Bobby Motzkin about you."

"That's not necessary," I said. It wasn't necessary, but it was wonderful. It was power. It was connections.

"I put on a great act, don't I," Lucinda said. She stood up and looked in the mirror. "My husband was just murdered in, in an apartment he kept for God knows what . . ." She corrected herself: "We do know what, don't we." She shook her hair out and brushed it into place with her fingers. "And the police want to say I did it. The papers are saying I did it. I am an object of great curiosity. I feel grief. I feel humiliation. And fear." She paused, took a breath, and announced: "But life goes on. The show must go on and now, now I have to be a sultry siren." She moved her hips and watched how the dress shaped on her, then shifted her shoulders to get her breasts working and walked out the door, in her obvious way, one of the vixens that America's mothers loved to hate one day and root for the next.

CHAPTER FOURTEEN

"I have a philosophy. Our first invention is ourselves."

—Shane Burke, actor

One of the really nice things about being a
detective—I had stopped expecting a rude
casting director to yell "Fine-next!" (one
word)—was the lack of supervision. Sonny and I were
doing our interviews of cast and crew from "Forever
and Ever." I had my voice-activated minirecorder in my
pocketbook. I would label the tapes and turn them in to
Duke whenever we caught up with him.

The information came at us in a very random way.
If someone wanted to, he could have taken our tapes
and by cutting and pasting them together he would
have been able to do an audio-only docudrama, *The
Lucinda Merrill Story*. If someone did, it would have been
something like this.

SHANE BURKE
(Mature Leading Man)
*I'm probably Lucinda's oldest friend on the
show. I was here before her, I'm the third Beaumont Ridley. The first two didn't last terribly long
and the show really found its legs, however short,*

*about when I came on, so you would think that
there's some longevity there, in that part, for me.*

*Arthur's friend too. That's another reason we
became friends, family friends, because I'm a heterosexual guy in a stable marital relationship, obviously one of the very few around here. Of course
we have kids, two of them, and Arthur and Lucinda,
well, never will, now.*

*Arthur wanted kids. I remember when they
came to my younger son's bar mitzvah . . .*

Like any businessman at the office, Shane had family photos in standing silver frames—the two sons and
his wife. He also had a shot of the whole family together
at what I took to be a temple. Shane and the boys all
wore yarmulke's and Shane had a white scarf draped
around his shoulders.

*. . . who is Shane Burke? He is a contraction of
Saul Burkowitz . . . People think of actors as people
who play other people, but our first role, the first
thing we have to create is that actor. Lucinda Merrill, sultry soap star, is a great example, terrific
example.*

*I know where she comes from, I even saw it
once. A suburb of Canton, Ohio. Nothing dramatic
and terrible. Just drab. Tract housing, four, five
streets, all the same. Small, dull. Her father, who
was dead she said, was a postman. And her real
name . . . Her name was Bernice Perlvukic.*

FAYE WRIGHT
(Character Actress)
*Oh hon, we go back, way back . . . all the way
to: Ber-nice! Her real name. Wormed it out of her*

one night. See she didn't become Lucinda right away. She was Jacqueline, Caitlin, Heather—Megan. Can you believe it? How many Jackies and Megans can the world stand?

We were Broadway babes. We were ready for those Big Shows! Only, of course, how many of them are there? Oh, I still get a musical from time to time, I did five weeks in Chorus Line just before this.

Back then, if you and I were making bets, I would have bet on myself over Lucinda. I mean, Jacqueline, Caitlin, Heather, Megan. But suddenly, it seems suddenly, she was on target. Moved right in, moved right on up.

ANNALISE CHRISTIAN
(Third Ingenue)
Artie claimed that he created Her. Totally.

FAYE WRIGHT
I wasn't in town when they met. I was in a road show of This Was Burlesque. Having a mad, passionate fling with the youngster who was our traveling techie. So physical, such fun. Where has fun gone, hon, where has it gone?

He was obsessed with her. Really, it was like something out of an obsession movie, like The Fan or Taxi Driver. Except that Arthur wasn't creepy. Very serious, of course, as befits an accountant.

ANNALISE CHRISTIAN
No, Artie didn't say that he made her name up. He had it made up. It was like something from . . . oh what's that famous story? It's mythology, you

know. Oh, Artie told me. You know the one, My Fair Lady *is about it.*

Pygmalion? *No. That's not it. It's something Greek.*

Artie got this marketing guy. That's like an advertising person. Did you ever hear of a focus group? A focus group is when they bring a group of people into one room and they give them different kinds of the same thing. Like the same soap but in a red wrapper and in a green wrapper and then the group says which one they like.

That's how Artie created Lucinda. Or how his marketing friend did, anyhow. With a focus group!

It was like a total make-over. They picked a name. And a hairstyle. Artie told me how they did that—this is really, really incredible—they had an artist draw a picture of Lucinda from her photograph, then they had him draw it over and over again with different hairstyles and the focus group picked the Lucinda they most wanted to watch.

They did it with everything, a total make-over. Her voice, her clothes, even her attitude, except I don't know how they could do that. An attitude is like a thing. It's complicated.

ESTHER LITVAK
(Casting Director)

What a load of rubbish. I never met an actor that was created by someone else. Who do you think Artie Hoffman was? Svengali? The Phantom of the Opera? Crap. He was an accountant.

If someone could create a star they could do it twice. And no one ever does. Look in Back Stage, *there are four hundred ads from people who claim they can make you a star. And let me tell you they can't. I know.*

Esther was—how shall I say this with delicacy—a lump of reality amidst the shallow glitter of the cast. Heavy, frumpy, smelling of the cigarettes she smoked. And she had the soul of a casting director as well.

> *I discovered Lucinda Merrill. It took me five seconds. I have the eye. I have the ear. I have the instinct. I know talent. I know it when someone's got it.*
> *That's my job. To be in touch. To see. To know.*

Esther asked Sonny if he'd ever done any acting. When Sonny said no, she suggested that he get a head shot and send it over to her. He was a good type and she thought she could use him.

She didn't say anything to me. Did that mean that I had gone so deep into my part—Nancy Drew, girl detective—that Annie McGrogan, actor, had become invisible inside it? Or did it mean that I did not have spottable talent of the kind that Esther Litvak was so expert in discovering? Did I want to have the sort of talent that someone as talentless as Esther could spot—the obvious, unidimensional, Johnny-one-note type of talent?

Being an out-of-acting-work actor is to be always on the defensive.

SHANE BURKE
There was a point when Lucinda moved from being a regular player to being a star, having fans, being able to make salary demands, that she changed. Their relationship also changed then and they stopped being as much fun to be around.

JENNIFER MCGUFFIN
(First Ingenue)

Oh Lord, I didn't know her way back when. Everyone who knew her way back when says she was so nice. I'm the kind of person who thinks the best of people. Call me naive, but it's true, I do. I'm a kind of Pollyanna. Until they prove me wrong.

Which Lucinda Merrill has.

Take this thing with Anthony, Anthony Oster who plays Jason, my intended on the show. Lucinda acts like we're really in competition for him. She's coming on to him off-stage, which is ridiculous because Anthony is strictly, but strictly, you know which way. I mean he's a dear sweet boy, but I for one wouldn't kiss him with my mouth open.

I, for one, believe in live and let live. People should be free to do what they want as long as they don't do it outside where they can frighten the horses, that's what my Grandma says, God bless her. She lives up in New Hampshire, in a small town. She raised me and she raised me right.

Lucinda acts, pardon the expression, Lucinda behaves, as if beauty and talent have made her a star. I for one, don't think so.

Let me tell you a story. You know the old joke about the Polish starlet? She went to Hollywood and blew the writer? Well on a soap it wouldn't be a joke. Oh, they have power. Write you in, write you out, write your part fatter or thinner, make you interesting or boring.

I'm not the kind of person who repeats stories. I hate gossip. I truly do. The way Lucinda Merrill took a very minor part and made a career out of it? There was a writer here then, he's since been fired, Harry Beinbruch, he was the head writer. Well, she sought him out and screwed him four ways from Sunday. Used to get him off right in her dressing room. Did him so much that he was walking funny. Whenever she took a break and lifted her head up she would make suggestions for how her part could be improved. Well, you can imagine that she had some influence.

Talent, my butt.

FAYE WRIGHT

Well, of course, Lucinda had her little affairs. What's a girl to do, hon, when men just love her so. Like bees to honey, hon.

But are they telling that one! Slept her way to the top? Just between us and the walls, hon, if a girl could sleep her way to the top, I'd be Meryl Streep. God, I wish it were that easy. And that much fun, hon.

Artie was probably messing around too. Oh I know he was. But I don't think he enjoyed it much. He was so, so serious. So many people are, you know. Serious. About sex.

Hey hon, I do know some juicy, juicy gossip about Artie Hoffman. It's old gossip but it is cute as can be. You know who they say Artie boffed— Samantha Trent, Dragon Lady.

SHANE BURKE

Of course Arthur changed too. And not for the better. It got progressively worse, I mean, he really was obsessed with the woman and she was getting progressively further away.

There was a real deterioration. In everything, business problems, financial problems.

JENNIFER MCGUFFIN

He came on to me. Now there are some women, in my position, who would have used the situation to make a point to Ms. Merrill. But not I. I was raised right, and my grandmother, she always said: "Even a dog knows enough not to do in his own dog house."

Besides, in my opinion, I hate to speak ill of the dead, it's a terrible thing to do, but why mince words and the word is cocaine. I hate to do it with coke fiends, too many problems.

FAYE WRIGHT

Oh, hon, sure Artie hit on me. But that doesn't mean anything. Men, they go through phases. One year it's baseball, the next monogomy, then it's grab anything that wiggles.

Well, sure, hon, I considered it. Out of mercy. But it was just too, too incestuous. I realized that after he came over to the apartment. There we were, I have a very romantic little place, high up, view of the city lights. I just love my little apartment to death.

There was music on. Sinatra. It's old-fashioned, I know, but don't you think it's time romance was back? Artie kept talking about Lucinda. Lucinda this, Lucinda that.

He even wanted me to do my Lucinda Merrill imitations. I am a great mimic and I do a Lucinda Merrill that'll crucify you, wanna hear?

ANNALISE CHRISTIAN

He was going to do for me what he had done for his wife. You know she was really nongrateful for all he had done.

I was going to get my own focus group.

Of course I remembered my friend Irene, who fit somewhere in this litany of extramarital activity. I asked Duke if he wanted me to track her down.

"What's the point," he said, "I think we pretty well nailed it that he was screwing around."

"She made it sound like he was particularly kinky," I said. I think I blushed.

"What do you mean?" Duke said.

"I don't know," I said.

"If we need it, I'll tell you," Duke said. "He already sounds pretty bad, don't he?"

CARMINE TOMASSO
(Gaffer)

You bet he was in trouble.

How do I know. I'll tell you how I know. A gentleman came to see him. The kind that say "your money or your legs." Maybe you know the guy. Morrie 'the Mule' Siegal.

I don't know if anyone else noticed. Actors are dweebs. They're not bad people, but they live in their own little world. And a narrow world it is. If it doesn't have something to do with how much screen time they're gettin' and light 'em so the wrinkles don't show, it doesn't penetrate, you unnerstand.

SAMANTHA TRENT

The rumor that I and Arthur Hoffman had any kind of relationship is categorically ridiculous.

Samantha made this denial without either of us asking about it. In fact, long before we heard any such rumor.

Arthur Hoffman approached every woman on this set. He was persistent and obnoxious. I also heard rumors of drug use and financial problems. I tried to be sympathetic. I really did. People have problems. They deserve every chance, as long as it doesn't affect the workplace.

There was absolutely nothing personal in my banning him from the studio.

SHANE BURKE

Does Samantha Trent hate Lucinda Merrill?

Samantha Trent hates low ratings, red ink, a bad P&L statement. Samantha Trent loves cost cutting, rising advertising revenues, and her picture in the annual report.

In other words, does Samantha Trent have any personal feelings at all? I am being catty, aren't I? I don't really think that the TV business was ever really nicer than it is now. But I tell you what, it felt as if it was. The corporate climate . . . you like that phrase? The corporate climate around here has changed.

Ever since the butchers from St. Louis took over UBS with junk bonds . . .

I didn't know exactly what he was talking about at the time, but it was later explained to me. The Wesley Brothers, St. Louis meat packers who owned Mid-America Meats, had become creative financers, taking over a host of other companies using bonds, a form of borrowing that paid very, very high interest. Along the way they changed the name of their company to Mid-AmeriCorp.

. . . things have become very cutthroat. They have to make something like twenty-three percent profit before they break even. It's a form of insanity. You feel the pressure everywhere.

CARMINE TOMASSO

The network is a cash cow. It's the only thing at this point that's keeping Mid-AmeriCorp from collapsing. They're draining the place, totally. If they don't do something soon, they're going to drag it right down to Chapter Eleven.

SAMANTHA TRENT

Daytime programming makes more net profit for this network than prime time. In fact you could say that we support many of the other operations. I'm proud of that.

It is impossible for this network to go bankrupt. Don't be ridiculous. That's beyond belief that anyone would say so.

CARMINE TOMASSO

Samantha Trent, she's a prime example of Wesley Brothers shark.

Her job is to find a way to get more cash out of here. If she can't, and they do go bankrupt, they'll use that to bust the unions.

VICKIE LAZLO
(Publicity Director)

Samantha Trent asked me to put together this little Fin-pack . . . that's our little joke up in Publicity. Mostly we send out Fan-packs, packages of gush for the fans who adore our daytime serial stars, so when we put together a business information package we call it a Fin-pack.

You know actors are very, very insecure people. Who can blame them? I certainly don't. I adore actors. So when someone's contract is not renewed or they get written out, they always, always come up with a story that makes it a deus ex machina. That's Greek for "God in a Machine." In the ancient days of Greek Theater whenever they got stuck in the plot they brought in a god, like Zeus or Athena, in a crane type of machine. The god would come down and fix it all. I majored in Theater in college.

That's why you've heard this latest story going around.

Actually, we hadn't heard it at that point. But I, for one, would believe an Actor over a Head of Publicity anytime.

It is not true that as soon as an actor demands over scale, we do not renew their contract. Nor are we eliminating all our higher priced players by writing them out.

Hey, and by the way, I have a really interesting story for you. Most people think that soaps are only popular with women. Not true. Anyone who has time to watch television during the day loves soaps. Including men. Two of the biggest groups of fans in America are pro sports teams and men in prison.

Well, they just did a prison poll. And for the first time ever, "Forever and Ever" has replaced "All My Children" as the number one show for our guys behind bars. Isn't that fabulous?

ANNALISE CHRISTIAN

I don't understand. Look at my fan mail. People like me. Why am I being dumped.

SHANE BURKE

I mean if they really wanted to just exploit poor Lucinda's problems they could have directed the writers to come up with a story in which Shanna McWarren kills her current husband. But her current husband is played by a guy who's only been with us two cycles. Scale. The sonuvabitch gets scale.

I'm the second highest paid actor on the show. So they wrote a story where I get killed.

I have to tell you, getting killed hurts. I've got two kids, two dogs, a current wife and an ex who refuses to get a goddamn job. She throws pots.

CARMINE CASSELA
(Sound Technician)

What you should know about Samantha Trent is that she did not come from television. She comes from Mid-AmeriCorp. She came in with the butchers.

She was with the Wesleys in St. Louis when they used goons to help them bust the meat packer's union. Next, she went to their real estate operations. There are some very nasty stories about that too. Wasn't Vinnie Toledo, our business agent, shot at just before the last contract negotiations? Now I can't say that it's connected, but it did happen.

What I'm telling you is that these are people who will do anything.

SHANE BURKE

Would Samantha Trent kill Arthur Hoffman and make it look like Lucinda did it—just for ratings points?

When I think that that's what happened, I call myself paranoid. I mean this is television. It's not the cement business or garbage hauling or casinos where that's expected.

CARMINE TOMASSO

Sure, she knows people who would do the business, or she knows people who know people. Carmine told you about what they did to the meat packers, and they own a casino in Vegas.

I saw her talking to Morrie "the Mule" once even.

"The Mule" was actually sort of famous. His real name was Morris Siegal. I'd read about him and seen his photograph in a *Metro* magazine article by Guido Pellegra "The Mob: An Italian Exclusive or Multiethnic!" He was a large man with a reputation for brutality and a very memorable face.

SHANE BURKE

However, if you think about Mid-AmeriCorp being on the verge of bankruptcy, which it is, it becomes conceivable.

Personally, I'd rather believe that than believe that Lucinda, who is a person I like, did it.

SAMANTHA TRENT

The only reason I had a conversation with Morris Siegal, who I have subsequently learned has been associated with organized crime, was to pro-

tect my cast and crew. Specifically, Ms. Merrill.
Apparently he approached her over one of her husband's debts. He tried to enter the studio. People like
that have no business here.

KENNY BAKER
(Security)

Well, you have to have specific permission to
enter more than being specifically banned if you
know what I mean though there are people who are
specifically banned of course you can't control
what happens out on the street which is public
property unless of course some member of the cast
specifically asks for an escort to a vehicle for example. As to the supposed-to-be loan-shark person I
think I know to whom you refer though I am not
an expert on organized crime wasn't he mentioned
in an article in Metro magazine, that rag, in an
article by Guido Pellegra about the "other ethnics."
I thought he was just a fan because he was here
quite often and I saw him speaking to Ms. Merrill
for example.

Our last two interviews were:

SAMANTHA TRENT

I had no personal relationship with Arthur Hoffman. Ratings are important but I would like to
think I could devise a better method of raising them
than having someone murdered.

I will sue you for slander if you do not cease
and desist this moment.

KENNY BAKER

Needless to say, I hardly relish the idea of conveying the information that you are barred from the

set, the studio, and all network premises I have an official network memo to that effect. This is one of the less salutory duties of security personnel such as myself but it is after all what we earn the big bucks for.

CHAPTER FIFTEEN

The problem in selecting a play for acting class was discovering a part that would suit Ralph's particular qualities.

I finally settled on a comedy, a one-act by George Bernard Shaw, *Man of Destiny*. Ralph's character was the Lieutenant, a sort of satirical version of the sort of dashing cavalry officer who died in the Charge of the Light Brigade. He must look very, very noble—like a horse on parade—but have no more irony, self-awareness or self-doubt than the statue he is certain should be erected of him.

The title character is Napoleon. As written by Shaw, a person full of irony and self-awareness, perfect for Andrew. I, of course, was the Mysterious Lady.

We held the rehearsals at my apartment. Convenient for me and for Ralph who was just upstairs. We have no intercom. So guests have to call from the corner, or, if they are unembarrassable, yell up from the street. Andrew preferred to yell from the street. It made him feel, he said, like he was Stanley to my Stella.

Nor is there an electronic way to let guests in. I have to run down and open the door or throw my keys down to the street.

The plot involves some letters of Josephine's that her

husband ought not to see, sent to Napoleon by the Lieutenant, intercepted (stolen) by the Mysterious Lady. She hides them beneath her dress. Next to her bosom. This is a Victorian play and surely no gentleman would search her there. But Shaw's Napoleon is not bound by convention and sham morality. According to the playwright, this is his genius!

Andrew was poised to rip my bodice when the phone rang.

"Hi," he said.

"Oh," I said.

"It's Rowdy," he said. I knew that. "I'm back in town."

"Oh," I said.

"I'm glad I caught you."

"Oh," I said.

"Hey, you know about the picture I'm doing? No. Of course not. We haven't spoken. But I did tell you on the machine. How about dinner?"

"Oh," I said.

"So when is good for you? How's tonight?"

"I'm rehearsing."

"Yeah? What, what? A movie? Off-Broadway show? I did a lot off Broadway myself. Lot of it. I miss you. I have a lead in this. Well, it's not *the* lead. Nobody stars. It's an ensemble piece. A group thing. I'm a streetwise cop."

"You miss me?" I said, having heard just three words out of forty-five.

"So how about tomorrow? Seven? I'm on expenses. We can go anywhere."

"OK," I said. He hung up.

"What's wrong?" Andrew said.

"I don't get this," Ralph said. "Is it supposed to be funny?"

"No, it's not funny," I said.

"It's not funny?" Ralph said.

"Oh, what am I going to do?" I said.

Ralph realized, at last, that we were having two different conversations. Nonetheless, he pressed on with what concerned him. "It's very wordy," he said.

I had no detecting, no auditions, no classes, nothing to do the next day except dwell on, moon over, worry about, be obsessed by that man, and shop. I had to have something to wear to dinner that would make him drop dead, but that wouldn't be grossly obvious about it.

I started at Nice Price, right on the corner. Of course I know better. I should end there, after I've discovered that there is nothing I like that I can remotely afford anywhere else. Everything was green, not even a khaki, sage, or olive, but bright kelly green, emerald green, and frog green, on a day when I didn't feel the least bit green.

So I browsed industriously south on Columbus Avenue, past Laura Ashley, which sells clothes that my mother would wear if she switched from double knits to cotton, to Kenneth Cole's shoe store. Where I stopped and tried on several things. But nothing that did It for me. Down past Charivari, altogether too trendy-yuppie, and stopped at Montmartre. Mostly because my friend Georgia works there. She's eighteen and terrifically avant-garde, clothes and hair.

None of this was remotely what I wanted. I wanted class and sass, allure with dignity, sexy *without* trashy. What any woman would want on an important date with a man who had wronged her.

Finally, I reached my favorite store, Henri Bendel on Fifty-seventh Street. Which is terribly expensive, yet each floor has sales racks filled with well-made imports that no one else liked. Which made them appealing to me. I like to like what no one else likes. Also, I'm a size five, a true size five, and there aren't many of us, especially for clothing made in France where fives are a little svelter than elsewhere.

But even Bendel's failed me.

I never have much luck in Bloomingdale's. Except for accessories and hats. I'm just not a Bloomie's kind of gal, there's too much to chose from, too much frenzy, and too many assaults by people peddling perfume. They lurk behind pillars, leap out from counters, aerosoling strangers with scents, the air thickens with civet and musk, castor and ambergris, attars, essences, and esters. I always leave smelling like four people I don't know and never want to be. I fled.

North, up Madison Avenue. Boutique Land, with clothing that tried and succeeded in conveying trendiness, great conservatism, and a sense of being truly overpriced all at once. Which is exactly the statement that most people with a great deal of money want to make about themselves.

At a loss, saddened, almost shopped out, I trudged across Central Park to try Amsterdam Avenue, a lower rent, quirkier version of Columbus. There, I spotted a leather store. Now I am not usually a leather kind of girl. At least not the black and shiny, zippers and buttons, motorcycle and pain thing. But this store went in for a softer look.

In the back, on the sale rack, there was a wonderful red deerskin suede skirt, handmade by a woman in Maine, $450 marked down to $200. Calf length, soft and flowing, not tough and leathery at all. A little more than I could afford, but, as the woman who was eager to sell it to me said, I would have it for twenty years. It went with my suede boots, and I had just the belt for it, handmade by the Masai, that I'd bought when I was in Africa.

All in all, irresistible.

I bathed, did my hair and my makeup. The skirt, with the boots and belt and a simple off-white silk blouse, had exactly the effect I'd been thinking of. The apartment was clean. What did that matter? And I was ready to go. Except, did I have a Duraflame log for my fireplace? I have a working fireplace, a precious thing indeed in New York and very rare. Not that I had any intention of ending up back at my place with Rowdy. But if I did, I wanted a fire in my fireplace.

I ran down to the market on the corner. They didn't have it. So I went to the supermarket across the street. They did. Standing on line to pay for it I discovered that Lucinda Merrill had, once again, made the covers of:

SOAP OPERA DIGEST

ELECTRIFYING DEVELOPMENTS
IN LUCINDA MERRILL'S REAL-LIFE SOAP
INSIDE: The Latest Sex & Drug Secrets
Revealed!

SOAP OPERA WEEKLY

SEX, LIES & DEAD HUBBY!
HOTTER THAN VIDEOTAPE!

ENQUIRER

REAL-LIFE CHEATIN' WIFE
AND HUSBAND!
INSIDE STORY OF LUCINDA MERRILL'S
MARRIAGE OF DISASTER

GLOBE

LUCINDA & ARTIE:
SHE SHOT HER MAN
BECAUSE HE DONE HER WRONG!

SIZZLING STARLETS REVEAL:
LUCINDA MERRILL'S HUSBAND
MADE A PASS AT ME TOO!

I bought them all.

"Getting some reading material, eh?" the girl at the checkout counter said. I had never been so embarrassed in my life.

"Yes," I said.

"Oh boy," she said, looking at the *Globe*, "I don't believe this one at all." She was referring to the publication, not to the specific article. She rang up the *Star*. "Lucinda Merrill must be hot stuff," she said. "She knocked Cher off the front cover." She rang them all up and my Duraflame log. "Sit home by the fire and read up on your favorite stars. That's nice," she said.

The actual story in the *Enquirer* was on page 42, opposite LOST FRISBEE POOCH IS HOME AGAIN—AFTER 4 YEARS! It was a fair synopsis of the work that Sonny and I had done. In the *Globe* it was next to AMERICA'S OLDEST BOWLER, 102 AND STILL ROLLING, but essentially the same story.

I read each and every one of them. As a result I was late for dinner with Rowdy. That made me feel good.

We ate at Memphis.

"I was talking to Don." Rowdy dropped the name, knowing I would know which Don he meant. Johnson. Rowdy had done a "Miami Vice" and they went to the same AA meetings. "Don said if you're going to New York, eat at Memphis. It's Carly's place. Don told me." Everybody knows it's Carly Simon's restaurant. She has fine publicity people and she's no dummy. She knows that a whole lot more people will eat there because of who owns it than ever would because of the food. "Mick hangs out here, that crowd, you know." I knew. Everyone knew. Carly has fine publicity people. She's not stupid. She knows more people will eat there if they think Mick Jagger might show up than ever would because of the food. "Order whatever you want." Which was what I was going to do anyway. How could I ever have loved someone this shallow? My heart, which has all the intellectual rigor of someone who would eat at Carly's place because Mick might show up, went "pitter-pat, pitter-pat, do you want me, love me, crave me passionately?

Forgive him, I said to myself, Don probably did tell him where to eat. I'd been in that Hollywood world. It was hard to escape making star names the reference points around which all the rest of existence is mapped. Since they have money beyond the meaning of money, the world assumes they buy only the best. Magical—their celebrity, salaries, and public adoration are beyond any other explanation—it is assumed that what they do, how and where they do it, is touched by the same magic. Everyone wants to buy laundry detergent from the same supermarket as Cher's housekeeper, get gas from the same pump as Jack Nicholson, go to the health club where Madonna's personal trainer used to work, have their toilets cleared by Liz Taylor's plumber.

"So?" I said. Meaning are you ready to explain why you always talked about marriage when I was married and never mentioned it after Patrick and I filed for divorce?

"So," he said, with that mischievous boyish smile that he figured would get him out of having to discuss it.

"So," I said, meaning, no I won't let it slide.

"So," he said, meaning would you like to look at the menu or order a drink first.

"Oh boy," I said, "nothing's changed."

"Well," he said. He made those love eyes that had seduced me in the first place.

"You still can't talk," I said.

"Oh boy," he said, "nothing's changed."

"I wrote you that eight-page letter. You must have heard from Ziggy how I felt. Everything that I was going through."

He signaled for the waiter.

"It was a difficult time for me," I said. I gave up my cats, home, and husband. The day I moved in, he went off to do an MOW in Minneapolis and didn't ask me to come with him. "You didn't like my cats. They committed suicide because I left them."

"Oh, Annie," he said, meaning that cats don't commit suicide, that if they do it wasn't his fault, that if it was his fault, it was long ago and I should forget about it.

"You have to say something," I said. "I always do all the talking."

"Um," he said. "Let's look at the menu. OK?"

"Not OK," I said.

He smiled one of his better smiles and reached across the table to take my hand. My hand tingled. Tears came to my eyes. Again. "Oh, Rowdy," I sighed. He took his name from the character that Clint Eastwood played on "Rawhide." His real name was Gordon. I held my breath. Held it. Held it. He did not speak.

"Talk to me, goddamn it," I said. "Or I'm walking out of here."

"Annie," he said. Meaning I wish you wouldn't and could you suggest a topic.

"Do you even know that you can't talk?"

"Annie," he said. Meaning why do you keep after me this way, can't we order.

"Do you have any thoughts? Do you have any feelings?"

"You look really good tonight," he said. "I miss you."

"Do you really?" I asked him.

"Yes," he said, surrounding the monosyllable with significance.

"Can I express some things to you," I said, wanting to speak of love and involvement and the nature of relationships.

"Yeah," he said. "Sure." Meaning that I could but that he preferred that I wait until we ordered.

"We were heavily involved in something together. You came into my house and pursued me for years, right in front of my husband, and I really fell in love with you. Was I just stupid and naive? Was it because I'd been with one man for thirteen years and didn't know better? You did. You knew better. You did this before. You preferred to get involved with married women, so you wouldn't have to take responsibility for a relationship. You asked me to leave him, but it must have blown your mind when I did. That's why you made sure it didn't work, why you left town . . ."

"Annie, I had a part," he said.

". . . and didn't even ask me to come with you."

"I'm sorry," he said.

Was there really something there or was he one of those blank faces in an Eisenstein montage to which the watcher could attach whatever meaning he wanted. Was he really sorry, did he really miss me, was I really beautiful in his eyes. I was convinced that he'd conveyed all that and—as they say on special TV offers—much, much more.

The waiter came and we ordered. The food had no taste. That could have been Carly, it could have been me. The waiter came again and gave us the check.

After Rowdy paid and took both receipts, the one at the bottom of the bill and the one from the credit card, he asked if he could walk me home. I said yes. We strolled up Columbus, which was filled with couples and pretty singles, new lovers and old, and dog walkers. We stopped at the Häagen-Dazs store and got a double cone, maple walnut and Swiss chocolate almond, which we shared.

The truth was that I hadn't gone out with anyone since Rowdy, who I'd cared for, who mattered at all, so it was good to be beside him, my arm through his, not laughing but seeming to be about to laugh, not at anything special, just a feeling that had been away. I had the taste of ice cream lingering in my mouth and a Duraflame log in the fireplace.

"Good night," I said at my front door.

"Annie," he said. I hardly need to explain what that meant.

"Call me," I said—meaning go away. But not forever. Just long enough to get your act together, become a better person, then feel free to try again—and kissed his cheek.

I put the key in the lock, opened the door, and shut it behind me before I could change my mind. I raced upstairs, and without turning on my lights, so I couldn't be seen, I peered down at the street to watch him walk away.

When he turned the corner I sat down in my armchair and started to cry. Not heaving, sobbing, or wailing. Just a few elegant teardrops, trembling down my cheeks. The phone rang. I snatched it up. It wasn't him, calling from the corner, begging.

"I'm sorry to call so late," Lucinda Merrill said, a voice full of desperation. "I hope I didn't wake you."

"No. I just got in."

"That's what I thought. I've been calling for a while. What am I going to do?"

"About what?"

"No one believes me," she said. "Can you imagine me in prison? Me. What am I going to do in prison? Start an acting group for fellow felons? Annie, please, help me."

"Lucinda, we're doing everything we can," I said. "Duke wants to solve this more than anything. You know how publicity hungry he is."

"Is he?"

"Mad for it. Worse than an actor."

"Is anybody worse than an actor?" She put a noise on the end of the line that was an almost laugh. Laughter was outside of her range, it's not something that soap opera people do. "What was that old thing, it doesn't matter what they say about you, good or bad, as long as they mention your name? Something like that. It's not true, Annie. They're making me look like a murderess and dragging out all this sleazy, sleazy stuff."

"I know, Lucinda, it must be painful." When I got to be a star, if some cheap tabloid dragged out my originally, at that time, adulterous affair with Rowdy Randolph, I would die. "Just too, too painful."

"I'm having lunch with Bobby Motzkin tomorrow," she said. "I'm going to speak to him about you."

"Thanks, Lucinda. It's kind of you to think of me when all of this is going on."

"Did anyone on the show stand up for me?" she asked. "Did anyone say Lucinda Merrill, I know her, she could never kill anyone? Did they?"

"Shane Burke had good things to say about you. And about Arthur."

"Poor Arthur. He was in so much pain, even before, you know."

"Someone said loan sharks were after him," I said. It was a question.

"He had financial problems," Lucinda said.

"Can I ask you something? Let me tell you why. I'm considering . . . there's this guy and it might get serious," I said, inventing as freely as I would in an acting exercise in order to draw her out. "But he used to be pretty wild and not great at holding on to money. I mean, he got in serious trouble a bunch of times, but he's really good-looking and we have something that seems pretty special. But if we got married, do you think I should keep my finances separate?"

"Control your own money," she said. "Absolutely. The only thing better is to control yours and his."

"Did you control yours?"

"It was almost too late when I did," she said. "Arthur was an accountant. He knew money. Like my trainer knows muscle tone. Like Edwina knows hair. So I let him handle things. Big mistake. But I caught it just in time."

"Just in time?"

"He was getting sloppy," she said. "He didn't care anymore. About money. He cared about . . . other things."

"Drugs?"

"I guess so. I tried not to notice. Willful blindness. If I knew, what would I do about it? Fire him? Turn him in? We were both adults. He handled his life, I handled mine."

"Did the other women bother you? You don't mind my asking you this, girl to girl."

"Oh Annie, is your guy one of those?" she said.

I knew that one of Rowdy's old girlfriends had flown

out to see him in Minneapolis. And stayed two weeks. I knew that. That was part of what made me leave him, and L.A. What if we had gotten back together? Would I have started getting phone calls where the caller hung up as soon as they heard my voice? "Maybe," I said.

"Do you love him?" she asked.

"Maybe," I said in a small voice. I did once. I could again.

"Stay away from him," she said. "He'll hurt you. Of course if it goes on long enough, you get to the point where you're just plain glad he's out of the house and you're grateful to anyone who'll keep him out all night."

"Was it that bad?"

"Oh yes and no. It was, but that twinge of jealousy never goes away. He loved me. I knew that. But our time was past. You watch "Forever and Ever," you know how tangled love can be."

"Yes, Lucinda," I said.

"Don't be like that," she said hearing the tone I thought I'd disguised. "I know the difference between television and reality. But soap opera reflects real emotions, real feeling, real life. More than any other form of TV, than any other form of drama. That's why millions of women watch us, care about us, feel for us. Because we are in touch with reality."

"I know a girl," I said, "who went out with Arthur." Irene. I remembered exactly what she'd said: *Hey, everyone is entitled to a little kink. Everyone's a little bent, right? But some people it gets out of hand. You know what I mean?* But I didn't quite know how to repeat that to Lucinda. "She said Arthur was . . . kinky. I didn't know what she meant by that, exactly."

"I don't either," she said.

"Oh," I said.

"It happens in a lot of marriages. Lots. We stopped

having relations quite some time ago. So, perhaps he developed some, whatever, after that when he started his . . . outside affairs."

"Oh," I said.

"Look into it, definitely. Maybe she knows something I don't know. Maybe she killed him. Somebody killed him, Annie, and it wasn't me! I don't want to go to the electric chair for killing a man I didn't kill. You know I didn't do it, you were there with me. Save me, save me, please!"

"I'll do everything I can," I said. There was no point in noting that New York State does not have a death penalty.

"You promise, promise?"

"Yes, I promise."

CHAPTER SIXTEEN

After breakfast the next morning I met Duke at the Stuyvesant Room of the Rensselaer. Sonny was already there.

"You owe me a coupla grand," Sonny said.

"I know what I owe ya," Duke said.

"How about it?"

"Hey, Annie, come on, sit down," Duke said. With big gestures.

"Hi, I hope I'm not interrupting anything."

"You want anything to eat or drink?" Duke said to me. "Hey did Lucinda Merrill call you last night?"

"Yes," I said. "How did you know?"

Sonny did not look content. Duke looked at him and said: "I pay you what I owe ya, you're off to Miami, someplace, the track."

"What do I work for? 'Cause I like workin'?"

"You get to hang around all them beautiful actresses on 'Forever and Ever,' best job you ever had." Duke said to Sonny. To me he said: "She called me too. At home. My wife thinks somethin' is happenin' wid us."

"I work so I can go off to Miami, someplace, the track," Sonny said.

"She call you too?" Duke asked Sonny.

"Yeah, but I wasn't home. She talked to my mother.

She was thrilled to death even though she watches one of them other ones, 'The Guiding Life,' I think."

"What'd she want?" Duke said to me. "Maybe I should have you tell my wife she called you too. But then I gotta explain to her that I got an actress working for me. Ever since that thing with the ankle bracelet, she thinks I'm sleeping around or somethin'."

"I told Caren I would come down," Sonny said. "To Miami."

"She's really upset," I said, referring to Lucinda. "She's frightened."

"I know," Duke said. "They want to indict her."

"She didn't say that," I said.

"It's not official yet," Duke said. "But she knows, and that's prob'bly what set her off." He took a fat roll of cash out of his jacket pocket, peeled off three hundred-dollar bills, and gave them to Sonny. "I need you workin' on this case. When this case is over, I'll give you all your money, you can go to Miami or wherever the ponies are." It was too much of a coincidence to be true, but the tune that came up on the bar's Muzak system was "Fugue for Tinhorns" from *Guys and Dolls*, and the gamblers sang "I got the horse right here."

"I know a girl," I said, hesitant because I had never suggested anything investigative before. It made me feel like I was challenging the dramatist, trying to write the scene as well as act in it. "Who went out with Arthur Hoffman. I mentioned it before." I had no idea how he would react to my temerity. Perhaps like the nuns did when I was in Catholic school and asked how we knew that someone didn't just make up the Bible like Margaret Mitchell made up *Gone with the Wind*.

"Yeah, why not," he said.

I breathed a sigh of relief. "I know her. But I don't

know her last name, so it might be difficult to find her,"
I said.

"You'll figure it out," Duke said.

"OK," I said, as cool and collected as if I knew what
I was doing.

I went over to Willie's. Andrew was working lunch.

"Do you remember, at your party here, a girl named
Irene?"

"Not offhand," he said. "Look, about rehearsing our
scene, I may not be able to make it."

"She's a blond. A little on the flashy side," I said.

"No," he said. "Did you look at the TV listings
today?"

"No. Why? Is Irene there?"

"Look at this," he said. He went behind the bar and
got two papers. Both were folded open to the television
page. Opposite the listings there was an advertisement.
It consisted of a quarter-page picture of Lucinda and
beneath her it said:

Lucinda Merrill—United Broadcasting System
and the "Forever and Ever" family, we believe in
her and stand behind her. Share the feeling, come
live with us, Monday to Friday at 1:00.

"What do you think? You think they're exploiting her?"

"Poor Lucinda," I said.

"It's not about acting," Andrew said, truly sad. "It's
not about acting. And you know what, I can't figure out
what it is about. I've tried, Annie, I really have. Forget
about just the acting classes and voice and body work.
Forget about that. On top of that I have a career counselor. I've taken How to Audition courses, a How to Get
an Agent and Make Him Work for You course. I've done

est. I've been through the Forum. I've had my picture and résumé redone too many times to count. I'm in a goddamn actor's support group. If going down on the casting couch would get me work, I would do it. I went to AA meetings to get close to Michelle Morris when she was the casting director at Heavenly Productions doing all that PBS work, and Annie, I don't even drink except at weddings and bar mitzvahs. I had to make up confessions."

"So you don't want to work on *Man of Destiny?*"

"Am I letting you down?"

"Do what you have to do," I said. I gave his hand an understanding squeeze. "Is Willie around?"

"In the kitchen," he said.

"Thanks," I said. "And Andrew, don't give up."

Willie was sweating over the stove, making a savory gravy and cursing steadily to herself.

"What are you doing back here?"

"Annie," Willie said. "Mother-raping cook. Look at me, I got sweat running down my tits, for God's sake. Did I leave Peculiar, Missouri, to be working in the kitchen? Jesus, if it's not one damn thing it's another. Some sonuvabitch came in here and claimed he was one of the Westies and tried to shake me down. I put a knife in his face and told him to get outta here. You think he really was one of the Westies?"

"I hope not," I said.

"I'm not an actress anymore. I don't have to take nothing from nobody."

"What happened to your cook?"

"He tried to rape a waitress. Dragged her into the freezer. Not what you call romantic. I had to let him go. Andrew was the only one would venture into the kitchen to pick up his orders anymore. Goddamn cooks. One before that was a thief. I'm talking about fifty percent wastage on steaks. For every goddamn steak we sold, he took one home. You hungry, sweetie? I'm making some great chicken."

"Do you remember a girl named Irene? She was here the night of Andrew's party. She went and had dinner with some guy and the guy's friend was coming on to me and you yelled at him."

"Blond, a little trashy, aging fast and wishes she was built like me?"

"That's the one," I said. "Is she a regular here?"

"She's a cokehead, right?"

"Yes," I said, remembering the way she'd snorted in the ad agency's ladies' room to get up for her audition.

"She comes in sometimes. When she's buying her own drinks, mostly," Willie said. "There are very few hip places with reasonable prices. Why waste them when a date's paying."

"Do you know her last name?"

Willie thought about it, then said, "No."

"Would you do me a favor? If she comes in here, would you call me right away?"

"Is this a case?"

"Yes."

"That's so exciting that you're a detective. Don't you ever get scared?"

"I don't do anything dangerous." I said.

"Oh, hell and damnation," Willie said. "Somethin's starting to burn."

The one place I thought I could find someone if I had a face but no last name was in the *Players Directory*. Provided that Irene had spent the forty-five dollars to list herself and had sent in a photograph that remotely resembled her appearance.

I went to the offices of SAG, the Screen Actors Guild, where it's kept on file. The book for women is divided into Ingenue, Leading Lady, and Character Actress. I didn't see her as an ingenue—an innocent, inexperienced, unworldly young woman—though I've known women thrice divorced, on their second lift and liposuction who've told me, "I always get cast in little-girl parts." I started with the Leading Lady section, five of us on each page, spiffy as we could afford to be, hair and makeup done, soft modeling light bounced out of a silver umbrella, hairlight from high and behind for separation and glamour. Back light, never get shot without it.

Did we really all look so alike?

I found two who could have passed for Irene—Ricki Pauli Canary and Darla Hensley—and four Irenes who didn't look like anyone I knew.

Then I went through ingenues. There I found five who looked like her—Shae MacIntire, Lisa Juliette, Nicolette Chamberlinn, Paige Lee Anderson, Shell Drake—one Irene, one Irena, and two Irinias. By then the images of actresses, all the desperate longing attempting to escape through the little black-and-white directory rectangles, had begun to blur in my eyes and in my consciousness. So I went outside and walked through the midtown bustle, breathing bus and car fumes to clear my head, viewing the flesh colors of real people to readjust my vision.

I went back upstairs and looked just at the seven—Ricki Pauli, Darla, Shae, Lisa, Nicolette, Paige Lee, and Shell. This time I was sure: she was Shell Drake, represented by Allan Dove at Trivers Talent Agency Ltd., 888 Seventh Avenue, New York, NY 10106, (212) 588-8000.

I called and asked for Mr. Dove.

"Can I ask what this is in reference to?"

"Sure," I said, inventing freely, "my name is Michelle Starkey, I'm with Backstreet Productions and we're casting a film to be shot in NY in June and we'd like to see your client Shell Drake, for the part of Dizzy. We'd like to see her tomorrow at ten A.M. At Two-ten West Fifty-seventh Street, Second floor." We're all hungry. She would show up, no questions asked, and assume, when there was no audition, that her agent had screwed up. Meanwhile, I would be waiting.

"One moment, please."

Someone else came on the phone and said, "Ed Lutzline."

I said: "Allan Dove, please."

"Can I ask what this is in reference to?"

I repeated my rap.

"I'm sorry," he said, "Shell Drake is no longer with us."

"Mr. Lutzline, could you tell us who she's with now?"

"My name is Ruben," he said.

"Sorry, how come you answered the phone Ed Lutzline?"

"I didn't," Ruben said.

"Oh, I thought you did."

"I answered it Ed Lutz's line. I'm his assistant."

"Well, could I speak to Mr. Dove," I said.

"He's no longer with the agency," Ruben said.

"Who's taken his place?"

"Ed Lutz."

"Great. Could I speak to Ed, please?"

"He's out."

"When can we reach him?"

"Is this about Shell Drake?"

"Yes," I said.

"Well, he would only turn that over to his assistant and I don't know."

"Thanks," I said, "anyway."

I called SAG and gave the same story to whoever answered the phone, adding that "our copy of the *Players Directory* lists Shell Drake as a client of Trivers Talent. She's no longer with them. Do you have more current information?"

"One moment," the person who answered the phone said.

"Yes?" a new voice said abruptly.

I repeated myself, emphasizing that I needed something more up to date than the Trivers Agency listing.

"One moment," the new voice said. I waited. It came back on the line. "Shell Drake is with the Trivers Talent Agency," the new voice said.

"I just spoke to them, she's not there anymore," I said, patiently.

"That's the information we have," she said.

"Thanks," I said, "anyway."

I tried Equity, the stage union, with the same result, and AFTRA, which overlaps SAG in radio and television. They had no listing for Shell Drake at all. I tried information for each of the boroughs in turn without success.

Andrew did show up to rehearse our scene that evening.

"Let's just improvise as the characters," I said.

"Fine," Andrew said.

"We should learn our lines first," Ralph said. "Shouldn't we?"

"I prefer not to," I said. "It's not about memorizing words. It's about context and learning what the ideas are beneath the lines."

"The art of rehearsal," Andrew said, "is the art of acting. If you learn by rote, you act by rote."

"Oh," Ralph said.

"Learning the lines too soon limits things. If we improvise, you get a chance to see how moved you can be by your own interpretation. It gets you closer to the nature of the moment," Andrew said.

"Oh," Ralph said, rather blankly.

I tried explaining it. "When we know the lines, we know what's coming. In real life a lot of the tension, the excitement, comes from not knowing. If I say hello, and I think there's an equal chance you'll kiss me or hit me, that has tension. But if I know the script says she says hello, then love and forgiveness fills his smile, I lose that whole dimension of living in the unexpected."

"Well," Ralph said, "I'll try it. But I think learning the lines is really important."

We broke down the scene, what our relationships were, where we were coming from, and what we wanted to achieve in it. Ralph lasted about ten minutes, then asked if we could go back to learning the lines. I liked Ralph, I really did, but it was like playing off a cigar-store Indian.

Rowdy called. I felt things I wanted to feel. But maybe didn't want to feel with him. Unless he felt them too. Felt them enough to unravel what happened to us in the past.

"What is it *you* feel?" I asked him.

"I would like to see you," he said.

"Are we going to be able to talk?" I said.

"I would ask you out tonight but I'm doing a ride-along. With some real cops. The producers set it up. So I get a real feel for the streets."

"Oh," I said.

"South Bronx, Spanish Harlem, I'm going to do it for a couple of nights. They said it might be dangerous. But don't worry about me. I'll be all right."

"OK," I said, "I won't worry about you."

"So," he said.

"Yes?"

"Maybe after that we could see a movie?"

He liked to take me to movies. It was in the dark. We didn't have to look at each other across a silent table. We didn't have to speak. It was safer. When we were together we went to hundreds of movies. "What is it that you want from me?"

"I want to see you . . ." He waited. Hoping that was enough. If it was enough he wouldn't have to make any further effort. It didn't cut it. I stayed silent. He tried, "I miss you." Why not? It had worked the last time.

"Why? What is it you miss?" I wasn't being difficult. That was a question I deserved to have answered if I was going to take the risk of seeing him again. A wonderful body, a good screen presence, boyish charm, the ability to convince others that he was witty even when he was silent—those seemed like sufficient qualities for me, if he would just give me some emotional connection, some communication in depth. Not even real deep to the bottom of the soul depth, just the normal, average depth you expect from a man who gets past being a one-night stand. Of which I have had my share. Well, it happened twice. Once in Paris. Where it should.

"You. I miss you, Annie. There's no one like you."

That wasn't it, but I said. "OK," because I was a pushover for easy flattery or I was lonely or I simply wanted him more than was good for me. There was no question that with a dozen roses, thorns and all, one big apology, and one moderate-length monologue lifted from any of the great love scenes in theatrical history,

Rowdy could sweep me off my feet and carry me off wherever whence he chose. He merely needed the will and a Cyrano to speak through his Christian.

The next evening, around 7:00 P.M., Willie called me. Unfortunately I was out. I got home at 7:45 and played my answering machine. I returned the call.

"She's here," Willie said.

"Make her stay, give her a free drink or something."

"OK," Willie said.

"And see if you can find out her name, her phone number, her agent, anything."

"What should I say?" Willie said.

"Tell her you've got a part for her and she'll do anything."

I hung up, grabbed my bag, threw on a coat, ran down the stairs, hailed a cab, and said "Willie's on Tenth, and step on it, driver."

I was too late.

By minutes, seconds even, according to Willie, who was very enthralled by my detecting. "But," Willie said breathlessly, followed by a big dramatic pause, which I waited out, ". . . she's going to come back. Or at least call!" Pause. Beat. Beat, another beat. "Because . . ."— two beats—". . . she forgot . . ."—one beat—". . . this!" The *this* that Willie had introduced so theatrically was a thick manila envelope containing—Willie had already opened it—one hundred new eight-by-ten glossies, head shots of Irene aka Shell Drake, plus the original negative and the retouched negative. What's a girl going to do when those little lines start to come?

While we waited, Willie wanted to talk about detecting. I wanted to talk about Rowdy and Los Angeles, losing my career and starting it anew. It was so damn hard to catch on again. I didn't understand it. Willie said there was just so much more work out on the coast. I talked about how I'd been mesmerized by him. Him, among a whole gang of friends, at my house, my house with my husband, for dinner. We always had dinner parties. So often that we called our regular group the Diners Club. Rowdy making eyes at me, love eyes, for over a year. Right in front of Patrick. Did I think she could be a detective too, Willie asked. I said of course, knowing that she spent so much time in the bar that she barely had enough time to go home, and did she think that Rowdy's MOW—which was also a pilot— might turn into a series and he would move to New York?

The phone rang, though I didn't hear it over the CD jukebox, but the bartender did and called out to Willie who went and took the call, me following.

"Hey, I got a great idea," Willie said into the phone. "Whereabouts do you live, Irene? . . . the Village . . . why don't I see if someone's going down that way . . . you give them the cab fare or something sweet like that and I'll ask them to drop it off. . . . Save you the trip and the expense of buying a round for the house if you come back . . . no, no that was a joke. . . . Hold on a sec- ond . . ." She put her hand over the phone and counted to ten. " . . . hi, Irene, you're in luck. My friend Annie, you know Annie . . . the redhead . . . yes the one who moonlights as a detective. . . . No she's got some off off off Broadway audition down there. . . . She's going down there in ten, fifteen minutes, give me the exact address and I'll have her drop it off . . . I'll check . . . Oh Ann-ee . . . you don't mind dropping this off for a poor dear fellow actress, do you?"

"Not at all," I said.

"See that," Willie said into the phone. She scribbled

the address on the envelope. "She'll be on her way shortly." She hung up, looked at me, and winked. "What do you think? Pretty good, huh?"

Irene lived on Eleventh Street just off of Third Avenue in an old factory building turned into apartments. Terribly trendy from back in the days when trendy was around. The name on the buzzer of apartment 3D said S. Drake.

I rang the intercom. There was a long pause before she answered. When she did and I identified myself, she said to come right up. Once I was inside I checked the mailboxes. The mail slot for 3D had two names. S. Drake and I. Rinna. Was her name Irene Rinna or was Irene sort of a contraction of Rinna and a still unknown first name starting with I? Or was it all made up?

She opened the door a crack when I rang the bell. She said. "Gee, thanks," and reached her hand out to get her pictures.

"Can I talk to you a minute," I said, not handing her her pictures.

"This is not a good time, Annie," she said.

"It's important."

"Could you call me?"

"I'm here now," I said. "Come on. I brought your head shots all the way downtown. I just need two minutes."

"Annie . . ."

"Two minutes," I said.

"Oh, all right," she said, "but really, just two minutes."

"Thanks," I said and opened the door.

She took the pictures from me. She was wearing a short robe wrapped tight, high heels, old-fashioned stockings and garter belt. The robe was for my benefit, the rest for someone else's. "What is it?"

"Artie Hoffman," I said. "You went out with him."

"I don't want to get involved."

"You said he was kinky."

"Never met him," she said.

"Look, we're doing a made-for-TV movie about him. We have the rights. I'll see to it you get a part."

"What a crock," she said.

"Yeah," I said, and smiled.

She smiled back.

"You did go out with him. You told me, at Andrew's party, 'Hey, everyone is entitled to a little kink. Everyone's a little bent, right? But some people it gets out of hand. You know what I mean?' That's what you said."

"You knew he was dead when I said that?"

"Hey!" a masculine voice called out from another room.

"Hold your horses," Irene said.

"You know what I'm holding," the masculine voice said.

"Just wait a minute," Irene called.

"I didn't know what you meant," I said. "What kind of bent? How was it out of hand?"

"What the hell is going on here?" The man who went with the masculine voice banged the bedroom door open. He was huge and blond and somehow shaggy. He was stark naked, somewhere between two hundred and fifty and three hundred pounds, with the small staring eyes of a murderous bovine and the attitude of a Viking asked to pause in mid-debauch. He looked at me. "Who the hell is this?"

"I told you, it's my friend, she brought my pictures down from the bar," Irene said. Very defensive, very nervous.

The naked man grew red in the face. "Who is she? Who is she? What's going on here?"

"Calm down, Ted, calm down," Irene said.

"You the detective?" he said to me, pointing, accusing. She must have told him something about me while I was on my way down. He came toward me.

"I better talk to you later," I said to Irene.

"I told you not to let her in here!"

"It's OK, Ted," Irene said in the soothing tones you might use if you were locked in a small room with a large dog you didn't trust.

"Come here, you," he said to me. "Come here." I was backing up, feeling behind me for the door. Suddenly he rushed forward. I shrieked. He got between me and the door. "Give me that!" he snatched at my bag. I tried to hold on to it, but I'm 102 pounds, a size five, a girl. He ripped the thing from my hands and dumped it out. "What you got, camera or tape recorder!"

"It's nothing to do with you, Ted," Irene said. "Nothing."

But he wasn't listening. He was dumping my life on the floor. When the tape recorder tumbled out, its little red light letting us all know that it was on, he screamed, "You bitch. You slimy sneaking bitch." I flinched. But he wasn't after me, he was after Irene. She retreated but he cornered her against the couch, big hands grabbing her soft and slender arm, applying casually brutal force the way a man can against a woman or a child. Just an overwhelming strength. She tried to pull away, but he twisted her arm and squeezed the flesh.

She started screaming. He slapped her. I grabbed my tape recorder and said "I got it," hoping that would pull him off Irene. It did. He came after me and I headed for the door. Irene was screaming, "No. No. No." I got to the door first. But this was New York. The door didn't open with a simple turn of the knob, it was a two-hand job, the lock above had to be turned simultaneously. He grabbed me by the hair, yanked me back, and flung me across the room. I was Dorothy caught in the tornado and whipped up to Oz. Not fun. I landed on my back. I twisted my neck. He was coming after me.

Irene, the ungrateful little twit, ran and locked herself in the bathroom. I was alone with an aging, berserk, overweight Viking. The only thing that I could think of that would save me was for him to have a quick heart attack.

He took the recorder, popped out the tiny cassette. He tried to pull the tape out of it, but it was too small for his fat fingers. In his frenzy, he put it in his mouth and chomped on it to break it. He must have cracked a cap or something because he clapped his hand to his mouth and started howling. Of course he blamed me. I was there. I was a woman. It was my fault. He came at me with paws extended and blood lust in his eyes. I squeaked and twisted out from under him as he lunged down. He missed. I escaped. I had a moment. I got my feet under me. I already knew the door was too complicated to open fast. So I went the other way. Into the kitchen. I saw two things in my hyperterrified state. Kitchen knives and a fire escape out the kitchen window.

The window did not stick, thank you Mary, Mother of God, all the saints and Jesus. I was scrambling out as he came in. I got out on the rickety metal and tried to slam the window back down. He caught it. He was stronger than me. We already knew that. He pushed it back open. I gave that struggle up. I turned and ran up the stairs. He followed me, I was half a flight ahead of him. I stopped, I took a deep breath, way down to my diaphragm where projection comes from and yelled:

"Help! Help!" He kept coming. I pointed at him and screamed, even louder, "Berserk naked man on the fire escape! Call the police. He's breaking into your apartment!"

That got them, those apartment dwellers who did not want to get involved. They had to look out and see whose apartment was being broken into so they could be sure it wasn't theirs. Faces appeared. Windows opened. That broke into his consciousness and he suddenly came out of his berserker rage and realized he was a naked fat man with his belly folds and withdrawn genitals hanging out in the cold for all the world to see. Embarrassment swept over him, withering his rage and leaving it limp. He retreated, in confusion, back toward Irene's apartment.

peeked my head back in. "Irene?" I called. There was silence. "Irene?" More silence. I leaned into the kitchen. No one visible. No sounds. My bag, my keys, my credit cards, my money, my bank card, my library card, my detective notebook, my tape recorder, were all inside. I stepped in. I moved forward cautiously. Still nothing.

Then I heard something. I froze. I waited. Silence. No. I could not hear, I could sense, someone breathing. I stopped breathing. I could hear my heart thudding away.

Someone was moving. Slowly, sneaking, shuffling along.

I breathed. It stopped. If it was that cautious, that frightened, it had to be a girl like me. Not the oversized man. I started to relax. Then I remembered that in every horror film I'd ever seen the point of relaxation was the moment the ax murderer attacked from behind.

He might have decided that he had to eliminate more than the tape recorder. He had to eliminate me. And Irene. I started to retreat. Better that I went back out the window, up the fire escape, to the roof or to someone else's kitchen, and walked home. At which point I would figure out some way to get into my apartment.

I heard someone moving toward me. I froze. "Annie," Irene said, tentatively.

"Irene?"

"Is he gone?" she said.

"Is he gone?" I said.

We both ran forward from our hiding places. The living room was empty.

"He's not in the bathroom," Irene said. "I was in the bathroom."

"He's not in the kitchen," I said.

"The bedroom," we said. It was more a gasp than a word. A fearful indrawn breath. We crept forward. The bedroom door was closed. I looked at the door. She looked. I looked at Irene. Irene looked at me. No, I didn't want to be the one to open the door. She didn't want to be the one who opened the door. I reached for the knob. My hand jerked back as if it knew something. Irene gasped.

She looked at me.

"I can do it," I said. I willed myself to put my hand on the knob. It was cool, not hot, as my hand seemed to fear. I closed my fingers around it and then turned it slowly.

The door swung open. I stepped back and held my breath. I closed my eyes and looked inside. I saw nothing.

I opened my eyes and still saw nothing.

Irene and I looked at each other and started to laugh.

"Did you see him bite the tape?" I said.

"Did he really go out naked? On the fire escape?"

"Uh-huh."

"The big fat pink behind on the fire escape."

"Big and fat."

"Did people see him?"

"Uh-huh."

"And that tiny little thing he has."

"I didn't look," I said.

"What are you, Catholic?" she said. "I gotta do a couple of lines. I hope he left his coke." She went into the bedroom.

"What was he so crazy about?" I asked her, standing in the doorway.

"Oh, thank God, he left his blow. You wanna toot?" She inhaled sharply twice. "Oh, that is better. He has such a little thing for such a big guy."

"He is big. How do you . . . ? Do you mind my asking, he must be terribly heavy."

"It's OK as long as he's moving. It's only when he stops." We started giggling again.

"I don't believe I asked you that."

"It's too funny."

"Why was he so crazy?"

"He's got a wife. He's got a million bucks or five million bucks. And he doesn't get laid at home. You sure you don't want any of this? Jesus, you'd think husbands'd wise up and say 'Honey, spread 'em or turn in your MasterCard.' Wimps. They're wimps at home and killers with us. Men. They're screwed up. He's afraid she's gonna nail him for alimony and punitive damages."

"Do you think he'll be back?"

"I don't think he'll be back."

"I'm sorry, I mean, do you care?"

"He took pretty good care of me. Once a guy admits he's got five million bucks he's gotta spend some of it on a girl, am I right or am I peeing without a potty? He won't be back. If you don't want any blow do you want a drink or a joint or something?"

"He's so fat," I said. "It all shook when he was running up the fire escape."

"Were you scared?"

"I was petrified. Irene, tell me about Arthur Hoffman."

"Another wimp. A kinky wimp." She rummaged through the mirrored table beside her bed and came up with a joint as she spoke.

"What do you mean?"

She lit up, inhaled, and held it a long time. When she exhaled she said, "You know, it's funny, it's almost a love story. If you like twisted love, and by the way, have you ever had any other kind?"

"Yes," I said, thinking of my husband, steady, faithful—I am certain—and true.

"Oh, lucky you." She offered me the joint. "What happened to it?"

I declined the marijuana. "I left him for another man."

Irene thought that was hilarious. And, for the first time, so did I.

"How was the other guy?"

"Not worth it," I said.

"So why didn't you go back to the first guy?"

"I didn't want to," I said.

"Would he have taken you back?"

"I think so. But . . ."

"But what?"

"Well, when the other man did what he did and I left him, I went away, that was in L.A., for a while. Six months or so. Then I came back. I've never told this to anyone before. I went to see him . . ."

"Which him?"

"Both of them," I said. "First I went to the lover's house. Ex-lover's house. Rowdy's house. And there she was in Lycra. Pink and green Lycra. 'Hi, I'm Tanya! Rowdy's not home! Who are you?' she squealed. She was an aerobics instructor. So then I went back to see Patrick."

"Your husband?"

"Ex by then, but yes, my husband. And he . . ."

". . . was living with an aerobics instructor," Irene said, and cracked up.

"Yes," I said.

"An L.A. love story."

"Please, Irene, tell me about Arthur Hoffman."

"I can't talk about that." She did some more coke. "I'm really glad Teddy Bear forgot his stash. I gotta be careful with stuff, I am careful with it, if I smoke, I binge. But I just snort usually, it's OK."

"Why not? I mean, why can't you talk about it?"

She didn't answer.

"Lucinda Merrill's in all kinds of trouble," I said. "But I know she didn't do it because I was with her. I'm in trouble because no one believes me. Anything you know about Arthur that could help clear her . . ."

"I didn't know he was dead when I told you about him," she said. "I swear it." The joint had gone out. She lit it again and inhaled.

"You did go out with him though?"

She nodded, holding the pungent smoke. She watched herself exhale to see how little came out, how much had been absorbed. "A New York love story," she said. "Poor bastard. We're all poor bastards, aren't we. All he did was love his wife. That's all he wanted. That and to get high and to hurt her, of course. He'd lay his rap on you: Come on, I'll help your career, come on, I got lots of blow up at my place, we'll snort it, smoke it, anything you want. Don't worry about cab fare home, I'll take care of it. A good-looking girl like you should have nice clothes. I'll help you get some clothes. Clothes. So you go up to his place, that rat trap over by York Avenue, and what the hell does he want?

"Hey," she said abruptly. "I'm not gonna have to testify about this or anything, am I?"

"Oh, I don't think so," I said, as if I had any way of knowing.

"Promise me I don't have to go to court. I'll tell you, but I don't need any trouble. I don't want to get involved in this."

"Don't worry about it," I said.

"Promise," she said.

"I can promise that I won't ask you to testify," I said, trying to make the statement narrow enough so that it wouldn't turn out to be a literal lie. If it became important for Irene to be deposed or speak in court, surely Duke or Petty could ask her, Sonny or Dom could subpoena her. So it was merely an intent to mislead, an opportunity for her to believe what she wanted due to a failure to elaborate and elucidate. I was learning to lie like a cop. "Tell me what Arthur wanted?"

"Jesus, I don't want any trouble."

"Irene, what did he want?"

"So you go up to his place and you're high, high enough to be horny. I'm telling this just to you. I don't want to talk about this to anyone else. But what does Artie want? He wants you to dress up as Lucinda Merrill.

"He's got everything there: a wig, dresses from 'Forever and Ever'—she gets great clothes on that show, gets to keep them too, it's part of her contract. And he has her makeup. Which he does for you."

"He'd do your makeup?"

"Yeah. He was really good at it, too. Boom, boom, boom, and you looked like her. I mean if you stood away from the mirror and took your contacts out so things got a little fuzzy. At this point he starts to want line readings. You're both pretty high by now, things are flying along, there's not much anymore that sounds like too much. All of that's OK. Sort of fun even, a little sad maybe."

"What's not fun?"

"But then he wants to think you're Lucinda, you know. He grabs you. He'd grab you by the hair, but it's a wig and it would come off. So he grabs your neck or your shoulders and starts to shake you and yell at you and tell you what a frosty bitch you are. Except he's calling you Lucinda."

"Oh," I said.

"Then you want it to stop and you tell him so. He doesn't want to stop, so he offers you money. 'Here, take this,' and he shoves a couple of hundred dollars at you, because he's fired up and really wants . . . he wants to hurt her. Except you are her. Hurt and humiliate. Too much for me. And hurters, they're dangerous, you know, you never know when it's going to really get out of hand. When, maybe, they want to see blood, or kill you maybe.

"I threw off the wig and started screaming. Once he got that I wasn't going to play, he backed off. See what I mean, though, he really loved her."

Before we went into the meeting Duke said to me, "You solved this case, kid, I'm proud of you. I'm giving you a raise, you're coming off the B scale. I'm putting you on the A scale. Twen'y bucks an hour from here on out."

It was more or less the same meeting with the same

characters in similar wardrobe. Naturally, I didn't tell my story, Duke did. He stood up and smirked.

While he spoke Lucinda sat like Queen Elizabeth.

"I told youse, I was gonna solve this screwy case. And I done it! Me and my operatives. Duke Investigations employs only the best of operatives, pardon me for the commercial.

"So what youse and everybody else was wondering was how the heck Lucinda Merrill could be at home, in bed, sleeping or whatever, and yet at the same time there was witnesses that seen her out of the house blocks away, buying cigarettes, running in the street, hailing taxicabs and so forth. With reliable witnesses to both.

"The answer, as it is to so many great mysteries, is not at all obtuse. It is simple in the extreme. What we got is one real Lucinda Merrill, at home, and a fake Lucinda Merrill at the scene of the crime. This explains all of that unexplained stuff that he conveyed to his pied-à-terre—the wig, the dresses, the women's accessories, and et cetera.

"Arthur Hoffman was in the kinky habituation of playin' dress-up games with his various amorata. His girlfriends and pickups and whatever. So he has this girlfriend over. They start to smoke what you call your crack or your free base. They get started with their kinked-up games. But they run out of butane for their torch. Said torch confiscated by the police as drug paraphernalia which it is. So Arthur sends down his girlfriend to the corner for a couple of Bics and a pack of cigarettes. They're right in the middle of things so she goes out in her wig, costume, and makeup. She looks enough like Ms. Merrill that the storekeeper he thinks it could be Ms. Merrill who after all is of a different ethnic origin than himself and he has only seen her sometimes on television. Which by the way is a small black-and-white one and has a lot of fuzzy lines. Then she goes upstairs. Whatever happens, happens, whether they fight or what, we wasn't there, how are we to know, but Artie, he winds up dead. This girl, all in her dress-up, she panics, runs out of the building, into the street, screaming, sees a cab, flags it down, jumps in, as witnessed by the lady across the street.

"I told you, Witte, you got no fuckin' case. Sorry everyone, pardon my French, but my sense of righteous outrage is overwhelmed. Our client here being in danger of being railroaded."

"What a hunk of hooey," Witte said. And snorted.

"Great, great, gurrr-rate story line," Stan Ruddiman said.

Samantha looked like gears were spinning in her skull, computing, calculating, finding the angles. Bobby Motzkin positively twinkled. Sonny looked around for an ashtray.

"I think that should settle things," Petty said.

"Where is this mystery broad?" Witte said.

"That's your problem isn't it," Duke said.

"The hell it is," Witte snapped. "It's her problem." He pointed a stubby tobacco-stained index finger at Lucinda.

"You know," Duke said to Witte, "you could use a manicure."

"You, wid yer mani-cu-ers and yer John Gotti suits," Witte barked at Duke. "Youse is too sharp for yer own good. And youse were too sharp when youse was on the force."

Duke was deeply offended. He said, "What are you sayin', asswipe?"

"Decorum, gentlemen, please," Petty said.

"Sorry," Duke said.

"I got nothin' to apologize for," Witte said.

"It does rather explain things," Samantha said, I think to goad Witte.

"It explains that Duke DeNobili don't know the truth from mayonnaise and he's got peoples working for him that'll make up anything he tells them to and swear to it on a stack of bibles because they's atheists wid no integrity. That's all it explains."

"Excuse me," Sonny said to Petty, "could we get an ashtray in here?"

"Yeah," Witte said, pulling a mangled pack of Kents from his pocket.

Petty sighed, picked up the phone, and made an internal call.

Duke rose back out of his chair, pointed his (manicured) finger at Witte, and said, "You're gonna eat that, Witte. I'm gonna take you a-part. Everybody in Duke Investigations is a good Catholic, except sometimes there's one Jew guy we use. Somebody from Duke Investigations swears on a Bible, you can take it right to St. Peter. We got no perjurers here, not like some cops I could speak about but discretion is the better part of gettin' along so I won't."

"Great, great, gurrr-rate story line." Stan Ruddiman said.

"You ain't got the girl." Witte sneered at Duke. "And if you ain't got the girl you got nothin'. Nothin' but a lotta wind."

"As I represent all of the parties involved," Bobby Motzkin said to Stan, "if you use this story, I think ve have to talk about rights."

"Ridiculous," Samantha Trent said.

"Quite," the network lawyer chimed in.

"Vell, I suggest that you meet with our legal department," Bobby said. "As representatives of Ms. Merrill ve represent the estate of Mr. Hoffman . . ."

"She don't inherit if she done it," Witte said. "Which she did."

A tiny flicker passed across the agent's smooth pink cheeks, a subtwitch, but he continued on as if he hadn't heard a word. "And it is upon Mr. Hoffman's life and death this story would be based. I think there are grounds for invasion of privacy. Also establishing commercial value to the story should not be difficult. And, naturally, ve represent the other important players here, Mr. DeNobili, Ms. McGrogan, and so on."

"You're an old fox, Bobby," Samantha said, "but this is unquestionably, unarguably, public domain."

"Vhut if it appears in the press, as an exclusive, under a byline, and I happen to represent the writer."

"What if I happen to have a draft, already in existence, weeks old, that has a very similar plot line."

"Then ve haff a very complicated matter. All kinds of questions for the lawyers. Vas there prior knowledge? Vas this something, this bizziness of the dress-up, something you already knew about and you vere vithholding from the police for making publicity and better ratings? That is probably criminal. And grounds for a lawsuit. Also writers are people of such vivid imaginations that the writer of this draft vould probably be so frightened of being charged with perjury that he would not testify very vell if ve haff to go to court over this. Not to vorry. I hate going to court. Ve are not in the business of suing people. Ve are in the business of making deals."

"I'm going to the DA," Witte said. "Tell him to take it to the grand jury. I think we'll get an indictment."

"I, for one," Lucinda Merrill said, still in her Queen Elizabeth mode, "would welcome the opportunity to settle this matter. Once and for all."

CHAPTER EIGHTEEN

The story was on the streets almost before we left the meeting.

Samantha Trent, who had rating points to win, fed it to the soap magazines and the tabloids. Duke, who was buddy-buddy with Guido Pellegra, leaked it to *Metro* magazine.

But Bobby Motzkin beat them out. He fed the story to Timmy Donohue, the crusading Pulitzer Prize–winning beer-guzzling street-talking garrulous investigative columnist who was also a client of the Motzkin Agency. Timmy's story was out first: written in the night, set by the printers in the wee hours, and delivered to the newsstands before dawn. Exclusive and copyrighted. It said so, right at the top of the page.

When you and I want to make love to our wives we approach it in what might be called normal fashion. "Hey honey, the kids asleep yet? Huh?" No, I'm just kidding. Personally, when that feeling of fondness comes over me I go out into the yard, pluck a rose, if they're in season, and bring it into the house like I thought of it special and brought it home. Then I put some

Sinatra on the old Victrola and turn the lights down low.

But then, I'm a regular working stiff, just like you.

There are some people who go about it real different. Mostly they're the ones who make too much, too easy, too fast. All that easy money gets them disconnected from reality and the goodness that comes from being plain working folks.

This is not usually, as you know, a gossip column. But when the gossip is as socially significant as this story is and tells us so much about where we are today as Americans and degenerates, this column is going to talk about it.

What am I talking about?

Lucinda Merrill and her husband, Arthur Hoffman. The late Arthur Hoffman. Shot full of holes and left for dead amidst the crack- and porn-strewn wreckage of his secret East Side rent-controlled love nest.

Now Arthur was an all-right guy, and a pretty good accountant, I'm told, until the wrong woman, drugs, and too much easy money brought him down.

So when Arthur wanted to make love to his wife, he got someone else to wear her clothes, wear a wig, put on makeup, and pretend to be her. Then came the drugs. After the drugs, the rough stuff. Like it always happens with drugs. They open up that secret rage that even us ordinary, regular Joes feel toward women, the kind that any decent fellow, raised in the Church, keeps under control. So Arthur tapped into the ugly place and wanted to do some hurting.

Was that what killed him?

We don't know. Yet. The police would like to tell you that it was Lucinda Merrill who did it. But the police like shortcuts too, too often. We all know that from my previous columns. And the police like to cover it up when they take shortcuts. That's how I won my Pulitzer.

But enough about me. Let's talk about Lucinda Merrill and Arthur Hoffman. Lucinda Merrill wasn't even there. She was at home. There were two detectives watching her. But was that alibi enough for a certain Detective Witte? Apparently not. Why not? Because Witte didn't want to go out and do the kind of hard work, the pavement-pounding, knocking-on-doors, endless-work-type work that you and I and every really good cop in the city of New York does. He went, automatically, reflexively, for the easy solution: "The wife done it!" He left it to retired Hero Cop Duke DeNobili, now a PI, to go out and unravel the real story. Which I have for you as an exclusive.

Somewhere, out there, on the mean streets, there's a Mystery Woman. She, herself, a victim. A victim of the excesses of our out-of-control moneyed class. Caught in the web of Arthur Hoffman's obsession, drugs, and rage, she—probably out of panic or a need to defend herself—reached for a gun. Maybe his gun, maybe hers, a .22, a woman's gun, and she shot Arthur Hoffman. Then, dressed as Lucinda Merrill, she ran from the fatal tryst, into the night. The black, rain-slicked streets swallowed her up. She disappeared.

But now I'm calling for her to come forward. Call me. Talk to me. I guarantee your anonymity while I tell your story. You have our sympathy, mystery woman, whoever you are. If you need a defense, we'll help you. If there's a book in it, we have an agent standing by. Call me. I'm from the streets, from the neighborhood. I understand.

Lester Petty wanted to get a sworn statement from Irene. Since I had found her and I "had a rapport" with her, I was the one given the job of asking her to testify. Exactly what I promised her I wouldn't do.

And I wouldn't ask. I would explain to her that other people were drawing up subpoenas which would be served and if she failed to respond they would send the police and they would force her to testify. But if she came forward she would have more control over the situation, she could be represented by a lawyer and so on. From this she would see the advantages of making a sworn deposition and decide to do it herself.

Sonny came with me this time. "Never go anywhere without backup," he said. "What happened the last time could happen again, worse. You think you're going to some guy to talk about apples. Apples, no big deal, nothing to get excited about. But he don't have apples, he's got oranges. Or a couple of kilos of dope. Or a murder warrant out on him from L.A. He doesn't know that you're just interested in apples."

But Irene wasn't there.

So we did what we always did. We parked the Silver Bullet, sat, waited, and talked.

Irene didn't show up that day. We told the Duke and he told us to stay on the place until she did. He put another team on so we could keep the building under round-the-clock surveillance. Sonny and I got the day shift, the other guys got nights. I was quite pleased with the state of affairs. I was making $240 per day for hanging out with Sonny. Which was fascinating. I wondered sometimes, when he talked about the frequency, volume, and duration of the female orgasm, whether some of his girlfriends might be playing up to his ego. But he didn't seem to doubt these extravagances at all. I told him a little about Rowdy and me and my husband. He listened quite uncritically, the first of my friends to see the triangle as a philosophical triviality, something on a par with having a bad day at the track or not studying for the sergeant's exam. That may have been because he saw me as one of The Guys and once you're one of The Guys whatever side of anything that you're on is an OK side.

Plus he never minded if I went on auditions. Suddenly there seemed to be quite a few of them. I was sent on a casting call for "Forever and Ever," among others. It turned out that everyone was being called for that one, including Ralph and Andrew. When we three met for our last rehearsal of our class scene, the talk was all of "Forever and Ever." The rumors of a purge were apparently true. While viewer interest, tied to the real-life travails of Lucinda Merrill, was at its peak, the high-priced players were being cleaned out, new story lines with new characters and new talent were being phased in. And after the Donohue article and the media storm that followed, ratings were high indeed. "Forever and Ever" rose to number two, surpassing, to the amazement of the industry, "General Hospital," even threatening the previously untouchable number one, "The Young and the Restless." A whole series of bad jokes were making the rounds: "Give me a part, *please*. I need the excuse to kill my wife"; "And the casting director said: 'But will you kill for this part?' "; and "The bad news is that the Screen Actors Guild pension fund will no longer insure the spouse of an actor. The good news is that the welfare fund pays for legal fees for any marital murder that's job related."

Samantha Trent was becoming something of a business celebrity. With cable and satellite dishes and the new mininetworks like Fox, all the networks had suffered a loss in viewers. The sole exception, the only gain in absolute numbers, rather than in audience shares in which a show merely got a bigger percentage of a diminishing pie, was on UBS daytime. Articles on Trent's success appeared in the trade press along with speculation that she would soon be named Head of Programming. That would make her a major player indeed. There are, after all, only four network heads of programming at any one time, and their decisions determine more of what the world sees and who makes how much money creating it than anyone else.

Ralph was very high on his audition. It was his first for a real part on a real soap. "She liked me, Annie. She really did. I could tell. I'm going to get this. You'll see." He'd read for Esther Litvak. As we all had.

Andrew had more reason for optimism. "Esther was so apologetic. About what happened the last time. Everybody up there, she said, loves me. 'From top to bottom.' That's how she said it. I don't know if she meant everybody from top to bottom or if everybody who loves me does so from top to bottom."

I had the least reason for optimism. I had just spent a week in the studio as a detective. I had interviewed Esther several times. Yet when I read for her she never once looked at me and never once acknowledged by word or gesture that she had ever seen me before.

I didn't care. I had an audition at the New York Shakespeare Festival for Portia, heroine of Shakespeare's *Merchant of Venice*, one of the absolutely premier roles in the all-too-short canon of women's parts in the classics. It is a role I know, that I have studied for years.

"Hey, you look pretty happy," Sonny said when I got back to the Watch on Irene.

"I got a call-back," I said. "They didn't even wait to phone me at home. They told me right there. I knew I nailed it. When I did my monologue I was right there. Defending a man I loved. I understood Shylock, sympathized with him. But I had to beat him. It was great."

"So what does a call-back mean?"

"That means you're one of the few that they're really interested in. They might see a couple of hundred people for the initial audition, then four or five, ten at the most, for the call-back."

"So what do they pay you for one of these call-backs?"

"Nothing," I said.

"Oh," he said.

Rowdy understood it without explanation. We had at least that going for us. We were, after all, both actors. In that we were kindred souls. Or was I so involved that I took some knowing looks and wise nods for communication. He took me out to dinner again. He said I should go back to Los Angeles. He was implying that that was where we could be together, though his actual words were that there was more work there, a lot more work. He asked what I'd done since I'd been in New York. I was forced to explain how all I'd done was acquire an agent, position myself to get a better agent, look for a manager to supplement the agent, go on a lot of auditions, mostly for things I didn't want to do, and get my head shots reshot, rejected, and reshot again. "I'm going at it in a businesslike way this time," I said.

"You never had to audition like that in L.A.," Rowdy said. "You're good and people knew it."

That warmed my heart to hear. I let him take my hand and hold it in a way that was meant to communicate eroticism, and did. I even sent a little back. Then we did the eye thing. There's lots of sex in the eyes.

"Do you still have that little car?" He asked me.

I thought of my little red roadster, a 1973 TR6. Although British cars have a very poor reputation, mine was a well-made machine, romantic and dramatic with the top down, quick off the start, tight in the corners, and powerful in the straights. My husband and I bought her new. For whatever reasons, both the original engine and the rebuilt we put in after ten years ran cool, which, with Triumphs, seemed to be the difference between a good car and a bad one.

"Yes," I said.

"Here?"

"No," I said. "It's in L.A."

"Oh," he said. "In storage?"

"No," I said. "Someone's taking care of it for me."

"Who?" Rowdy asked. Now that he'd finally found something he wanted to communicate about, of course it was the wrong thing.

"Patrick," I said. The man we both betrayed.

"Oh," he said.

"He's taking good care of it," I said brightly. But everything had gone cold. The eros had left our fingertips and the love light died in our eyes. "He always takes good care of things." I realized that the word had an unintentional ambiguity. It was his failure to take care of things that left me looking for trouble and finding it in the first place. "Of thing things," I said. "Cars, houses, all his sports stuff."

"Uh-huh," Rowdy said.

He did the gentlemanly thing and escorted me home. He didn't try to come upstairs with me. I was prepared to write it—him—off, good-bye and good riddance to the confusion and the temptation to move backward.

"Let's try again," he said.

"What do you mean?" I asked. My confusion instantly rearoused, temptation immediately reanimated.

"We could have dinner. Maybe a movie," he said.

"A movie?"

"Or something else. If you want."

"Can't you ever open up? Don't you ever have anything real to say? What if I told you you treated me like yesterday's news and I don't understand it? And I can't deal with you or be with you until I understand it."

"What's there to say?"

"What's there to say? Do you have a heart? A feeling? An idea? Did you ever read *Romeo and Juliet? The Comedy of Errors? Much Ado About Nothing?* Steal something from them to say . . ."

"Come on, Annie . . ."

"Do I want to be loved in monosyllables? Does anything go on in your pretty little head? Or did I make it all up and there's nothing there except what I put there? What happened to us? Won't you talk about it?"

"That's a lot of different questions," Rowdy said, sounding little boy lost.

"Don't give me that little-boy-lost act. I don't buy it," I said.

"Well, I guess . . ."

"You guess what?"

"I guess . . . Look, could we . . . why don't I . . ."

"Why don't you what?"

"Uh, call you."

"Call me," I said.

"I will," he said.

When I went up to my apartment I felt sad or something very like it, nostalgic or lost. I decided that I missed my car and I should check in on her so I called Patrick. He answered the phone himself.

"Hi," I said. "No aerobics instructor?"

"Oh, hello Annie," he said. "How are you?"

"I'm fine," I said. "How are you?"

"OK, I guess."

"I mean for real," I said. "How is your heart? Your mental condition?"

"I'm OK," he said. Patiently.

"Is this a Pinter piece?" I said.

"A what?"

"Pinter. Harold Pinter. Remember I did two of his short plays at the Garden Theater? Everybody speaks only in complete banalities and everything is buried deep in the subtext."

"Things are fine, really. There hasn't been much smog. Lately. It's nice."

"My mother and father were like that. They never said anything. Did we ever say anything?"

"You always had a lot to say," Patrick said.

"Do you forgive me," I said. "Really and truly?"

"I never was angry with you," he said.

How could that be? "How's my car?" I said.

"Fine. I run it once every couple of weeks. I just had it tuned. The top is drying out, but it'll last another season."

"But it runs all right?"

"Oh yeah, runs great."

"Sometimes I think of going back to L.A."

"Oh," he said.

"Maybe just to visit. Maybe to stay. If I come, I'll come by and see you. As well as to pick up the car."

"Sure. That's OK," he said.

"Well, take care of the car," I said.

"I will," my ex-husband said. And he would.

"Good-bye. Take care of yourself," I said.

"You too," he said.

We hung up more or less simultaneously. It was nice to know my car was running well.

CHAPTER NINETEEN

In a soap opera every desire is an ultimate. The One
that will bring Complete Happiness or Total Despair.
Every love is the one that one cannot live without.
But the drama must go on, day after day, and therefore
the characters have neither history nor future. Neither
memory nor consequences place any restraint on the
constant churning. Even the dead return. The loss of
one husband leads to another who will be lost in turn,
and it doesn't matter—because all passions are equal.

The great classical tragedies are about that one
moment out of all the ordinary ones—to murder like
Macbeth, to avenge like Hamlet, to go mad like Ophelia,
to test the love of one's children like Lear—after which
there will be no sameness.

Real life is normally less absolute, less terminal than
tragedy. But it's not soap opera either. We do have
personal histories. They compel us toward certain
choices. Once we have made them, they will have consequences, and those consequences will change us.

In what direction would my life change if I started
in again with Rowdy? From east to west, New York back
to L.A.? Did that mean more than geography? Was it in
some sense an acknowledgment of defeat? To choose to
go where (I think) the work is, rather than where (I

hope) the art is? To depend on a man, however undependable, rather than on myself? And the truth was that with my detective work I was totally supporting myself without family or husband, for the first time in my life. This is not to say that I did not make more, at times, than my husband. I did. But there were times when I made nothing and knew I could depend on him. And shouldn't a new life mean a new man, if any man at all?

Over the next several days many things conspired to bring me to the point where I let Rowdy Randolph come upstairs with me and enter my bedroom.

Our scene went brilliantly. The class laughed where it should and applauded when we were done, a spontaneous, enthusiastic applause. Even Geraldine Page joined in. Though she spotted the way we had used Ralph's limitations as an advantage and told him that for his next scene he ought to choose a part that stretched his abilities instead of one that masked his stiffness.

It put me in the right mood for my call-back for Portia. Geraldine even agreed to help me with the part. "Never forget," she said, "that *The Merchant of Venice* is a comedy."

The next day Ralph got a part in "Forever and Ever." He was to be an undercover cop brought in to investigate the murder of Beaumont Ridley. As such he was to have a love affair with the chief suspect—probably Shanna McWarren, unless something radically new happened in the real case of Lucinda Merrill. It was clearly intended to be a continuing part.

I asked him if he was going to look for a real apartment. Move out of his tiny cell upstairs from me. He hadn't thought about it. The room sort of suited him.

We went to Willie's to have a celebration dinner.

Andrew and Willie were sitting in a corner talking when we went over to share the good news. Andrew didn't look like he wanted good news. He looked stricken.

"Hey, everybody, join us for dinner," Ralph said. "I got a part."

"I know," Andrew said, very flatly.

"Oh," Ralph said, confused.

"Congratulations," Andrew said with an effort.

"Thanks," Ralph said. "How'd you do?"

"Andrew's leaving us," Willie said.

"What's wrong?" I asked.

"Oh gee," Ralph said. "That's too bad."

"I got an offer I couldn't refuse," Andrew said with what was supposed to be flippancy.

"His father's not feeling well," Willie said.

"I'm going home to go to work in the family furniture store."

"I'll miss you," I said. And I really was going to.

"The truth is," Andrew said, "that I just can't take it anymore."

"Take what?" Ralph said.

"Being an actor. Or trying to be an actor. Being a waiter who thinks he's an actor. Going up for parts and seeing people who I know can't act get them. So at a certain point I have to accept that I'm wrong. That I don't get it. I don't want to be rude, but look at me and Ralph. Now by my standards, I'm a better actor than Ralph. But he's working, or will be shortly—and I wish you a long and happy career, I really do, Ralph, you're a nice guy—and I'm not working."

"They thought he was the right type," I said. "It's not saying that Ralph's a better actor."

"It's saying he's a more *employable* actor, I'm not an

employable actor. I'm not as dedicated as you are, Annie. You'll go on acting as an artist for the rest of your life, whether you get cast or not cast, no matter what. But it's just not the same thing for me. I'm heading for complete dining room sets, ninety-nine dollars down, easy monthly payments, no one's credit refused, in Cedar Rapids, Iowa. I can fit in. I know I can. Perhaps I'll even become a heterosexual. Get married and have children. This profession of ours, it hurts."

The next day I left our surveillance of Irene's building—she still hadn't shown up—earlier than I had to. I wanted the Portia more than I'd wanted anything in a long, long time. More than anything since when I was married and I wanted Rowdy Randolph, who was not my husband.

When I act I prepare as much as I can. I read aloud and listen. I break down the script. I research the part. I search for clues. I research the play and the playwright. Where does it come from in terms of the events of its time and in terms of the writer's intentions. But when all of that is done, I go somewhere, into some other place, and the performance happens. That is what I wanted to occur with that audition.

I was ready.

A young girl, an aspiring actress no doubt, sent me to the small stage at the appointed time.

A voice from the dark seats said my name with a question mark in his voice. I admitted I was who I was and peered out. It wasn't that dim and I realized that my audience was only one person, the casting director. In this case a heavy balding man who swirled long side locks over the barren spot on top.

Something was quite wrong. If this was for real there would have to be at least five people out there. No director was going to permit someone else, least of all a casting director, to select his leading lady in a Shake-spearean production. The producer would insist on be-ing present, and where the director and producer went, assistants always followed. A minimum of one a piece. Last, and least, would be the casting person.

"You may be-gin," he proclaimed in a fey and high-pitched voice.

"The quality of mercy is not strain'd. It droppeth as the gentle rain from heaven upon the place beneath. . . . it is twice blest: it blesseth him that gives and him that takes. 'Tis mightiest in the mightiest; it becomes the throned monarch better than his crown. What is going on here?"

Silence. No reply.

I took two steps down stage and pointed in his direction. "You," I cried, not as gentle Portia but as domineering Mrs. Macbeth, "what game's afoot?"

"Huh?" Crieth he.

"What falseness? What untruth lieth there in that barren empty oval where should sit they who sitteth in judgement. Why have they sent a mere minion in pre-tence guileful . . ."

"Huh?" he said.

"I would have thought," I said, "that this being the call-backs, the director would be here."

"Well, I'm here."

"Does that mean that there will be second call-backs for the director and producer?"

"It's none of your business what it means. I'm here, you do your audition for me. Or you can leave if you don't want to."

"I think I should know what's going on. Is that asking too, too much?"

"Yes," he said. "It is."

I took a deep breath and began again. I was proud that I didn't let the altercation affect my performance, but I was ashamed that I didn't walk out. When I was done I took what dignity I had with me, found a pay phone, and called my agent. I told her what had happened.

"Well, you know, they're probably not really serious about the call-backs now."

"What do you mean?"

"You didn't know?" Martha Fiel said.

"Know what?"

"Carrie Fisher wants to play it."

"Princess Lea?"

"I think the director is in L.A. being interviewed by her now."

"Why did they waste my time? What's going on?"

"Well, it might not be a waste of time. It's good for you to be seen down there. For them to get to know you. And what if Carrie doesn't lilke the director and they can't find someone she likes to replace him and the deal falls through? Then they have to use a regular actress."

Back on surveillance—Irene still hadn't showed up—Sonny said, "You look depressed."

"I am depressed. That's why I look depressed. I could cover it with makeup but I'm too depressed to bother."

"What's the matter?"

"Forget about it," I said. "Who's running at the track?"

"If you were a guy, what I would say, I would say you should go out and get laid tonight. Get your mind off whatever it is that's bothering you."

So I let Rowdy order a sparkling wine with dinner. I even smoked two cigarettes. Something I do from time to time when I want to feel particularly debauched. It conveys a party atmosphere to me. I let looks and touches substitute for declarations and explanations. I tried to convince myself that he really was enigmatic, not shallow, repressed in a torturously romantic way rather than boring.

I'm such a good actress that it worked. I believed what the character I was being believed and laughed and had a good time. I felt warm and tingling, sweet and ever so touchable. We necked in the back of the cab on the way to my apartment and I let his hands float over the tender parts of my body.

We had to stop to enter my building. Both downstairs locks on the inner door have to be opened simultaneously and it takes two hands. This low-tech instead of high-cost approach to building security is typical of Lidie our landlady. It's the Mississippi country cunning answer to New York street smarts.

Ralph likes to hang out in the hall sometimes, when his room gets too small for him, and look down the stairwell to watch his neighbors come and go. I was relieved that he wasn't there, watching, to see that I'd given in.

When we entered my apartment Rowdy took me in his arms and kicked the door shut while he was kissing me. I really wanted to talk and establish some more intimacy, but I knew if I insisted on that we would founder on the same old rocks. So I let him lead me into the bedroom.

I thought he undressed in much too familiar a fashion, marital and practical, as if we were a couple, two people who'd seen each other before and were ready to get down to business. Disrobing should be desperate and passionate or slow and seductive to get the right effect. However, he still had an excellent body, naturally muscled and firm, not all pumped up with Nautilus machines. It was nice to see him naked.

I was still dressed.

"Come on," he said.

"Help me," I said, throatily.

He began to unbutton my buttons. The phone rang. Rang and rang.

"Dammit," I said.

"Ignore it," he said.

"I can't. You know noise drives me crazy."

He looked around for the phone. Saw it, went to it, lifted the receiver, then hung it up.

"At least put the machine on," I said.

"Isn't the machine on?"

"If the machine were on, it would've picked up."

"Where is it?"

"Over there."

He was annoyed, but enough in heat to do what he was told. He turned it on and came back to me. His fingers found my buttons. The phone began to ring. We tensed. But after two rings the machine kicked in. We both heaved sighs of relief and started to melt back into each other.

"Annie! Annie," cried a woman's voice when my announcement was done and the beep had gone off. "It's Irene. I know you're there. Please be there. I'm desperate. I need help. Please, please."

"What is it?" I said, picking up.

"Help me," she said.

"How can I help you?"

"Let me in. Hide me."

"Are you in some kind of trouble? What's going on?"

"I'm downstairs. You gotta let me in. I tried to buzz but you got no buzzer. Jesus Christ what kind of weird place you live in, got no buzzer."

"This really isn't a good time."

"Bet your bootie, it's not a good time. They're gonna kill me. Let me in."

"Irene . . ."

"Please."

"No," Rowdy said.

"How far away are you?"

"On the corner. I'm coming now. OK?"

"Can it wait a little while?"

"No," she said.

"OK," I said.

"Dammit, Annie," Rowdy said. "What's that about?"

"We'll find out," I said, buttoning the few buttons he'd gotten to. "You better get dressed."

"Why don't I just wait in here, undressed," he said.

"Suit yourself, but don't get impatient."

I closed the bedroom door behind me and went downstairs to let Irene in. She was already racing up the stoop when I got there. She clutched a shopping bag and looked like hell.

Once she was in she turned and looked back out through the etched glass. "Oh no," she said. I looked out also. Eighty-fourth is one way, west to east. Irene had come running from the east, against traffic. Now a large black BMW was coming from the other direction. "Did they see me? Did they see me? Did they see me come in?" Irene cried.

CHAPTER TWENTY

Don't turn on the light," Irene said when I opened the door to my apartment.

"Why not?"

"Then they'll know I'm here."

I left the switch alone. There was enough ambient light from the street to move around without tripping on the furniture. "Would you like a cup of tea? You look terribly stressed," I said.

"You got a gun?"

"What would I do with a gun? Come on, sit down."

"You gotta give me something. You got any downers. Anything, even Tylenol with codeine." Still clutching her shopping bag, she backed up to the wall, as close as she could get, and then moved sideways to the window. She peered out. "I don't see them," she said. "But you got this thing here . . ." My apartment faces the front and looks out on the street. There is a stone balustrade and balcony that runs the width of the building. It's only two feet deep, not big enough for anything much except to stand and watch a parade if there ever was one on our street. ". . . I can't see all the way down. They could be hiding there. They could be. Come on, you must have some kind of downers."

"Irene, tell me what's going on?"

"It's your fault. All your fault. You got me into this. You get me out."

"Let's sit down and calm down and we'll talk."

"We're trapped here, aren't we. Is there a back way out?"

"I'm going to make some tea," I said, moving away from her into the tiny kitchen at the back of my apartment. I put water on. I looked through my herbal teas. Camomile would be just the thing, I thought.

"How about some percs?" she said, trailing along behind me. The shopping bag never left her hands. She stood by the doorless door frame that led to the kitchen. "Maybe your dentist gave you some percs? Mine gives them to me all the time. Even some reefer would help. You got a jay? A roach stashed away somewhere? I'm crashing. It hurts, Annie. Do I smell bad? Do I? I haven't slept in a while. And I'm under a lot of tension. Are we the same size? Maybe I can borrow some of your clothes?" She looked down. "I'm tired of these shoes. What size do you wear?" She scratched at her scalp up behind her ear. "Don't bother with cooking. I can't eat anything anyway. We did a lot of blow, as if you couldn't guess, right?"

"Take a deep breath and slow down," I said as the water started to boil. I packed the loose tea in a metal steeper, took down two cups, and found some honey.

"I think I should get out of town, but I don't have any money left. They're going to kill me. I've been hiding out. Getting high a little bit to pass the time. OK, more than a little bit, maybe, but I'm scared, right? So get me out of here, 'cause it's your fault." Holding the shopping bag to her chest, she made her way along the wall back to the front window and peered out.

"This useless thing you have," she said, trying to

look past the balustrade without being seen. "I can't tell if they're here or not."

"Who, Irene, who? Who's out there? Who's trying to kill you?"

"What do you think, you think this is cocaine paranoia or something? This isn't paranoia. They know who I am. Thanks to you."

"Who?"

"The guys who killed Artie," she said as if that should have been clear to me.

"What guys?"

"Don't you have anything in this goddamn apartment? I need, that's N-E-E-D something to bring me down."

"Don't insult my apartment," I said.

"I'm sorry," she said, truly contrite. She looked around. "It's really cute. Is that a working fireplace. That's cool. They're hard to find. And that wicker couch. I like that. It looks feminine. That's nice. Couches in guys' apartments, they're always big, heavy, ugly things. Fold-out beds. Lumpy fold-out beds, yuchhh."

"Come over here," I said, taking her arm. She twitched, moving the bag away from me, but I touched her again gently and led her to the table.

She sat and went limp. "I'm so tired," she said. And she was, for a moment, then she was wired again. "OK. We gotta make a plan. You can do that, you're good at that."

"You say the man who killed Artie wants to kill you? Can you tell me who that is? Can you tell me why?"

"How in hell would I know his name? Huh? How would I know that?"

"Slow down. Have some tea," I said, trying to calm her. I poured.

"That stupid article of yours. That's what did it. The

mystery woman. The whole damn world is looking for me."

"You're the mystery woman? You were there that night?"

"Why the hell else would they want to kill me?!"

"You were there that night?" I repeated. I was having trouble accepting this particular revelation.

"I can prove it," Irene said.

Then the light came on.

"What's going on?" an irritated but very good-looking Rowdy Randolph said. He'd had the decency to put his pants on, but he was shirtless and his hair was lovingly tousled.

"Hi," Irene said, all attention. "Oh God, I must look a mess. I know you."

"Hey, no. I don't think we ever met," Rowdy said.

"Yes," Irene said, getting all throaty. "You must remember."

"Maybe you're mixing me up with . . ."

"Come on, Rowdy. I was pretty high," Irene said, running her fingers through her dirty hair, trying to fluff and comb it out. Might as well use a twig to groom a dog that'd been rolling in the mud. "And so were you. But how can you forget." She fluttered her lashes over her bloodshot eyes. "Remember you were going to introduce me to your agent and everything."

"Forget what?" I snapped at Rowdy.

"Annie, I . . ."

"Annie, I . . ." I mimicked him. "I don't believe you did it with her."

"It's a mistake. Uh. Umm. You and I . . ."

"You were going to touch me with something you put in her?"

"Uhhh. How can you be . . . We weren't . . . Not then."

"So you don't deny it!" I said.

"Don't talk about me like that," Irene said. "I am somebody."

"I think you better leave," I said. To Rowdy.

"I am somebody. I'm the Mystery Woman. Look!" Irene said. She reached into her shopping bag and pulled out the Lucinda Merrill wig followed by the crumbled Shanna McWarren dress that she'd worn the night she'd run out of Arthur Hoffman's building, to be seen by Anne Lynn Murphy, nurse, who lived across the street. That she'd worn when they'd run out of butane and she'd gone down to the corner newsstand to get cigarettes and four lighters.

"Oh," I said. Not the most intellectually penetrating statement that could have been made in regard to this new piece of evidence. But an acknowledgment that suddenly made a great deal of sense and that a lot of what might have been drug-abusing babble should be taken quite seriously. Maybe there was someone outside and maybe he did want to kill her. If he tried to kill her in my apartment it suggested that I might get hurt as well. I was very much out of my depth.

"Huh?" Rowdy said. "The mystery woman?"

"Don't you read the papers? Or watch TV?" Irene said, fiddling with the buttons of her stained blouse to draw attention to her overused breasts.

I picked up the telephone. "Sip your tea, put a little honey in it," I said to Irene while I dialed the Duke. At the office I got his machine. At his house I got his wife.

"He's not here," she snapped. "And who are you, calling so late?"

"I work for Mr. DeNobili," I said. "As a detective."

"He didn't tell me he had a girl working for him," his wife said.

"I think he thought you might think the wrong thing."

"You bet. I'm married to that sonuvabitch. I know him."

"But it's not what you might think. It's strictly business."

"Sure it is. Get any ankle bracelets lately?"

"Look," I thought I heard Rowdy say to Irene, "tell her you mistook me for someone else. I'm sure you did."

"Mrs. DeNobili," I said on the phone, "I'm sorry you're getting the wrong idea here, but please, listen to me. If you see or hear from your husband tell him I found Irene."

"You got a joint, anything?" Irene said to Rowdy. "I like to party when I get high. You know what I mean?"

"Irene?" Duke's wife said. "Is she the one got the diamond-encrusted ankle bracelet? I heard, from friendsa mine, she was some Puerto Rican tramp."

"Please, listen. This has got to do with the Lucinda Merrill case. I found Irene. She's the mystery woman. She was with Arthur Hoffman when he was killed. She says. And there may be people after her to kill her. She's at my house. They're downstairs."

"Who's downstairs?"

"The people who want to kill Irene?"

"This is for real?"

"Yes, Mrs. DeNobili, it is."

"OK, honey, I'll tell him, if I talk to him. And you can call me Anita."

I hung up and said to Rowdy, "At least put your shirt on."

He gave me a look but retreated to the bedroom. I started dialing Sonny's number.

"I hate that," Irene said. "Sleep with a guy and he

wants to pretend he doesn't know you. That's cheap. That's what I call cheap."

Sonny's mother answered. I said hello—she knew who I was, at least, Sonny wasn't afraid to tell his mother about me—and asked for Sonny.

"I only slept with him," Irene said about Rowdy, "'cause he said we would meet his agent, you know?"

"Sonny," I said, when he came on the line. "Irene's here. She's the mystery woman, and she thinks someone's in the street going to kill her."

"I'll be right there," he said and hung up.

I called 911. I reported a man with a gun downstairs. I said he'd threatened my roommate, the girl who'd run into my apartment. After taking my name, very slowly, and my address, very slowly, and my phone number, the voice paused to take a healthy chew of her gum and said, very slowly, "We'll send somebody."

"Tell me what happened," I said to Irene.

"I was going out with Artie," she said. "Artie could have had lots of girls. But he chose me."

"Irene, tell me what happened the night that Artie was shot."

"OK. Yeah. OK. I was out. I was there. We were getting high, you know, smokin'. He had good stuff that night. Really good stuff. But then he ran out of butane. So he sent me out. The newsstand, on the corner, it's open twenty-four hours, round the clock. I was already dressed up." She stood up and held the dress in front of her, trying to smooth the wrinkles out with her hands. It had probably been in the shopping bag, with the wig, since the night it happened, and short of steaming and pressing, it was a hopeless, sort of pathetic effort. "We were kind of in a hurry. So I went out with everything on. The wig and all. And my purse, thank God. And the shoes." She dug into the bag again and came out with

Lucinda Merrill/Shanna McWarren spike heels. "So I go. I buy the lighters, the cigarettes, and everything. And I get back to the building, and even from downstairs I knew something was weird. I am so tired, Annie. So . . . you got some kind of pick-me-up?"

"Some people are coming, they'll have stuff, anything you want. Uppers, downers, grass," I said, stalling.

"Some weed sounds really nice. Mellow me out, you know. But some downers, maybe that would be better."

Rowdy came back in. Fully dressed and pouting.

"You got a jay?" Irene asked him. "One lousy goddamn jay? A goddamn roach?"

"Look, uh . . ." Rowdy said, shuffling his feet.

"Uh what?" I said.

"Listen, Annie, I better go."

"You what?"

"I got . . . uh . . . pre-pro. Early morning pre-pro meeting."

"Come on, Rowdy," I said. "I don't like you a whole lot right now, but don't you think it would be a good idea if there were a guy here to protect us? Don't you think that?"

"From what?" he said sarcastically.

"Whoever is out there trying to kill Irene."

"Annie, honey, she's crazy."

"I am not. I'm the mystery woman. I was there," Irene said.

"If I thought you were in any danger, I would stay. I would be here for you. But she is . . . wacky. And I . . . am outta here."

"You are a cowardly pig," I said.

"Come on, Annie. One thing you are is an actress. Through and through. And you get caught up in dramas.

You make everything into a big . . . thing. So. So, I'm sure everything is OK. And I'm going now."

"I hate you," I said. Simply, "Get out of here."

"I'll call you in the morning," he said, backing out.

"He's a pig," I said, seething, when he closed the door behind him.

"All of them are," Irene said. "And he didn't even have a joint."

"Let's forget about him. Can you believe I ever . . . Oh! Come on," I said, "tell me the story."

"Well, sure. Sure. Listen."

"I'm listening."

"I knew it as soon as I walked upstairs and saw the door."

"The apartment door?"

"Yes. It was open a little bit. That was all wrong."

"Maybe you didn't close it behind you when you went out."

"I did. I did. I did. I know I did. Also I heard Artie lock it behind me, like he always did. Twice. Two locks. Right? So why would it be open. But it was. But I went up anyway. Maybe it was his friends or something. Right, I was high and wanted to keep going. You know what it's like. You get going and going and you don't ever wanna stop. Well I got upstairs and I saw there was another set of keys in the lock . . ."

"What do you mean, another set?"

"Well, I had Artie's set, right?"

"He only had one?"

"That's all that I ever saw. One. But, you know, who's looking at keys. When you got smoke."

"Then what?"

"I was, I was real nervous. So I kinda crept up. Then I heard them. I swear to God, Annie, I never been this scared in my life. Every time, whenever I try to go to sleep I hear them over and over. I'm afraid to go to sleep. That's why I've been up. Partying. So I don't hear them."

"Tell me what they said. Go on."

"I was just peeking in . . ."

"What did they say?"

"There were two of them. One said . . . One said: 'Where's the bitch? There's supposed to be a bitch here.' Then the next one said, 'Fo'get about it. If she ain't here, she ain't here.' Then the first one said, 'You said we was gettin' paid for two, I don't wanna end up paid for one.' Then the second one said, 'Fo'get about it. Don't be greedy. Let's get outta here.'

"I was frozen, listening to them. Frozen. I couldn't move. Then I realized they were going to come out. I turned and ran down the steps and out to the street. I tripped on these stupid shoes. Who can run in heels? And there was a cab. Thank God, there was a cab and I ran out in the street and he stopped."

"These guys, whoever they were, they had a key?"

"Yeah, I told you, I saw it hanging in the lock."

"One key, or a whole set?"

"There was a bunch, you would need a bunch, upstairs and downstairs too."

"And they expected you, a girl anyway, to be there?"

"I told you, Annie, I told you."

"Tell me something else. Arthur talked about his wife?"

"Yeah, all the time."

"Did he ever say that she knew about him and you dressing up as her?"

"Oh yeah. And she was vicious about it, the things she said to him."

I could see it. Lucinda Merrill taking the keys out of her husband's pockets. Down to the locksmith, make a

second set, put the keys back. Finding someone—
who?—what kind of people do that kind of thing and
how do you find them?—giving them the keys and
telling them there would be two people in the apartment. Even figuring that something might go wrong
and the girl would get away, like Irene did. Or simply
that Arthur was not that discreet anyway and his girlfriends, disguised as her, had been seen around. So she
needed witnesses that she'd been home all night. Could
that be true? Was it too fantastic? Too soap opera?

Then Morrie "the Mule" Siegal kicked the door in.

rene shrieked.

He looked just like his picture in *Metro* magazine. Except uglier and twice as big.

He slammed the door shut, moved into the room, grabbed Irene by the throat with one hand, and slapped her across the face with the other.

"Stop it, stop it," I cried.

Irene was crying and whimpering. She went half limp like a little girl, pushing herself away from him. She wasn't going anywhere.

I backed up to the mantel. I keep my dad's old bayonet there, from World War II. Not that I'd ever expected to use it. It's actually sort of blunt and I doubt if it could slice cheese. Never mind. I was outraged to see anyone treat a woman like that. I grabbed it and pulled it out of the scabbard.

The big man laughed. He pulled out a gun. It had a silencer attached. I'd never seen one in person before. The whole assemblage looked gigantic and terribly deadly.

"I got nothin' against you," he said. "Just put it down. Nobody get's hurt. Your girlfriend comes with me." He released Irene's throat and put his big hands in her hair, grabbing her hard. She made frightened whimpering sounds and looked at me with big, helpless eyes. "Say bye-bye." He backed out the door like some cartoon Neanderthal, a primitive dragging a female victim by the hair, whatever it was that he wanted from her, rape or murder or both.

"No," I screamed insanely, and charged at him.

I don't know why I did that. I don't know why he didn't shoot me. Maybe he thought I was cute. He released Irene and grabbed my hand easily. He moved very fast. And just took my arm and twisted. The old bayonet fell out of my fingers. But he kept twisting and I went to my knees. He twisted even harder. "Come on, girlie," he said. "Don't be stupid. I don't wanna kill you."

I glared up at him. The fight was out of me.

The phone started to ring. I looked over to it as if help would come over the wire. It rang twice. Then my answering machine picked up.

Irene had not taken the opportunity to run. Silly cow. She just crouched there, on the floor, in terror.

I heard Rowdy's voice. I felt great relief. He'd come back.

"Annie," he said, "some guy shoved his way into the building when I went out." I realized I was hearing him talk to my machine. "I just thought I'd alert you. Call you in the morning."

By then, Morrie had grabbed her again and yanked her to her feet. He had her under total control now and moved her effortlessly with him as he strolled out my door. I had no idea how to stop him.

Horrified at what might happen to her, I poked my head out the door, then looked over the banister as he moved her, unprotesting, down the stairs, his hand holding her by the hair, a dog on a very tight leash. I sensed someone else and I looked up. There was Ralph looking down.

"Annie, are you all right?"

"Help me, Ralph, help me," I cried.

He came galloping down the stairs to my doorway. "What is it?"

"Oh God," I said.

"What is it?"

Suddenly, I had an idea. It was insane. But at least it was what I do. "Listen to me. That man. With that girl. Who just went out. Delay them. Stop them. Just for a few minutes. Please."

"How?"

"I don't know how," I said. "Just do something."

Ralph turned and ran down the stairs, off to do battle, as valiant as the fool I'd had him play in *Man of Destiny*. No doubt about it, and Shaw acknowledged it even as he made fun of the character, our not-quite-bright lieutenant was the sort to ride into the cannon's mouth armed only with a saber. "Be careful," I cried after Ralph. "He's got a gun."

I tossed off my clothes as quickly as I could. Faster even than that useless posturing actor Rowdy would have wanted. I whipped into the dress that Irene had brought with her. And the shoes. Then the wig. It was amazing how much Lucinda Merrill's look was a look. Even with the pieces wrinkled and crushed I looked something like her. If you didn't actually look at me. I just needed three strokes of makeup; crimson lips and two slaps of heavy contour on my cheekbones.

I heard yelling from the street even as I did it. It was Ralph. Yelling for the police. Screaming about kidnapping and murdering and such.

I ran downstairs.

When I opened the front door the noise had stopped.

Ralph was lying half on the sidewalk and half in the street against a tire. He was bleeding from the side of his head. Morrie was shoving Irene into his car.

When all the rehearsing is said and done, all the background, all the preparation, if there is to be a really good performance, the actor goes someplace else. Someplace where it just happens. I suppose it works that way for other things as well, for athletes, painters, maybe even politicians.

This time my preparation was not specific. It was just all the training I'd been doing all these years, never anticipating this role or betting our lives on it. I'd watched Lucinda Merrill and heard her and recorded her in my actor's memory bank, perhaps thinking I would use some bits and pieces of her someday. If I thought of it at all consciously, I would have supposed I would use her sarcastically, to mock a character full of herself, or even to play a "bad" actress.

It was absurd to think that I could transcend the wrinkled dress and the tawdry wig and convince someone who had met her that I was her. I could do the voice, I could do the posture and the style of movement. But sheer mimicry wouldn't carry it. I would simply have to *be* her.

I dashed down the steps before he saw me coming from the house and got to the sidewalk making sure the streetlight was behind me, so I was backlit, my face shadowed, more silhouette than detail.

"Morrie, Morrie," I called out. Even in my own ear it sounded like her.

"Lucinda? What are you doin' here?" he said, looking up at me.

"Morrie, let her go. You're making it worse," I said.

"But, but you tol' me . . ."

"It's a mess, let me take care of it. Money will take care of it."

"Hey, speakin' o' money, you owe . . ." His mouth sort of hung open. "You ain't Lucinda Merrill, you're that broad from upstairs." He sneered and reached into his jacket for his gun.

I yelped—as I remember it—and dove behind the nearest car. Full of adrenaline, which I understand is the biological term for terror, I shuffled around on my hands and knees trying to get away from him.

I never saw Sonny arrive. I didn't hear the Silver Bullet's brakes slam on. Or the door open. But his voice registered.

"All right, Morrie, it's all over."

"Fuck you, Gandolfo," Morrie said in a contemptuous way. "You've retired."

I looked around at that point. There was the Silver Bullet, casually double-parked, not more than ten feet away from me. I cautiously lifted my head. There was Sonny in the shooter's position, a gun in his hands—I certainly don't know what kind—pointed at Morrie.

"The girl's my partner," Sonny said.

A rush went through me. Something like true love, but better. I wanted to curl up on a great big sofa with great big arms around me and cry for a while. Happily.

"Drop it," Sonny said.

"Hey, you and me, let's talk this out. We can work something out here. I don't wanna hurt your partner. Ask her. She'll tell you so. Hey, girlie, didn't I tell you I din't want to hurt you."

Suddenly there was noise behind me. Morrie looked, I looked, but fortunately Sonny didn't. It was the Duke's Seville, doing forty miles an hour, the wrong way, down Eighty-fourth street. He slammed on his brakes, making lots of noise—something he enjoyed—leaving skid marks.

He leapt out in his John Gotti suit. "OK, I'm takin' charge here." He walked right up to Morrie, even though the oversize loan shark still held a gun. "This the perp," he said over his shoulder to Sonny.

"Yeah," Sonny said.

"Gimme the gun," Duke said.

"Screw you," Morrie said, sneering.

I watched awestruck. These people were not real. Duke shoved Morrie's gun hand aside with his left hand, stepped in and hit him with his right. Morrie doubled over, gagging and coughing. Duke hit him again. This time drawing his arm all the way back and slamming in into the side of Morrie's face. Morrie went down to his hands and knees. Duke kicked his gun hand and the gun skittered away. Then Duke stomped on his hand, breaking the fingers. For good measure.

Sonny strolled over and picked up the gun with the silencer. He did so delicately, touching it as little as possible, and put it in his jacket pocket.

"I told you we'd crack this one," Duke said. "So where's the fuckin' mystery woman, you got her for me?"

CHAPTER TWENTY-TWO

Ralph was alive. Hit, not shot. Knocked semiconscious, knot on the head, split lip, but alive.

"You're a hero," I said to him.

We all went upstairs. Me helping Ralph, Sonny herding Irene—who wanted to slink away—Morrie in handcuffs, and Duke in triumph.

"Where's the phone?" Duke asked the minute we opened the door.

I pointed. "Are you all right?" I asked Ralph, leading him to the couch. He sat. Even dazed and bloody he looked noble enough for television.

"Are you OK?" Sonny asked me.

"You can't arrest me, you ain't even a cop," Morrie "the Mule" Siegal said to the Duke.

"Hey, Guido," Duke said into the phone. "Hey, hey, hey . . . they hung up on me." Incapable of believing that someone didn't want to be bothered at two in the morning, he redialed.

"You look like a nice guy," Irene said to Sonny. "Maybe you could do me a favor. I've been having a really rough couple of days and I could really use something that would help me smooth the rough spots, you know?"

I went to get Ralph a cup of tea. Actually, it was the only thing I had in the house, except tap water.

"Hey, I wanna talk to Guido Pellegra," Duke barked into the phone. "You tell him it's Duke DeNobili and I got the story of the year for him." He put his hand over the phone. "That'll bring him running."

"Annie, Annie," Ralph said when I gave him the tea. "Tell me . . ."

"What?"

"My face . . . is it . . . ?"

"Pretty as ever, Ralph. You just got a big lump on your head and a swollen lip. When are you scheduled to start shooting?"

"Next week," Ralph said.

"You'll make it," I said.

He sat back and sighed. "I'm going to take a nap." His eyes closed.

"That could be a sign of concussion," Sonny said. "Hey Duke . . . Duke . . ."

"Hold on," Duke said to Sonny. Back on the phone he gave out my address to Guido Pellegra. He hung up. "What'd I say? On his way."

"You wanna call EMS," Sonny said. "Somebody should take a look at our boy here. He shouldn't be going to sleep like that."

"Jesus, you got a second line here? Annie, you got a second line?"

"Maybe upstairs, you could use Ralph's phone," I said.

"What the Sam Hill is going on here?" Lidie Murphy, my five-feet-two-inches-tall landlady, cried out in a deep Mississippi accent. She was standing in my doorway in one of her transparent negligees. This one was lime.

"Tim. Timmy Donohue," Duke said into the phone, "have I got a story for you."

"I asked a question," Lidie said.

"Come in," I said to Lidie.

"Well, I'm already in," she said and she was. "Now I want to know what in tarnation is this carryin' on. And Annie, what have you got on your head?"

"Oh this," I said, suddenly remembering that I had my Lucinda Merrill wig on. I reached to take it off.

"No, leave it," Duke cried. "It's a great photo opportunity. The press is gonna love it."

"Oh my word," Lidie said. "What did you do to Ralph?"

"Ma'am," Sonny said, "would you do us, and Ralph, a big favor?"

"It depends what it is, don't it," she said, hands on hips looking at Sonny square in the eye.

"Would you call EMS for Ralph? Then call the police."

"Police won't come," Lidie said. "I call them all the time, and they never come. But I'll do it."

"WNEW?" I heard Duke say, "Give me the newsroom, I got a hot, hot story for you."

Lidie was more or less right. The police did come, but not until after half the press in New York had piled into my tiny apartment. Even then, it was not the local precinct in response to the man in the street yelling about kidnapping or Morrie waving his gun around or even my 911 call from forever earlier, it was Detective Witte, and he came because he got a call from CBS News. Somebody sent out for beer. And lots of them were smoking, stinking up my apartment and dribbling ashes on the floor.

Duke was right about the photo opportunity. I stood

in my wig and Lucinda Merrill dress, then took off the wig for every cameraman in the room. They loved it.

When Witte arrived, Duke made the boys photograph them together, shaking hands. Witte clearly didn't want to do it, but things were moving too fast for him.

"OK, here's the scoop, boys," Duke said when everyone was there. "When the Duke says he's gonna solve a case, then the Duke solves a case. This here is Morrie 'the Mule' Siegal, he's the guy who hit Arthur Hoffman, Lucinda Merrill's husband. As you know, Lucinda Merrill is my client who has been the victim of malignment and unfounded accusation.

"This man is a notorious loan shark well listed on many police blotters in this city. In addition, tonight, he committed many acts of violence and brutality attempting to assassinate this woman: Shell Drake! A beautiful young actress and model who was a witness to the slaying in the love-nest apartment on the East Side."

When Irene had understood that people with cameras were coming she disappeared into the bathroom. She went through my makeup and applied it to herself with a lavish hand. So she didn't look as bad as when she first arrived, although the bathroom looked much worse. Also she scored a pill from one of the ABC guys and that mellowed her out. When the Duke cued her, she stepped up and preened.

"This attempt was foiled by myself and my associates, Sonny Gandolfo and Annie McGrogan. Step up here and get your pictures taken, Sonny and Annie.

"Tonight the Duke solved the case and made a citizen's arrest of the perpetrator whom I will now transpose over to the duly constituted authorities and representative of the NYPD—greatest police department in the world, though I am no longer among them—Detective Witte."

The reporters asked Witte what he had to say.

"No comment," Witte said, clearly boiling.

Did he resent the interference? "No comment." Did he believe Morrie Siegal was the killer? "No comment." Was he happy to be working with Duke DeNobili? "No comment." Did this mean that Lucinda Merrill was cleared? "No comment."

EMS came for Ralph. Lidie ushered them in. They shouldered their way through the crowd and took him out on a stretcher. I asked Lidie to lock up. She said she would.

Irene was starting to snooze on the couch by then.

I went upstairs, got Ralph's personal phone book, then went with him to the hospital.

I called his mother when he got there. I'd never met her, or even spoken to her before, but apparently Ralph had spoken to her about me. She knew who I was immediately. When I told her what had happened she went into action. His private doctor showed up within the hour. He was followed shortly by Ralph's mother, who was followed shortly thereafter by the family priest. I felt like I had done all I could. I made her promise to call me.

Then I went home and went to sleep.

By morning, the story was everywhere.

Duke was the absolute darling of the media. According to them he'd solved the case and apprehended the perpetrator and more or less made the world safe for American womanhood. He upstaged both Morrie "the Mule" and the newly unmasked mystery women, Irene Rinna, aka Shell Drake.

When I was mentioned at all, it was about fourth

billing. Duke had been absolutely right about the wig thing. It was what the media loved, and when I was shown, that was the shot. I was "the detective-actress."

I got a call of thanks from Lucinda Merrill. It was brief, but heartfelt.

Almost as soon as she hung up, Bobby Motzkin rang. I don't know if it was connected to Lucinda or my new notoriety. There was reason to believe both or either.

"It has come to my attention that you are a very, very talented young lady, but that you have no agent," he said.

"Actually, I do have representation, at the moment," I said.

"Oh, who is it that represents you?"

"Martha Fiel," I said.

"Vell then, that comes to the same thing, doesn't it." That would have sounded cutting and nasty coming from most people, but Bobby had an impish way of saying those things that made them sound light and amusing instead. "Vould you like to haff lunch with me?"

"When?"

"I am certain you must be very, very veary from all your activities that have been so excitingly covered by the television and newspapers, you must need your rest, so today is out, but if you are available, perhaps tomorrow?"

I agreed. He said one-thirty at the Russian Tea Room. Who could argue with that.

Morrie was charged, at his first arraignment, with attempted kidnapping (of Irene), of assault and battery (on Ralph, Irene, and me), assault with a deadly weapon, and possession of an unlicensed firearm. He had a high-powered attorney who argued, of course, for bail. The DA pointed out that Mr. Siegal had been arrested while attempting to kidnap a witness to another crime. Bail was denied.

By the following day, things looked even worse for the loan shark. A parking ticket, for blocking a fire hydrant, placed him at Arthur Hoffman's at approximately the right time. Irene claimed she could identify his voice. Anne Lynn Murphy claimed she had seen him leave Arthur Hoffman's building, walking calmly, after Irene—dressed as Lucinda—had come running into the street. Although the murder weapon was not found, a shell casing of the same caliber was found in the crack between the backrest and the seat of Morrie's car. In addition, there were the witnesses that we had found earlier, as well as others, who would testify that Arthur owed money to the loan shark who had made threats.

Ralph's mother came by the apartment. She wanted to tell me in person that Ralph was fine. He'd had a concussion but there was no fracture or permanent damage.

"Did you know," she asked, "that he thinks he's a homosexual?"

"Yes," I said.

"I think that it's just a phase and I think he is very much in love with you. You two could be very good for each other."

"Thank you," I said. "He's lucky to have a mother who cares so much for him. And is so effective in getting things done."

"Then you'll think about it?"

"I don't think it's what Ralph wants," I said gently. "Best to let things take their course. Naturally."

"All right," she said, and kissed my cheek.

* * *

I had lunch with Bobby Motzkin. He urged me to have the blinis with caviar and sour cream. He said he could tell I had a great deal to offer, a special something. He loved, he said, the detective-actress thing. Much could be done with it.

"I just want to act," I said.

"Excellent, my dear, excellent. We shall see to it."

"Do you want to represent me?" I asked.

"My dear, that is what we have been discussing."

"Fine. I would like that," I said.

"Oddly enough, NBC is just now casting a pilot. About a young woman who vas a reporter who becomes a private investigator. Or maybe it's a private investigator who becomes a reporter? No. I'm sure it is the first one, she becomes a private investigator. I vill see to it that you are called for that. The description fits you very, very well."

The next day Morrie "the Mule" Siegal dropped his bombshell. He faced a charge of murder two—murder one is only for killing cops and corrections officers—and a host of other felonies. He was a predicate felon, current legal jargon for three-time loser, and would probably max out on all the sentences leaving him in jail for life.

He offered a plea bargain that would give him just three to nine years in return for testifying against his coconspirator. Since there was little else to link the coconspirator to the killing, since the coconspirator would not even be charged otherwise, since it was a very high-profile case indeed, the police department and district attorney's office agreed to cut Morrie a deal for naming Lucinda Merrill.

Various summations and versions of what he had to say were leaked to the media. But Sonny somehow got an actual tape of what Morrie told the DA. Though Sonny had told me intimacies that I'd never heard from anyone else, he was absolutely silent on the source of the tape.

"I was hittin' on her for the dough," Morrie told the DA. " 'Cause she's the one with the dough, he ain't got no dough by now, it's all up the pipe, stupid crackhead. Dopers, they're all unreliable, you unnerstand? So the spouse is the only source of recouping in this situation. She tells me millions for defense not one penny for tribute or somethin' hysterical like that that someone famous once said, I don't know who.

"I try to explain to her rational like, no threats, I never does threats right off unless it's required, that family is family and debts are a family responsibility.

"We get to talking and she says if I were to off her husband who is a big drain, which is true, he's pretty worthless, and she would collect the insurance, which she doesn't even need, she would pay me what I am owed. I said 'No way. No goddamn way, lady. If I hit your husband I want double what I'm owed, which was twenny-five original, fifty with vig, so now we're talking about hunnert grand. A nice round even full kind of number. My kind of number. She says 'no way, fifty gees, max.' I hold out for the full century. We negotiate. Hey, I'm flexible. We settle on eighty-five. Which is not bad. I get my capital out, plus hunnert percent markup—people say that's high or somethin' but I tell you what, I'm one savings and loan that ain't goin' under. No scumbag Fed'ral government has to bail Morrie 'the Mule' Siegal out, am I right or am I right? You put me in charge of them banks and you ain't gotta worry. But that's wishful thinkin' in the too-true-to-be-good category. So where was I? Oh yeah, we cut a deal at eighty-five. So figure that's thirty-five for a whack.

Not bad at all. For that kinda bread I'll do it myself, make sure it gets done right.

"So she tells me where the husband's pussy pad is and gives me the keys. She says I gotta tell her when I'm gonna do it so she's got an alibi. I says I can't give her no exact-to-the-moment hour, like it's a TV show, life in crime ain't like that, as we here all know. 'Just tell me the night,' she says, 'and I'll make sure I got an airtight for the whole P.M.' Which, I got to hand it to her, she does. She scams these two dicks to sit there and watch her. I heared they even passed a polygraph that she was snugabug in bed while Artie took his dive."

I read for NBC and thought I did a very creditable job.

We had a meeting with Mr. Petty. Now that Lucinda Merrill was actually being charged, he'd brought in Bernie Auerbach, a real criminal-law hotshot. The basic line of defense would be that Morrie Siegal would say anything in order to get off and that this was a made-up story.

Which sounded very believable, and Morrie might have made up a story about Lucinda Merrill, if it hadn't been true.

Our job would be to collect information to discredit Morrie. It should be easy enough, Duke said. It appeared there would be plenty of detective work. If I were available to do it. Everyone was confident that Lucinda would get off scot-free. After spending a considerable amount of money, of course. The network was "on board," full support, including picking up a portion of the legal fees.

* * *

Bobby Motzkin was indeed a powerful agent. Power-ful enough to get on the phone and find out what happened to my casting at NBC. "She's just not the type," the casting director said. "This is a new type of show. We're going for realism. She doesn't have that reality look."

"They are so funny," Bobby said to me.

I went home and called Patrick. Maybe the Coast was the place to be. He answered the phone himself.

"How are things out there?" I said.

"Oh, fine," he said.

"Honey, do you want to eat Mex tonight?" a female voice said in the background.

I really didn't want to go back. That was the truth.

"My car," I said.

"Yeah?"

"I was thinking, if you know someone reliable, com-ing to the East Coast, could they drive it out here to me? Can it make the trip?"